COME HELL OR HIGH DESIRE

MISTY DIETZ

COME HELL OR HIGH DESIRE
COPYRIGHT © 2015 by MISTY DIETZ

MISTY MEDIA
REPRINT: OCTOBER 2015
ORIGINAL PUBLICATION: AUGUST 2013

eBook ISBN: 978-1-943716-02-9
Print ISBN: 978-1-943716-03-6

Cover designer: Misty Dietz
Edited by: Denise Dittus
Interior design by: Top-ePublishing Services

For Mae, an extraordinary grandmother.
I treasure you.

To the hard-working and all-around awesome Fargo Police Department, especially Officers Melissa Westby and Phil Swan (the pub crawl ride-along was an eye-opener!), as well as all the instructors of the Fargo Citizen's Police Academy. Every officer I interacted with was helpful, detailed, and prompt. For that and everything you do for the community, thank you.

To mom and dad, for your sense of adventure and open-mindedness.

And to David, for challenging me to spread my wings.

ONE

FARGO, NORTH DAKOTA
SUNDAY MORNING, AUGUST

Zack Goldman slapped at a mosquito and leaned against his truck as Morgan Sawyer sashayed down his rutted gravel driveway like she'd driven up in a limo instead of a Corolla sporting a spare tire. She was the sister he'd never had, earning her PhD in urban wiles and tomfoolery when they were adolescents—alone, but not so innocent—on the streets.

He'd bet his river-side acreage that she'd left the cryptic *WHERE IS SHE* note on his door this morning to punk him. Something was definitely going on if she was up—and put together—this early. "I was on my way into town. After my errands, I was going to stop by your place to see if you were still alive. Haven't seen you in weeks. How'd you manage to crawl out of bed before noon?"

Her red-painted lips tilted up at the corners. "Haven't gone to bed yet."

He pushed away from the truck and ruffled her pixie-short blonde hair. "*Brat.* You come all the way out here to spy on me, or are you finally going to ask me for a job?"

She shook her head. "You're too boring to spy on nowadays. But damn, I'd pay good money to watch you roll somebody over a pool table again."

"Those days are long gone, Morgan."

"Never say never."

The way she said it made Zack's shoulders tense. *I should*

1

have brought you to Sunday suppers with John more often. A mistake he'd never be able to fix since John, his plain-speaking, charismatic mentor—the only person he'd ever strived to emulate—had been buried for almost a year now.

Zack battened down the lid of his grief. "Nice try with the mysterious note you left on my door. You should know by now I don't bring women out here." Didn't bring *anyone.* He appreciated his five acres of elbow room.

Morgan's eyebrows rose. "What note?"

A cold sensation rippled through him. She looked too intrigued to be lying. "Never mind." His thoughts raced. If Morgan hadn't left the note, who had? And why? It had to be either a mistake, or a joke. His inner circle was two men and three women. Five people who didn't share his blood but were the only family he'd ever known. The only ones who'd never betrayed him.

His mentor, John Samuels, was dead. Morgan was here. Twyla and Archie Raessler were at home as of fifteen minutes ago when Archie had texted him...

The only one not accounted for was John's daughter, Ann. She hadn't answered his phone call a half hour ago when he'd first found the note. Zack's pulse throbbed in his neck.

Don't miss the sun today by worrying about the rain coming tomorrow. One of John's positive affirmations.

Maybe Ann had finally taken his advice and unglued her phone from her hand.

Time to get on with the day. "What do you need, Morgan, I should get going."

"Can't I simply come to visit?"

He crossed his arms. "At six-thirty on a Sunday morning?"

"Maybe I'm turning over a new leaf." When he smirked, she sighed. "*Fine.* I want to have a shindig for Ann out here in the boonies. When she's ready to share the news, that is. We'll have a bonfire, drinks, and cookies in the shape of baby bottles. Isn't that the cutest thing you've ever heard? They make them at the deli on 32nd."

He'd derailed about a mile back. "Baby bottles?" Her expression indicated he was a member of the forty watt club, but he still couldn't wrap his mind around baby bottle cookies. "Why would you—"

No.

Morgan cringed. "Oh, damn. How can you *not* know?"

His throat dried. "Stop bullshitting, brat. If Ann's pregnant, so am I."

"Well, in that case, we'll get more cookies."

Her grin fueled his alarm. He drummed his fingers on top of his head, but that didn't help, so he cussed. A lot.

"Sorry, big guy. Guess she knew you'd react this way so she was obviously waiting to tell you. She'll probably thank me for breaking it to you, now that I think about it. But yeah, she got knocked up."

Morgan's voice faded into the background while questions ran circles in his mind. *Who? When?* He was ready to throttle Ann for not telling him right away. But first, maybe he'd better throw himself under a bus. Not fifteen minutes ago he was wondering if she had a boyfriend so he could do a background check on the guy, and now he finds out she's having a *baby?*

She's just a kid herself.

No way. "All right, joke's on me. Give it up, Morgan." She was probably lying about the *WHERE IS SHE* note, too.

Her dimples deepened. "Better get your mad out before you see her."

"I'm *not* mad." Really, he wasn't. Just shocked. And guilty. John had made him promise to look out for Ann when he was dust because she had no one else. His pulse pounded in his neck. *John's grandchild.* "How is it she told you before me?"

Morgan's face went blank for a second. "She didn't exactly tell me. I kinda guessed with her feeling sick so much lately."

Oh, that. He'd chalked it up to the stress of her recent move and the coming anniversary of John's death. But then, he hadn't asked, had he?

What were they going to do with a *baby*? He was acting like a stereotypical idiot bachelor, but *damn*. What if the sperm donor wasn't there for her? He couldn't let Ann's kid grow up without a father figure. John hadn't come into his life until he was an adult and look how messed up *his* adolescence had been.

He checked the time on his phone. *Six-forty-one.* He tried Ann's home and cell numbers again, leaving messages when voicemail picked up. Then he slipped the phone into his pocket. "Who is it?"

Morgan had been squinting across the river. Her gaze scooted back to him. "Who?"

"The boogey man. Who else, Morgan? The *father*."

She shrugged. "No idea. Sure is a secretive little bug, huh?"

He frowned at her grin, and his gut cartwheeled. "I'll get back to you on that party thing, okay?"

"No sweat, big guy."

He heard her laugh as he slid into his truck and gunned it down the gravel driveway.

The only thing he hated worse than a coward was a deserter. And deserter dads topped the list. Somebody's head was gonna roll.

TWO

Zack had his blood pressure under control by the time he pulled up to the service entrance of Skinny Dipping, a frou frou home furnishings boutique where Ann had recently scored the part-time job of her dreams. Or so she'd claimed. He hadn't been here yet, but he'd been curious about it, not only because Ann talked it up, but also because a moniker like that conjured good mojo.

He cut the engine and stepped into the spill of sunshine, industrial sounds from the front of the mall reassuring him that his construction crew was still on the job. On a Sunday. Early. Hopefully wrapping things up because the amusement park addition was scheduled to open in two days. Two more days of burning the candle on both ends, and he'd give all his crew fat bonuses.

Skinny Dipping's plain steel door looked no different from any of the others along the back of the mall, except this one was propped open. He knocked and peered inside. Finding no one, he zigzagged through stacks of boxes toward a door that presumably led to the showroom.

While the back room blazed with ugly fluorescent lighting, the store itself was like the backdrop for a chick flick, glowing with strategically placed lamps, wall lanterns, and lights that dripped crystals.

Getting no response to repeated calls, he continued deeper into the store. Silly, sparkling things—paperweights?—sat on fat wooden candlesticks any self-respecting Boy Scout could carve.

He kept his hands in his pockets as he carefully bypassed chunky necklaces draped over stilettos, fuzzy blankets that wouldn't keep anyone warm, tiny pots that reeked, painted and beat-up furniture, smelly candles, and a ridiculous assortment of gaudy accessories. Honest to God, the sensory smorgasbord made him lightheaded.

This place is an epic fire hazard.

Ann's motive for working here *had* to be educational since she didn't need the money. She wanted to enroll in NDSU's interior design program but was conflicted about walking away from her father's construction business. Zack had told her she could do both, but so far she hadn't made any moves.

Though with a baby coming, who knew when that would happen—*or if.*

He frowned, reaching for a flimsy blue scarf on impulse. He ran his fingers down the sheer length, turned a corner, and almost collided with a pair of legs on a ladder.

His eyes traveled from the three-inch heeled sandals with ribbons that wound up delicate ankles, inch by satiny inch, until—*Jesus*—what had to be almost three and a half feet later his eyes feasted on an ass in white denim.

"Hey there, be with you in a sec." Her voice was like caramel. The kind you suck on. And her scent, warm vanilla. He twisted the scarf between his fists. *Say something.* The woman went up on her toes to arrange a feather boa on a shelf and damned if those Daisy Dukes didn't raise several tantalizing centimeters, exposing the generous swell of her buttocks.

And no tan line. He stifled a groan.

She started down the ladder, and he rubbed a hand over his heart and backed up. He hadn't had such a visceral response to a woman since...*ever?*

"Thanks for waiting. You here for the daybed pickup?" she

asked.

"Yeah. *No!* Ah, sorry. That's not why I'm here." *Tongue-tied even?* The woman stood with one brow raised, arms crossed under her small breasts, the billowy-type shirt doing nothing to conceal the flare of her hips.

Hips just begging for...

He shut his eyes on a slow blink, forcing himself to focus on his purpose. His face heated before he set the scarf on a table and extended his hand. "I'm Zack Goldman. I work with Ann at Samuel's Construction."

The woman looked at his hand, hesitating. Yeah, his hands were rough, but they were clean. Maybe she was a germophobe or something.

A second later, though, she placed her hand in his, and the jolt must have been mutual. Her eyes widened. Weren't they an unusual gray-brown? The color he'd imagine on a she-wolf.

Purpose. Ann. Baby. "The back door was open. Ann told me she'd be here early one of these mornings to help out, but I couldn't remember when," he said.

"Ann was scheduled to be here by six to help with yesterday's freight, but she hasn't arrived yet. Have you tried her at home? I figured she'd slept in. I'm Sloane Swift, by the way."

Flamboyant clothing and enough noisy arm bangles to accessorize a band of gypsies... Her name matched the package. Large, darkly-lashed eyes anchored an oval face above cheekbones sculpted by a master. And all that soft, smooth skin...

Was frowning.

He looked down at their joined hands, let go, and shoved his own in his pockets. "Ann's not answering her phone."

Sloane was about to say something when a tiny blonde

whizzed around the corner. "Hey, boss." The woman's eyes moved from Sloane to Zack, her smile warming a hundred degrees. "Hey handsome, don't let me chase you away. I'm Tori Daily—the manager."

"Zack Goldman. I work with Ann."

A brief disturbance crossed her features before she pinned the smile back in place. "So *you're* Zack. Ann told me you're donating a kidney to a friend's wife. When are you doing that?"

Sloane raised her eyebrows, and his face warmed again. "They hope to do the transplant shortly after Twyla has the baby. Anyway—"

"I hadn't heard the woman was pregnant. That's cool. I'm sure Ann will keep us posted." Tori turned back to Sloane. "Where is she anyway? She was pumped to see the new stuff."

"She's not here yet." Sloane gazed steadily at Zack.

Don't be afraid of women with balls or brains. You don't want no box of rocks. John had been down on his knees trowling concrete with Zack's crew of eight when he'd shared that bit of counsel so long ago.

Zack shifted his weight, then realized how weak that made him look. He could really do without all the unbidden Johnisms today.

"That's not like her. She sick?" Tori asked.

Ann was usually conscientious to a fault. So where was she? That cryptic note was making him more bent by the minute. "I'm sure there's a reasonable excuse."

"Yeah, you're probably right." Tori studied her nails.

She's lying.

Either she knew where Ann was, or she sucked at reassuring people. Maybe both. Zack's phone chirped to signal an incoming text from his CFO. *Benji's irate. Better be here in 20 or better.*

Now what? Once he was done with Timothy Benjamin's mall amusement park and the sub-contractors were paid, he was never going to work with a scumbag like him again. He frowned at Sloane. "Sorry for the trouble. I'm sure Ann will feel terrible about being late."

"We'll be fine. But maybe you should stop by her place to check on her? She could be ill or something."

It was the *or something* he didn't care to think about. But since he needed to deal with Benjamin, and the Samuel's office wasn't far from Ann's, he might as well stop over there. "Yeah, I'll drop by her place in an hour or so."

"Be sure to have her call us so we know everything's okay. And hey, the transplant thing's pretty neat." Sloane's eyes smiled, making something warm pass through his chest. He nodded and made his way outside, itching to run for miles. He couldn't decide who frustrated him more—Benjamin for making his crew hate their jobs, himself for being in the dark about Ann's mystery man and his gut-level response to Sloane, and John, for making him care about it all in the first place.

THREE

Sloane continued to look at the back door for several moments after Zack's departure, not sure what to think. Tori wrestled a box off a dolly and drew a box cutter across the packing tape. "Quite the eye candy, eh?"

Sloane rubbed her hands on her forearms. "Silky black hair, stormy green eyes, and five o'clock shadow. Tall, built, and moody. In a word? Yummy."

Tori smirked. "Yeah, he seems like the whole package. Besides being gorgeous and obviously altruistic, he's successful. Samuel's Construction is one of the largest contractors in the upper Midwest. Ann's father could have had any number of front runners take over the business, but Zack's been the man running the show these last few years even before John died. Weird thing is, Ann says women fawn all over him, but he doesn't even seem to notice. I bet he's gay."

"He's not gay."

"I have several male friends who you'd never think—"

"So do I. The hetero vibe was in full force, Tori. Your loss if you missed it."

Tori paused in the act of lifting an ivory reproduction of *Nymph and Satyr Carousing*. "We've been friends for fifteen years, and I've never seen you so instantly gaga over a guy." She pointed the carved model at Sloane. "I'd hate to see you disappointed if he's not in your market."

Sloane eased the satyr out of her manager's grasp. *Definitely time to change the topic.* "Speaking of men, when will Teddy be in town? You guys have been dating for a month now, and I still haven't met him. You're making him up, aren't you?"

She relaxed when Tori took the bait and launched into a diatribe about her busy, out of town boyfriend. Sloane set *Nymph and Satyr* on a velvet-covered pedestal and drifted from box to box, unloading freight, barely noticing the beautiful objects that normally gave her so much pleasure.

Truth, she was unnerved by her response to Zack Goldman. Sure, the man was a looker and—wow, obviously unselfish—but even more than that...

He'd sent her energy. And she hadn't even touched anything metallic. Her nerve endings were still sparking like they were having an orgy. That unexpected encounter of his energy was all...*beach heat, rolling waves, and oil-slicked bodies sliding together in a dim cabana.*

It had felt delicious.

Carnal.

That unsettled her more than anything.

She couldn't remember the last time she'd physically touched someone who didn't require her to envision her energy shield—that unfortunate but necessary layer of protection that prevented people from short-circuiting her equanimity. No one could see it, but Lordy, she could feel it. Especially if she was too late to initiate her shield.

So what the heck had happened with Zack? That encounter left her...*hungry.* And wasn't that interesting?

Crap. What was she thinking? He was one apple she wasn't biting. If he'd instigated that kind of reaction in her, she couldn't—*wouldn't*—do that to him. Anyone who glided that effortlessly through her barriers always ended up burned. Her gift was largely uncontrollable.

A curse.

And a source of danger to anyone who got too close.

The cascading trickle of water in the fountain broke her reflection, and she looked up to find herself snared in one of Tori's scowls. The *I know there's something going on and I'm going to hound you until it's on the table* kind of stare that had Sloane's heart revving. Tori was one of a handful of people who knew about her object reading burden—that whacked liability her mother referred to as a "gift."

Unlike shielding herself from people's energies, which she struggled to manage, Sloane had become quite masterful at silencing this other ability. But because Tori knew what she was capable of—touching metallic objects to infer information about their history via latent energy fields—Sloane let her guard down more easily around her. Except for times like now when it made her feel...over-exposed. Because, wow, it was really creepy when you thought about it.

She forced a smile and moved to arrange a pile of pillows to give her hands something to do. "When Teddy's back in town, I'll have you guys over for supper."

Tori pursed her lips. "Knock it off. I saw you shake Zack's hand. You read something when you touched him, didn't you?"

"You know I don't like it when you bring that up."

Tori leaned forward. "I *knew* it."

Sloane's hands started to sweat. She wanted away. From this conversation. From this despicable affliction that required so much effort to ignore. She marched through the storeroom and out the back door. The August air clung heavy and damp to her skin. Did this classify as pouting?

Lord, she hated pouters.

"Sloane?"

She turned to find Tori's head peeking around the steel

12

door.

"Your lip's dragging. Pick it up and—" Tori burst into laughter. Sloane looked back at the parking lot to see her part-time employee Carmen Miller sauntering up in a straining-at-the-seams leopard print dress, wheeling an enormous purple suitcase.

"*Whew*. So hot out here I nearly left my ass on the leather car seat. Shake a leg, girlies. I wanna see the loot."

Sloane closed her eyes, breathed deep, and concentrated on the beat of her heart, using the rhythm to summon the energy required to raise her protection shield before she put an arm around Tori to follow the wide-hipped redhead inside. Carmen leaned the suitcase against the wall, grabbed a handful of Kleenexes, and stuffed them into her pillowy cleavage before opening the staff refrigerator.

Sloane gestured to the luggage. "Mind me asking what you plan to do with the mobile unit, Carm?"

Carmen rubbed a pop can against her cheek. "I'm facing reality. No way am I gonna be able to pass up a lot of this new stuff. And I don't trust Miss Salad Shooter over there to not poach my digs until I can get it all home. Hence, the carry-on."

"*Carry-on?* More like semi-truck trailer. And a fugly one at that." Tori wrinkled her nose at the beat up baggage.

"You're just sorry you didn't think of it yourself, short stuff. So where's Annie? Bet that twit's already on the floor, huh? She was happy as a hooker on sailor's payday to see what was comin' in."

Sloane took a water bottle from the fridge. "She isn't here yet. She's not answering her cell or home numbers either."

"Really? I busted my rump to get here early so she wouldn't get all the good stuff first. That girl likes to shop more than I do. I hope her big doin' last night went alright."

Sloane frowned. "What was she going to do?"

"Wouldn't say. She blushed pinker than a sunburned tittie, though, which means it had to be about a *man*."

Tori began to pace. "I don't like this."

Sloane didn't either. "Oh, stop it. I'm sure she's fine. You girls head out onto the floor and get as much unloaded as you can. I'll help as soon as I have this paperwork in order. I want the store to look less like a war zone by the time Mr. Benjamin stops in later."

Sloane plopped into her desk chair, tucked a lock of hair behind her ear, and reached for a clipboard. "Oh, and Tori? Speaking of Mr. Benjamin, can you pull the new numbered Swarovski rhino? He wants to add it to his collection, which is excellent, since he has all but committed to sponsoring Project Broken Wings. Anything at the store he wants, he gets. Okay?"

Not getting a response, she set the clipboard down and swiveled in her seat to find her manager staring at her. "Tori?"

"Oh, God."

Sloane's neck tingled. "Something happen to the rhino?"

"I, Ann, we… Ah, *crap*. Ann wanted to see how the crystal would look in her curio when it was all lit up. So, I told her you wouldn't mind if she took it out on loan, to see if it would fit in with her…other…pretty things." Tori twisted her fingers in her skirt. "But, you do mind, don't you?"

Sloane tried not to panic. Really, it wasn't a big deal. Or it wouldn't be, if so much wasn't riding on maintaining a relationship with Timothy Benjamin. She'd have to start looking for sponsors all over again if he wouldn't sponsor Project Broken Wings—the suicide support alliance that she'd dreamt of founding since her sister Megan's tragic death.

She rubbed a hand on her stomach. "So you're sure Ann has it at home?"

"Yes. I'm sorry, Sloane. I didn't know Benjamin wanted it."

"No, of course you didn't." Sloane chewed on her lip and looked at her watch. It wasn't even eight o'clock yet. Benjamin most likely wouldn't be here before the store opened at noon. Then again, it wouldn't be out of character for him to come earlier and demand a private showing.

Tori plucked at her skirt. "Call Ann. Even if she's not home, Zack said he was going to stop at her place in about an hour. By the time you grab a latte, he'll probably be there. Ann told me he has a key. You could ask to go in and have a look around."

"I'll call, but how about you go?" *Please.*

"I can't, two college summer school students are interviewing me for a class project at nine."

Dang. "Right. Okay, would you ask Carmen to go?" Sloane mentally crossed her fingers, toes, and any other body parts that were crossable.

"Naw. She hasn't seen the crystal yet. Why does it matter who goe— Oh. *Zack.*"

"Zip it. There's no 'oh, Zack.'" Sloane pretended to dig into her paperwork. After a few long seconds, Tori slipped out the door, and Sloane picked up the phone.

Four minutes later, she sat with her head in her hands. Ann still wasn't answering either number.

The day was rapidly deteriorating. Her choices? Face the beefcake who made her body remember she was a freak, or show up empty-handed to the man with the money and connections to make her dream come true. A dream that could help heal so many other families affected by suicide.

A dream that straddled the fence with a secret that would never release her.

A secret Tori didn't even know.

It had taken two years to get a bite from a sponsor. She *had* to stay in good graces with Benjamin. He would deny her the money to start her foundation if she couldn't produce the rhino. It was exactly the sort of control game he enjoyed. So she'd either have to get used to crap like that, or start all over.

Her legs felt wobbly as she stood. She grabbed her purse and walked to the back door, praying for a low-consequence encounter with Zack. And knowing somehow it wouldn't be.

FOUR

Long legs, shiny golden hair, and eyes too sexy for their own good haunted Zack until he turned the corner to Ann's block. A black Bentley that cost as much as a decent starter home dominated her driveway. A heavy weight settled in Zack's gut when he parked at the curb and noted Timothy Benjamin's startled expression as he spun away from Ann's closed front door. Zack unclenched his teeth and stepped out of the truck.

The holding company executive flashed a practiced smile. "Well, well, look who's come to call. Good to know you aren't a total recluse, Goldman, but I could've saved you the trouble had I known you were on your way. The lady's not in this morning."

"Was she expecting you?"

Something flickered in Benjamin's eyes. "Not entirely."

"What's that supposed to mean? Either she invited you, or she didn't."

"My wife is organizing a charity fashion show and asked me to help find models. Of course, I thought of Ann immediately."

"And you thought you'd drive right over to ask in person on a Sunday morning instead of calling or asking any of the next hundred times you walk into the Samuel's office? How remarkably inefficient of you, Tim."

The loose skin around Benjamin's eyes crinkled as his eyes narrowed. "And that's remarkably rude of you to say. But then, I don't really expect more out of someone like you."

Zack forced himself to relax his shoulders as Benjamin brushed by him. Thinly veiled references to the past didn't hurt

17

so much anymore. *Yeah, right.* He watched the back of Benjamin's head until the car's tail lights vanished around the block. Then Zack turned back to Ann's front door feeling his shoulder muscles ball up again—the way they always had when bad shit was about to go down.

***

Sloane slid her SUV into park in Ann's driveway and sat there for a moment, willing herself to open the door and get it over with. Zack pushed away from where he'd been leaning near Ann's front door, and started walking toward her car. Her heart gave a curious tug at the lost-little-boy look he masked before halting near her front bumper.

He waited there, one big hand scraping across his stubble, until she exited the vehicle. "What are you doing here? Did Ann call or show up at the store yet?" he asked.

"No, but one of my part-timers came in after you left and said Ann had a date last night. Do you know her boyfriend? Maybe you could give him a call." Lordy, were his eyes ever a complex mixture of greens. Saturated shades of rich color like the underside of a sunlit leaf.

Those mesmerizing eyes clouded over. "You came here to tell me she had a date last night?"

"Isn't it likely they're still together?"

His arms folded across his chest. A really, really nice chest. And...other parts. "I don't know about any date Ann may have had last night. Was there anything else you needed here?"

A spurt of heat warmed her cheeks. "Actually, yes. Ann has something from the store that I need to get back for a client. Have you been inside? To make sure she's—you know—*actually gone*?"

His eyes darkened, but a bit of his bluster dissipated. "There's nothing wrong. No sign of forced entry. No missing luggage, jewelry, art. Not even any dirty dishes in the sink to tell me the last time she ate. And her car is sitting in the damn garage."

"So she was picked up and stayed overnight with him." Sloane looked to Ann's front door, fixing on the door handle. Her vision flickered, and she staggered forward until Zack's warm hands grasped her arms, dispelling the gray haze in her mind. She blinked up at him. Subtle waves of energy poured into her where his hands made contact with her skin.

"You okay?" His speech wrapped around her, warm and comforting. The sudden change in his attitude was almost as disconcerting as the psychic jolt.

Or whatever that had been.

"Yeah, I'm fine. Thanks." She stepped back as far as good manners allowed and rubbed her upper arms. "Mind if I go inside to get what I need for the store? It's a Limited Edition crystal rhino, about *yea-big*."

"How'd you know I'd even be here?" he asked.

"I didn't, but I hoped if Ann wasn't, you might be." He didn't respond, and heat crept up her neck. "Look, I really need to get that rhino back. At the store, you said you were coming here after your meeting, and I took you at your word. You have a problem with that?"

He didn't say anything for a long while, but took her measure with those gorgeous eyes. Then he blinked, and she could breathe again.

Until he shoved his hands in his front pockets. *Oh*, but the man was well-made.

"My word's good. But what's this really about?" he asked.

"What is your problem? I just told you—"

"Lies are for cowards."

Her breath seized at his quiet words. If he only knew how many lies she'd had to tell over the years to protect her—

Sssecretsss.

She glanced to the side, looking for the source of the echoing sound, then back at Zack, but he didn't seem to have heard it. She clasped her icy hands and faced Ann's front door. Her peripheral vision glimmered. A rolling tightness crept from her stomach toward her esophagus. *Oh, Lord, something's really wrong here.*

And Zack was watching her. *Think about Ann. Ask a few helpful questions, then you can leave in good conscience.* "Is there anyone else you can call? Any other family or friends she could possibly be with?"

He looked down at his scuffed work boots. "No. I'm not blood, but I'm all she's got."

One of his elbows brushed her shoulder when he raked a hand through his hair, turned, and started up Ann's walkway. A blast of negative energy radiated off him, leaving her nerves vibrating in awareness. That kind of damaging aura from anyone else required use of her psychic energy shield. Why not from him? Her nausea had abated as well. "What did you just do?" she asked, trailing after him.

"What?" He halted on the walkway arranged with brimming petunia pots, his hair sticking out at all angles from hand-worrying it.

Her heart slugged away at her chest like it had in high school when she got those sideways glimpses from the teachers. "Nothing. I, uh, I'm gonna head back to the store now. I'm sure Ann's fine."

But Zack's glower told her he didn't believe it either. Which left them where? Mother had always told her ignoring her gut was equivalent to playing Russian roulette with only one empty chamber. But that didn't make her any less determined to ignore the compulsion telling her to walk up to Ann's front door and hold on for the ride.

Crap, crap, crap.

A woman moseyed down the walkway from the condo next door, making poor pretense of waiting for her tiny fur ball to pee while she angled her ear their direction. Zack moved closer to whisper. "If you see Ann first, have her call me."

She'd never seen such expressive eyes in her life. Right now they were so earnest. What would it be like to have a man that concerned for your welfare? *Why couldn't you affect me differently?*

He seemed to storm her defenses without even trying, so he *had* to be off limits. Just the thought of hurting someone again...

Suddenly his eyes crinkled at the corners and the color lightened to that sparkling green once more. They were saying something entirely different now. Butterflies began a mass migration from the pit of her belly to her chest.

He cleared his throat.

Right. Her turn to speak. "Call you. Sure thing. Bye now." She turned to walk back to her SUV.

"What about the rhino?" he called.

She stopped mid-stride. *Lord, thunder, and Jesus.* She hadn't made such a dolt of herself in front of a guy since the tenth grade when she'd tripped on her prom dress and landed in the punch bowl. She'd sworn off high heels for the most part since then. Besides, towering over your dates didn't do much for their egos.

But when she turned around to face Zack, she realized this wouldn't be a problem with him. Standing in her wear-once-in-a-blue-moon three inch espadrilles, she matched up mouth to mouth with him. Her eyes dropped lower. From the contours of his black T-shirt, she discerned powerful shoulders and a solid chest that made her fingers itch.

Yummy.

A dog yipped. She jumped like a teenager caught in the backseat, and Zack's grin stopped her heart for a split second. Then he turned, running to catch up to the neighbor lady with the stupid pooch.

Sloane brought her hands to her hot cheeks and watched his spectacular ass jog across the lawn. Ms. Pink Polyester tugged the leash, nearly air walking the dog in her hurry to return inside. Sloane looked at her SUV longingly, but she had to retrieve the rhino first, deal with Benjamin second, and hopefully somewhere down the line launch Project Broken Wings.

Maybe in the process of helping others, she could mend herself, too.

She cut across the lawns to catch up. She'd ask his permission to go inside, get the rhino, then split.

"Excuse me, ma'am. Mrs. Bailey, right? I remember your excellent oatmeal cookies from when I helped Ann move in. I'm Zack Goldman."

The woman stopped abruptly and the dog rammed its nose into her calf. Her faded blue eyes beamed. "Why, thank you. You can call me Agnes."

While Zack and Agnes talked, Sloane couldn't help looking at Ann's portico again. All the cheerful flower pots couldn't dispel the unease emanating from the house. Particularly the door.

Leave now.

Oh, she wanted to, but without Benjamin's backing, she'd

have to put the foundation on hold. Find another sponsor. There *was* one other possible benefactor, but he didn't have nearly the resources Benjamin did.

She rubbed her forehead. She'd finally been able to put the past behind her and had been making all the right choices. Because her store was her passion, her employees were more than overhead. She hired deliberately, carefully, and made an effort to really get to know her people.

People first.

Problem was, this time the ideology seemed to be calling upon her gift.

Why? She couldn't help anyone. Not like her mother who worked with the FBI. *Oh, no.* Hers was a broken gift with the power to hurt, not heal

And the closer you are to me, the more you stand to lose.

She peered at Ann's door once more, then started toward her vehicle. She'd find an excuse for Benjamin and get the rhino later because even if the door handle could tell her where Ann had been going, what would she tell Zack? *Hey Zack, Ann went to such-and-such place, and this is how I know...?*

The skin on her neck burned. Chest, too. *Please no hives this time. Almost to the car.*

There was no way she could do this. That door would have to keep its secrets. She closed her eyes as guilt and relief warred within.

"Sloane."

Startled, she thrust a hand out to steady herself, touching the metal door handle of Zack's truck. In an instant, her peripheral vision grayed, and she was sucked into another dimension. She tried to hold on to reality, imagining a bright pulse of light rapidly enveloping her body like a white blood cell encasing a virus.

But it was too late. Contact with the door had been made before she could seal the protection shield.

A tsunami roared in her ears. She experienced the blow of residual emotion first. Frustration, anger, and anxiety slammed into her system, forming a tight knot in her belly. Then images rolled through her mind, one after the other so fast she felt nauseous.

A well-muscled man in a suit. Sandy blond hair. Attractive. He speaks to Zack: You can handle this. *He has such a nice inflection.*

Zack strides past the man and enters a well-appointed conference room with floor to ceiling windows. Two men in sport coats rise and extend soft hands. Zack's disgust tastes like acid in her mouth. Their conversation swirls through her head, making her so dizzy she can't keep up with Zack's cascade of emotion.

Disappointment. Shame. Guilt.

She hears his thoughts. Who left the note? Why? Where, Ann? Where can you be?

Her soul wants to bleed at the pain in his tone.

"Sloane."

The bright afternoon sunlight punched through the vision. She swayed, heard a moan, and then her stomach heaved, emptying until there was nothing left. Spent, she was on her hands and knees. Something firm braced her ribcage below her breasts. Holding her up. *Zack.*

Oh, Lord. She'd just puked. In. Front. Of. Him.

She tried to stand.

"Easy." Zack's husky drawl stirred the hair by her ear, sending goose bumps on a painful relay across her arms. Her skin, already so sensitized by the vision, tingled at the touch of the hard male curved around her.

"Fine! I'm fine. Can you...I need to sit down." When he swung her up into his arms, her heart galloped, and her stomach quavered all over again. She wanted to cry. And Sloane Petra Swift didn't do crying in front of an audience.

"Just put me down! On the ground. Please. In the grass. I want to sit in the grass. Now!"

Her voice cracked on the last word. Zack eased her down beside the rampant red blooms of a weigela bush. She wiped at her mouth and thrust her fingers into the grass until her nails found rich soil. She closed her eyes to imagine a pathway traveling from the center of her body through her fingertip connection to the earth. The sudden discharge of energy made her weak.

She'd avoided this shit for six years. Envisioning the aftermath of a girl's murder as she had would probably make anyone averse. Sure, the results of this vision weren't nearly as horrific, but what good had come of it?

Zero, zilch, zippo. Only a raging headache. And don't forget about the heaping dose of mortification. You knew it was a pointless "gift." Now knock it off.

A large shadow fell across her lap. She didn't have to look up to wonder what he was probably thinking. Weirdo came to mind. How about freak? That had been a crowd favorite during her hellish puberty years.

Agnes hurried over to them, water sloshing over the sides of a glass. She thrust it at Sloane, then pressed her hands to her chest, her breathing so labored Sloane wondered who needed the water more.

Zack extended a hand to help Sloane up, his eyes questioning as his hand curled around hers. Once on her feet, she walked to her vehicle to wet-wipe her hands, swill some water, and swallow half a dozen breath mints. She returned to the site of her gutting and poured what remained of her water bottle onto the sloped pavement.

Sucked to have someone you wanted to impress witness your humiliation. Sucked worse when that same someone pulled you through it.

And wasn't it petty to be pissed about that?

She watched the pair talking on the grass between the two condos when suddenly Agnes pointed at the logo on his tinted truck window. Her words carried all the way over to Ann's driveway. "Oh would you look at that! Samuel's Construction. No wonder Ann's name always niggled at the back of my brain. John was her father, wasn't he?"

Sloane plucked up her courage and headed their way. Agnes was on a roll now. "That Johnny Samuel was quite the catch in his day. Didn't he court that high fallutin' belladonna who was a visiting professor at North Dakota State? Sang opera or something. I met her once at a banquet. Prissy as all get-out. He never did marry her, though. Wait! Ann...was she?" Agnes blinked, then smiled, nodding and posturing like a rooster in a henhouse. "*Ah.* John and the opera diva ate supper before they said grace. Happens to the best of 'em. But, don't you worry, the family secret is safe with me."

Sloane snorted. *And safe with her bridge club, and her knitting cronies and...*

Zack elbowed Sloane. "Listen, Mrs. Bailey, have you spoken with Ann today?"

"I haven't seen her since yesterday. I saw her looking out her front window when my son picked me up. It was right when that storm was rolling in."

"So, that would have been about six-thirty. Did you see her again when you got home?"

"No. She wasn't home. I noticed right away that only the

26

front door light was on. She usually has them *all* on. And I mean every last light. Real wasteful-like, you know." Agnes sniffed, and Sloane felt Zack go very still.

"Do you remember what time you got home?" he asked.

"Maybe around ten. What's this about, anyway?"

"I'm just taking care of a few things for Ann. I appreciate your time," he said.

After Agnes returned inside, Zack stepped away from Sloane. "I'm sure Ann'll show up soon."

She wondered if he was reassuring her or himself. "No you're not."

He jammed his hands in his pockets in a gesture she was coming to realize he used when he was disconcerted. "It's a good thing you own your own business because you're not only bossy, but nosy as well."

They observed each other for a few moments. Important moments. See-under-the-skin moments. *People often attack when they feel most vulnerable.* Funny how so many of her mother's words were coming back to her today.

He apologized, and though his jaw was still set, his eyes had softened. "I'm used to working alone."

"Working alone isn't always good for a person."

He arched a brow. "Oh, I don't know. Beats getting tangled up in other people's BS."

"That's not only a lousy attitude, but one guaranteed to make you lonely."

"Probably." The warmth seeped from his eyes, leaving her strangely sad.

He turned toward Ann's front door. "If you want to take a look around for that rhino, now's your chance." They had started up the walkway when a thud and shattering glass rang out from the garage.

FIVE

Damn cat. Zack wondered how he could have forgotten about Ann's scrawny tom. He and Sloane had entered Ann's front door that he'd left unlocked and hurried through her massive kitchen into the garage to find the trash can upended with colored glass, white plastic, and a mish-mash of garbage strewn across the concrete floor. The cat perched on the lone intact bag, staring at Sloane. When Zack shooed him away to chuck the bag in the can, the tomcat ambled toward Sloane to rub against her golden legs.

"Naughty kitty, look how dirty you are. Ann's going to scold you for sure." She scratched his head as his motor sawed.

Zack forced his gaze away from Sloane's legs. "He doesn't belong to her."

"Why's he here then?"

"How should I know? When I broke in earlier, he was just here."

Sloane's hand paused on the cat's back. "*Broke* in? I thought you had a key."

"I didn't stop home to get it." Which was dumb because he needed to let his dogs out pretty soon.

She frowned. "Oh, look, the poor thing only has two claws in his right front paw."

"No wonder he's so scrawny. Can't hunt."

She raised an eyebrow. "This is a real drawback if he's an outside cat and can't properly defend himself." She continued petting the cat. "So, when was the last time you spoke with

Ann?"

"Last night after the storm. Around seven-thirty." Had she left with her date after that? Maybe that was who'd left the note on his door this morning. He could take that note to the cops, but what could they do when there was no evidence of foul play?

Sloane came over, standing close enough that he got a whiff of vanilla. He wondered where she applied it—in the valley between her breasts, a spritz across her neck, lathered into her hair? She had really pretty hair. So silky and shiny a man could probably run his fingers through it without snagging on any calluses.

She bent over the garbage on the garage floor, searching for who knew what, but careful not to touch anything. He made himself look away. "This isn't your problem, you know."

"You want me to leave?" she asked.

Why couldn't he say yes? He didn't want another female to worry about, and he certainly didn't want any extra complications. The deeper you let someone in, the more opportunity they'd have to deceive you. He managed a slight nod. From the corner of his eye he saw her stand and place her hands on her hips.

"You want to be alone then?"

"I can take care of this myself," he replied.

"Lose the attitude. I'm concerned about her, too."

How was he going to make her leave? He kicked at a piece of broken glass. "Ann was upset when I talked to her on the phone last night."

"Something you did?"

Her tone was neutral. His shoulders unwound. "No. She didn't talk about it, and I didn't ask."

"Then how do you know she was upset?"

He thought about it for a moment. "She had that stuffy-nose, bright-voice combo that doesn't fool anyone, but everyone plays along because aren't we all so proud to be stoic? You know how it is."

She nodded, but didn't say anything. He'd learned a long time ago never to take things at face value. What someone presents on the outside generally provides no indication of the subtext buried within.

When Ann had returned his call, she'd assured him everything was all right, so he'd taken the easy way out and didn't press. Now, he wished he would've done what was right.

Driven over to her place and found out what had made her cry.

Gotta be present to mine the subtext.

Birds chirped outside. They sounded so content. A long-ago memory of black plastic-covered basement windows chased the warmth from his hands. He looked back at Sloane, wishing she would just go. She was making him think.

And he was better off not thinking.

Or feeling. *Dammit.*

"We'll figure this out," she said.

Her soft murmur punched a hole in his gut. "Why do you care anyway?"

He saw an intriguing spark of irritation come and go in her eyes. "Because Ann's more than an employee, she's a friend." She watched the cat crash his wiry body into her shins. "And maybe because I get the feeling there aren't too many others you reach out to."

"You think I'm reaching out to you?" If she only knew how much, she'd be as surprised as he was.

"Totally. Whether you realize it or not." She looked around. "Okay, I'm going to look for the rhino, then let's review what we know about Ann." Without waiting for a response, she turned and walked through the garage door into the house.

He followed and waited in the kitchen, listening to her poke around until the silence indicated she'd moved on to another room.

He'd hurt her feelings. But when most women would've either flipped the bitch switch or subsided into an all-out pout, she hit back with a good dose of reason that made a man tuck his tail between his legs.

The more sides of this woman he saw, the more he was charmed. And that kind of landmine he *didn't* want.

"Zack."

He hurried into Ann's bedroom where Sloane stood holding a photograph, her face as gray as a corpse's. "What's wrong?"

"What's that on Ann's sweater?"

Her whisper raised the hair on the back of his neck. He looked at her for a moment before glancing at the picture of Ann, John, and himself. "The pin? John had it custom made with nineteen tiny crystals for her nineteenth birthday last year."

Sloane visibly swallowed. "So there's probably only one like it?"

"Yeah. John always said Ann was one of a kind, so her jewelry should be, too. What's going on?"

"Probably nothing. I thought...wondered if maybe I'd seen it somewhere before." She chewed on her lower lip and set the frame back on the nightstand with trembling hands.

"If you know something about Ann, you'd better tell me now." The old fashioned wind-up clock on Ann's nightstand ticked off at least half a minute in the quiet room.

"Tori—my manager—found *that brooch* at the store under a display table. We thought a customer had lost it, so we kept it at the store for weeks. When no one claimed it, I finally brought it home." She swung toward him, her eyes a gunmetal gray. "Why didn't Ann tell me it was hers? It was lying in plain sight in the stock room."

The uptick in her voice made his pulse climb. "You know something." She moved to the bedroom door. He realized he wanted her to stay as much as he wanted her to leave. "Out with it. Don't be a coward, Sloane."

She stopped in her tracks. He rubbed a hand on the back of his neck. Twenty bucks said she'd start crying any minute. He looked around the room for something to distract her, something else to say, but came up with nothing. He'd always sucked at words. His gut all but ordered him to pull her into his arms and soothe her fear—because she was afraid of something—but he'd kick his own ass before he pulled a stupid move like that.

Which left no safe options, so he stared at her bent head. When she moved gracefully back to the bedroom's French doors to peer outside, he felt like Neanderthal man trying to understand modern Homo sapiens.

Coarse. Bush-league.

Still, he couldn't stand seeing her so upset. There was just something about her that made him want to *act*. Hold her hand. Slay her demons.

Something about her told him she deserved that. Big hearts always had a way of showing themselves. She wouldn't be here otherwise.

He rubbed his chest and made himself look away from where she stood by the door, because this was all getting a little too close. *Remember what Kasey did.*

He'd trusted her, and she'd lured him into the lion's den.

Needing some outlet for his restlessness, he left the room.

Soon he returned with the tomcat in a football hold and walked to stand beside Sloane. As soon as he transferred the tom into her arms, the cat's motor fired. She brought him up to her neck for a snuggle, grungy as he was. Then she glanced at Zack and back out the French doors. "I sometimes have these...uh, dreams?" She cleared her throat. "Dreams about things I really shouldn't know about."

"Dreams. Like when you're asleep?"

"No."

"You dream awake?"

"Not exactly," she said.

"Daydreams."

"No."

"Fantasies?"

She massaged her forehead. "No."

"Delusions."

"Oh, for heaven sakes, no!"

"Dreams that aren't night dreams, daydreams, fantasies, or delusions. Help me out here, Sloane."

"Oh!" She swung toward him, tears on the verge of spilling over. She swiped at them with one hand, looking at the wetness on her fingers like it was offensive. *"Shit."*

His lips curled upward in spite of himself. "My sentiments exactly."

She closed her eyes. "Okay." She gathered a deep breath, and Zack had second thoughts about hearing what she seemed ready to confess.

"That brooch on Ann's sweater? Two nights ago I dreamt about it. In the dream, I heard someone say, *'Help her. She's in trouble.'* At the time, I didn't know who the voice was talking about. Now..." She looked at the floor.

What? He wanted to laugh. "That's crazy."

33

Her head whipped up, her eyes darkening to nearly black. A sliver of energy ran down the length of his spine. Creepy, but exciting in a fucked up sort of way. Maybe she was part of that new group the Fargo PD had their eye on. Some weird cult activity was attracting notice a few miles south of his place. He made a mental note to keep his dogs inside at night from now on. They'd love that. He smiled.

It seemed to piss her off more.

"You don't want to believe me, that's your problem. But know this, Goldman. In all my life, my visions have never been wrong."

"*Visions?* Now you're calling this...this dream-business...a vision?" Nothing in all his soul-sucking years of living on the streets could have prepared him for this. She was talking about some kind of ESP. It was so farfetched he had trouble even imagining it. What did he say to *that* without offending her?

"Zack, when I touched your truck door handle, I saw a beefy, blond man in a navy pin-stripe suit encourage you before you stormed into a floor-to-ceiling windowed conference room. There were two older men in sport coats—one gray in tweed, the other in beige. I felt your contempt for them. Those were the most recent memories of the person who last touched the door handle, which I'm assuming was you. Now you tell me, how accurate are my visions?"

What the hell? How perfectly accurate, indeed? No way could she know those details. And if she was spot-on about his earlier meeting with Benjamin's subordinates, that meant there was either some logical explanation for how she knew...

Or, Ann was in a scrape.

"*WHERE IS SHE?*" the note had said. Good goddamn question. "Well...*huh.*"

The fight went out of Sloane so fast her shoulders slumped

and her eyes fluttered shut. When she finally opened her eyes, they were that intriguing gray-brown again, though more brown than gray this time, like felled tree trunks, long forgotten on the forest floor. The knots loosened in his gut in spite of his growing anxiety about Ann.

"Thank you." She resumed petting the cat, blinking rapidly as though trying to hold back some big emotion.

His heart kicked. "For?"

"For believing me," she whispered.

He nodded vaguely, but did he? It simply wasn't logical. Yet, there was no other way she could know about his meeting at the office unless she'd talked to Ross. But his CFO had never mentioned her. Then again, Ross wasn't known for gossip.

He watched Sloane pet the cat. She seemed so unsettled—scared even—of revealing herself to him. No surprise there, though. An ability like that would pretty much ostracize you from the rest of society. But did that mean he really believed her? He'd have to proceed carefully here. "Ann can't be in trouble. She would've told me."

"You really want me to believe you're her confidante? Based on things Ann has mentioned at the store, Tori doesn't think you two are exactly BFFs."

Direct hit. He felt the blow rattle him from the inside out. The worst part was that someone else—someone who was making him feel things, *dangerous things*, he hadn't felt in a long time—had finally verbalized his failure to carry out his duty to John's daughter.

It was time to stop being so selfish. There was a baby in the equation now, too.

He swallowed past the lump in his throat. "In your...vision? How did it end? Did it tell you anything about who or where..." God, this conversation couldn't possibly be about Ann.

"No, I'm sorry."

He made a sound of frustration, then turned to walk to the kitchen. Sloane murmured to the tomcat and followed him. He could feel her even though she wasn't touching him. Was that part of her "ability"? She must radiate low-level energy or something. Couldn't have been easy growing up knowing you were different like that.

Man, he was probably imagining all this kooky stuff. Energy and fucking ESP. *How?* The question rolled around in his mind as he rifled through Ann's cabinets until he found some instant coffee and mugs. When the water was hot, he stirred in the coffee and handed the cup to Sloane. "Look, I've never met someone before who has...powers like yours." She winced, but he had to know. "Can you...I don't know...hear other people's thoughts?"

"Oh my God, no!"

Well, that's a hell of a relief. "But you can touch something and know its back story."

"I..." She looked ready to bolt. Her gaze kept wandering to the front door.

"Tell me."

When her eyes met his, they were luminous. "Yes."

"Yes?"

"It's called psychometry. Every object has a soul that retains a memory of sorts. If I try, I can usually...read the most evocative impressions of an object's history. Especially if the object is metal, and only when it has received strong emotion. But I *don't*. I can usually control it now that I'm older. It's not who I am. I...I *hate it*. It has never, *ever,* served a useful or happy p-purpose. It's only brought...pain."

Her chest was heaving, tears were spilling, and, man, how he wished he'd never asked her. Besides his employees, he made it a point to never ask personal questions. But with this woman, he couldn't seem to stop.

"I'm s-so sorry. I'm not usually this emo-emotional."

Dark rose stained those striking cheekbones. Her gift obviously terrified her. But then, who the hell wouldn't be afraid?

Don't you dare touch her. He retrieved a box of tissues from the bathroom and handed it to her. "What else can you do?"

"You don't think that's freaky enough?" She blew her nose like a circus clown.

He couldn't help but smile. "You're not very scary. Can you dial up your powers to find someone?"

She looked at him like he was crazy. Which was hilarious, really. This whole thing had to be a dream. Maybe he'd eaten some bad fish yesterday. In a while he'd wake up, go to work, and see Ann at the front desk as always.

"No. I can't...what I mean is...I can't call it up whenever I want. A vision, that is. They sometimes come to me when I'm over-tired and stressed. When I'm too exhausted to keep my protection shield at full strength." By the end she was whispering, and he had no idea what she was talking about.

"Protection shield," he repeated.

She nodded at the floor.

"As in some invisible energy field that wraps around you to, what? Keep bad things away?"

She nodded again.

"So you have object reading abilities if the object receives strong emotions by the person who touches it, but you have visions only sometimes? Like they're involuntary?"

She hesitated. "Ye-ah."

She couldn't meet his eyes. She was either snowing him or flat out petrified. He didn't like either possibility.

Time to go for broke.

"Someone—I don't know who—left a note on my door this morning." He pulled it out of his pocket, held it up, and watched her carefully. Sloane fussed with a canister on the countertop. All the beautiful color she'd had on her face leached to white.

"Something's going on here, and it's not good. This isn't metal, but can you somehow help me find Ann?"

Her mouth worked for a moment. "I'd rather not."

He scrubbed a hand behind his neck, not sure if he was ready to laugh himself into the loony bin for overreacting to Ann being uncommunicative for less than twenty-four hours, or pound the wall in frustration over a dogging intuition that she was really in trouble.

But he was alive today because of his gut.

He looked at Sloane, his mind choosing words his mouth refused to form. To tell her to go. That she was full of shit, and he didn't believe her. Couldn't believe her.

Could he?

Yet...how far was intuition from ESP when you got right down to it?

"Please help me find Ann."

"You don't understand. I *can't*. This could...*hurt you*." Her words ended on a whisper.

"Tell me how?"

"You just have to trust me on this."

That was the worst thing she could have said. Zack knew all about people who encouraged others to trust them. They were the most betraying bastards on the planet.

They regarded each other in Ann's kitchen. Suddenly, a loud crack sounded from the condo wall expanding in the heat of the sun. Sloane flinched violently. Zack's pulse picked up.

He saw the instant she made her decision.

"I'm sorry!" She snagged a dish towel off the counter and sprinted to the front door like the place was ablaze. She wrapped the towel over her hand, reached toward the door handle...

And went to her knees.

SIX

"No, no, no, no, no!"

The words had come out of Sloane's mouth, but they seemed so far away. Reality was slipping. Icy pressure began to scrape and claw at her skull. The landscape in her mind grayed. She turned in a circle, looking, straining into the smoky palette. Where was she?

A chill wind teased her hair and picked up detritus as it moved beyond her, swirling, congealing to form a single tornado. Then two of them, three, and she lost count. Twirling, mesmerizing, a curtain of tornadoes as far as she could see, fading, fading into gray.

She looked up and her head swam. More gray. An endless ocean of it. She put her head between her legs so the dizziness would ease. *Oh, sick. Don't wanna be sick again.*

The whirling winds stopped. The curtain parted. And she whimpered at the view of a brown-haired girl's broken body, her blood a crimson rug beneath her in a pristine bed of snow. The girl swiveled her head until she was staring at Sloane with bulging, bloodied eyes. She lifted swollen, rope-burned arms and in a low, hollow sound keened a song of torment.

Hickory dickory dock,
Her blood is on the rock.
The clock struck one,
The girl came down.
Hickory dickory dock.

The girl's unearthly voice, childlike in pitch, but empty,

empty, empty, echoing with a sea of sadness, tore into Sloane. She rocked on her knees, trying to block the noise with her hands, but the sound was coming from within.

A shadow coiled up in the midst of the grizzly vision, a new soundless tornado sweeping up the snow, defiling it, and then expelling it over the mangled body in a blanket of darkness. The swirling winds swallowed the gruesome scene, creating a new murky backdrop for what was to come.

Sloane panted on her knees in Ann's foyer, reaching out with her hand until the gray swallowed her arm up to her elbow. She blinked back sweat as it rolled into her eyes. Maybe she'd start laughing now and never stop.

Sloane, come back.

Through the disorder of her mind, she heard it. A deep rumbling like thunder after a lightning bolt, spearing light into the shadows. She extended her hand in front of her, wiggling her fingers. The gray had eased back. She whipped her head around, honing in on a chink of light through the gloom. Slowly, as though dragging her arm through quicksand, her hand strained toward that light. She braced for a new nightmare and—

Touched the sun.

Heat settled in her bones, unclamped her muscles, and traveled in fiery waves through each sinew, cell, and capillary until the warmth scorched away every last trace of darkness inside her. She was weightless, adrift on a current of positive, white energy. It had never been like this. She'd stay here forever.

Dammit, Sloane, get back here!

God. *It has to be God.* Only God could swear in a voice like that. His bass timbre vibrated along the white currents, slid into her body, and pushed roots into her very soul, filling her with a peace like she'd never known. Warm bands came around her, gathering her to the source of the light, and oh, surely this was Heaven. She pressed nearer that heat, wanting to simply be absorbed into the warmth, but—

The light had substance. And a heartbeat. And smelled vaguely of woods and...

Soap?

Her eyes gradually cleared, and she soon realized the heartbeat was coming from beneath her cheek, which rested on a black T-shirt, which covered a rock-hard chest.

Zack.

Her head popped up so fast it bumped into his chin. His eyes, a turbulent green, held hers for a second before he guided her head back down to rest against his chest once more. He kept his hand under the curtain of her hair, using the pad of his thumb to softly brush the side of her neck. Up and down, that warm thumb slipped across her skin. *It's okay. You're okay. Safe. I won't let anyone hurt you,* that thumb told her. His arms, too. She inhaled deeply, trying to match his steady breathing.

Lord. She was attached to him. Like literally Saran Wrapped around his body. Even her legs were scissored intimately between his. She should be mortified, but she wasn't. She felt...

Content.

She wanted to sneak a look at him again, but was afraid he'd be able to read her naked emotions. He felt so good, his chest solid and warm beneath her cheek. And he wasn't doing that awkward back pat when two people are so uncomfortable to be in each others' personal space. One arm wrapped around her waist and the other braced her back, his palm sliding across her upper shoulder and then against the nape of her neck in a motion meant to soothe.

She inhaled and took him into her lungs, her body, her mind. She wanted to stay like that for hours, to be held so tenderly, almost possessively, by someone who knew—if not understood—what she—

"Oh!" She drew back from his arms so suddenly she clipped her head against his chin again. "Sorry! Oh my gosh, do you know what just happened here?"

"You saw something bad," he said.

"A bad vision, yes, the start of one anyway, which was rolling into another one, but then— You touched me, right? When I was reaching for the door handle?"

He smoothed her eyebrow with his thumb. "How do you stand it?"

"Did you touch me or not?"

"I did."

Her mind spun as she processed this information. Was it possible that he was some sort of psychic anchor for her? She'd read about that once, but had dismissed the idea as farfetched because even her mother, renowned psychic that she was, didn't have any such thing.

Or person.

"That's never happened to me before," she said.

"And what exactly was *that*?"

"I didn't even touch the door handle, but as I got closer, a huge wave of negative energy blew through me, and as scared as I was when I was about to leave, I didn't think to put up my shield."

"So, what happened? Where the hell did you go?"

That was apt. *Yes, Hell.* Sloane-style. But she couldn't tell him that. "Uh, usually, as a vision grabs me, I'm a passive conduit, helpless to stop the flow of images until the vision ends. I can't wake myself up or push it away. I'm stuck. But just now…" She paused and looked down at the hardwood floor.

She'd never shared her failed attempt at working with law enforcement to find Abigail, a missing five-year-old, with anyone. Not even with her parents, as much as they had tried to get her to open up about it. But how do you explain something you couldn't control—something that seemed to be a Pandora's Box of tragedy?

Did the visions make bad things happen? Or would they happen whether she saw them or not?

A cause and effect question she'd wrestled with for years and still didn't know the answer to.

Better to keep it battened down. Locked away.

Just in case.

She looked at the front door, her eyes fixing on the door handle not three feet away. A new wave of fear froze her muscles. Zack squeezed her shoulder, bringing her eyes to his.

"I'm good for secrets," he whispered.

Oh Lord, she believed him. She didn't know why. She'd only met him a few hours ago, but after all he'd seen of her, he was still here. And it seemed as though he believed her, too.

But her fear was stronger than her trust.

Stop it. Here she was worried about herself when Heaven only knew where Ann was. She slowly stood, feeling a chill on her skin where he'd touched her. She watched as he unfolded his long legs and stood next to her. Then it hit her.

He'd gone to the floor with her. Taken her in his arms to comfort her. He hadn't moved, pushed her away, or acted uncomfortable with her drama.

God.

"I…I need a second." She turned toward the bathroom before he had a chance to reply, and it was all she could do not

44

to run like a four-year-old on the verge of peeing herself.

Inside, she locked the door and rested against the heavy wood for several long moments. Going to the sink, her skin came alive as the water sluiced between her fingers. She cupped her hands and drank, then methodically dried her face.

Where was this road going to lead? What was she still doing here? And where was Ann? Every supersensory cell in her body told her that wretched front door held secrets.

But could she go there? Would it give any clues as to Ann's whereabouts?

More important, could she live with herself if she did nothing to try to help?

It feels different with Zack. Somehow the experience was...buffered?

She combed at her tangled hair with her fingers and opened the bathroom door to find him standing there.

"You okay now?" The concern in his eyes made a lump settle in her throat. She tried and failed to smile.

Ann was missing, and something was definitely wrong. Plus, she couldn't find the crystal rhino, so Timothy Benjamin would probably never back her foundation—out of spite, if nothing else. And it could be months if not years before she could secure another sponsor. Add to that, she'd blown her cover with this man who had so many contacts in town. If he wanted to, he could completely discredit her. Her business could be devastated.

Worst of all, her psychic sensitivities seemed to be growing.

Total. Nightmare.

But...

But.

She could still recover from all of that as long as she kept the most important secret.

She looked at Zack and wondered what might have happened if they'd met under different circumstances.

But it wasn't to be. His concern was for Ann, whose very life—not merely her reputation, nor her career—was in the balance.

It's different with him.

Try me, his eyes seemed to say.

It wouldn't jeopardize her secret. The two situations were unrelated.

So be it.

She wrapped her arms around herself and prayed for a cast iron stomach. "I need to go back to the door."

SEVEN

Zack used the side of his index finger to bring Sloane's chin up. "We'll do this together, okay?"

His voice was a steadying caress over her skin. Locked in the profound green of his eyes, she felt—for the first time in her twenty-five years—that maybe, with him there to anchor her, she might put her psychic gift to use without such debilitating consequences.

She rubbed her arms, established her protection shield, and led the way back to Ann's foyer, where she stopped before the door. A tremor passed through her, and she started again when Zack's warm, tough palm swallowed her own.

He looked as surprised as she felt. "I won't let go, if that's what you want."

She'd blubber like a moron if she opened her mouth so she nodded, then focused on the door handle, using the golden color to build a flower in her mind. As the edges of the petals unfurled, the perimeter of her vision glittered in a million silver sprays of light, heavy with waves of negativity. She took in Zack's calm face, twined her fingers more solidly with his, and reached for the door handle with her free hand.

Darkness swept around her so suddenly she faltered. Wind slapped at her and she slipped down, whirling, spinning away into a whirlpool of stygian clouds shuddering with malevolence. The clouds were alive, pulsing with lightning, reverberating with thunder, raising goose bumps all over her body.

Zack! She scanned the darkness for his light anchor but her

47

cry boomeranged against the tornadic winds. Then she was sucked through the storm's eye into the murkiness on the other side, a ragdoll tossed in a tug of war between rogue winds.

Ssseee meee.

Heart pounding in her throat, she pushed at the hair whipping her face and looked up. Could that have been him? Where was he?

Panic bloomed in her chest. She squeezed her eyelids shut and imagined Zack's face, his eyes—the green reaching out to save her. Her heartbeat grew louder, drowning out the fury of the storm around her. She called out for him again and felt a moment of zero gravity at the wind's sudden calm.

Her breath whooshed out as she landed in a crouch in a midnight forest filled with mist, night sounds, and moving shadows. Dank earth and stagnant water clogged her nostrils with tangy scents of death and decay. She straightened as gasps and groans spilled from the shadows.

This isn't real. Not real. Sooo not real.

She saw an opening between the shadows and ran deeper into the forest. She ran, underbrush tearing at her shins and tree limbs scraping her cheeks until her legs and chest burned. *Calm down. Calm. Down.* She had to stay focused or she'd lose all control.

Sloane.

Zack's voice rolled through her—composed, centered—ripping her from the grip of hysteria so suddenly she tripped over a fallen log and slid into a dusky bower of wildflowers. She reared up, brushing leaves from her hair to squint through the darkness. She rubbed a hand over the wild beating of her heart and looked around.

There!

A tiny pinprick of light above her. But it seemed so

COME HELL OR HIGH DESIRE

hopelessly far away. She inhaled deliberately, then let the breath out slowly, each subsequent exhale murmuring Zack's name, a mantra to release the disturbing images.

Immediately, the forest floor gave way, dropping her once more into a silent void, a blackout so complete she couldn't see her hands in front of her face. She struggled to her feet, panning out with her fingers to find substance, but encountered only cobwebs that snagged in her hair, stuck on her clothes, and caught at her skin. She heard a squeak, then something cool feathered against her cheek. Her system flooded with adrenaline. She spun in a circle, alone in the eclipse.

Sloane. I'm here. Stay with me.

Panting, she looked up. The pinprick of light had become a stream of energy, pulsing white directly above her head. The vise around her chest loosened slightly, and she reached out for the light with her mind, drawing it to her. Sweat poured down her temples and between her breasts. Her arms quivered. In her head, a buzzing began.

That's it. You're doing fine.

The closer she came to the light, the louder the buzzing grew until it filled every corner of her mind, amplifying until she thought her skull would rupture. She tried to stymie the noise, squinting, focusing on the light. *No good!* The buzzing vibrated down her spinal cord and rippled across her skin like a league of beetles. Her hands raked at her skin to try to dislodge the phantom bugs and the light slipped. *No!*

She couldn't breathe. *No air!*

Come on, Sloane! Beat it!

His presence dimmed the buzzing to a low drone. Enough to gather herself for one last desperate jump. Her thigh muscles shook as she squatted, then leapt toward the light. Dozens of bony fingers grabbed at her ankles. She kicked with her legs as

49

her arms gathered the light to her body.

Suddenly, a pulse of warmth flooded her brain, flashed down her torso, and singed the demons clutching her bloody ankles. Their screams faded into oblivion along with the buzzing, leaving her momentarily dazed in the too loud silence. She felt weightless, floating on a current of heat, the light so brilliant against her eyelids she brought an arm up to shield her eyes. She counted to ten and then back to zero.

Holy.

Holy, holy, holy *crap.*

Her vision self sat up and took stock of her body. No bloody ankles, ripped shins, torn clothes, or Bride of Frankenstein hair. Not even any queasiness. Instead, a low pulse of power thrummed in her veins. More remarkably, she was in control—not of the secrets the door might ultimately reveal, but of herself. Her sanity.

That was new.

Because of Zack.

He'd pulled her through the gauntlet. The dark scary place she always had to tread to bring forth a vision. Her pulse drummed steady, nerves and excitement bringing her to her feet in the panorama of white. Zack's white light. Her heart constricted thinking of him. He hadn't left her. He'd talked to her. Kept her with him. She would thank him. So many ways she could do that.

Later.

She looked around, wondering what to do next.

Okay, Ann. Don't you dare make me come all this way for nothing.

Concentrating, she brought up an image of Ann's face. Ebony hair framing her delicate features, the upturned nose. So beautiful, so kind, so impossibly shy.

Sloane filled her mind with positive thoughts, letting her genuine affection for Ann guide whatever vision needed to come forth. Soft as a gentle rain, vocalizations began filtering through her consciousness. She squinted, trying to place the muffled sounds. The pitches sounded angry, but curiously the negativity didn't overwhelm her.

As she approached the image of Ann, her face began to waver, blurring like waves from a heat mirage until the cameo dissolved completely, leaving behind a gray-blue mist, a curtain of secrets.

This is it. Beyond that mist were the answers they needed.

Sloane braced herself, gathered light to her until it was a living thing hammering inside her, and stepped into the fog.

Echoes of anguish, fear, and desperation throbbed in the silence, push-pulling at her, yet she identified the emotions only on an intellectual level. Moving faster now, she parted the curtain of gray mist and found herself—

In Ann's foyer. In a different time.

Late in the evening, lightning putting on an awesome display through the windows. An expensive Tiffany lamp glowing in gorgeous reds, oranges, and golds on the table next to the door. A show house room, but the aura, oh so wrong. A desperate pall seemed woven into the fabric of the home. Sloane jerked when Ann's voice broke through the silence.

Please, please stay. We have to talk. The man with her is tall, movie-star handsome in an old-fashioned way. Trim and dapper. So appealing. Until Sloane looks in his eyes. They spill over with rage and disgust. Thunder shakes the walls of the house in time with his reply. *Not now.*

Sloane felt Ann's shock before the image short-circuited and immediately picked up in an explosion of pain. Sloane moaned, clutching the side of her head, the coppery taste of blood filling her mouth.

Zack!

Here. I'm here. I won't leave you.

In the vision, Ann's foyer filled with shadows and frequent pulses of lightning through the front windows. Shards of glass from the lamp lay in a hundred pieces across the hardwood floor. An upturned bowl of rose potpourri drifted pungently through the humid air. Sickeningly sweet.

Sloane panned in every direction trying to locate Ann and her attacker. *There.* Ann lay in darkness, curled on the floor, thin shoulders quaking with the strength of her sobs. Her sadness pulled at Sloane, so insistent even through Zack's anchor that she felt compelled to lie down next to her and take her into her arms.

But it was only a vision of what had been.

Ann was no longer there.

Sloane breathed through the vision, focusing all her senses on the man. He was still there, swamping the room with rancor. She waited for the next pulse of lightning, her muscles cramping with motionlessness. When she saw his face again, she would need to remember every line, every mole, every scar, so they could find him.

When electricity sliced through the air, his back was to the window, his face in shadows. A shiver rocked her frame as he spoke. *It had better be gone by the time I come back.*

He moved, the light shifted, and she saw his face. *Trim, dapper, movie-star handsome. Older than Ann.*

Then he vanished, and the vision winked out, replaced by a new picture of Ann. Time had passed. She had changed her clothes and fixed her make-up. She was composed, but at the touch of her fine-boned fingers on the door handle, Sloane registered a sorrow more profound than when she'd been a crumbled heap on the floor.

Ann said something over her shoulder Sloane couldn't hear. Then she grabbed her purse and stepped through the front door into the smothering night.

No, Ann! Please, please stay home tonight.

But of course she didn't hear.

And then the world went black. The door handle had reached the end of its memory.

EIGHT

Zack caught Sloane as she collapsed. He carried her away from the foyer into the living room where he hunkered down, filling up two thirds of Ann's sofa. He could see faint blue veins beneath Sloane's cheeks. His hands wobbled as he smoothed her hair back from her forehead. "It's okay. I've got you. You're okay."

She'd scared the ever-living hell out of him when she'd first gone into the vision. Her face had lost all animation, as if she'd up and died right in front of him.

His arms tightened around her, and she curled toward his chest. Her scent drifted over him, peeling away his last defenses. He studied the dark crescent her eyelashes formed against the upper part of her cheek. The splash of freckles, barely noticeable, on the bridge of her nose. The subtle color variations of her hair as the strands shifted when he breathed. Her smooth, soft skin, too pale, way too pale...

He forced himself to look out the front window. He was lucky she'd fallen into a light sleep because it wouldn't do to let her to see him this rattled, though she'd probably attribute it to his concern for Ann. Which would be right, but...

Something about Sloane pulled at him, dredging up feelings that unsettled him. Made him vulnerable again. And being vulnerable usually led to heartbreak.

Chill out. These restless feelings were obviously the result of this crazy-ass episode. That made a lot more sense.

ESP. What a racket. It mucked up his foundation of

possibility. More than once, he'd wanted to jerk her out of the vision, to just shut it down because he could feel it damaging her on a level he didn't understand.

But he was afraid of what might happen if he did something wrong. What if he couldn't bring her back? Could she somehow lose her way in that other realm? Never a gambling man, he'd done the only thing he was sure of and clutched her hand so tightly he feared he'd fracture her long, graceful fingers.

Then something around her had begun to change. He'd known the moment their spirits joined because he'd felt jacked in, amped up. Every hair on his body had sparked with awareness. Currents of power crackled along his nervous system, and he was hypersensitive to the rush of her blood.

On the couch, he shifted uncomfortably beneath her weight as his body remembered the sensation. Her eyelashes fluttered and her color was finally returning in that delicious golden shade he knew covered so much of her landscape.

So beautiful and brave. So full of secrets.

He forced himself to look away. This was no time to be getting hard. She'd risked her soul to find answers about Ann. The least he could do was not poke her in the hip with a steel rod. He stared at the ceiling, inhaled deeply, and wondered if he was dreaming when he felt a hand on his cheek. He glanced down and lost himself in the liquid brown of her eyes.

"You all right?" she asked.

"You're asking me? *Jesus*, Sloane."

She sat up and quickly moved off his lap to sit beside him. Her eyes glowed. "You're my psychic anchor, Zack. You grounded me through the vision. You can't imagine how big this is. I never believed it would be possible. Other than a mild headache, I don't feel sick at all. My *mother* doesn't even have anyone who can do that for her." Her eyes flickered as her fingers tunneled into her hair. "I found some answers, but not nearly enough, I'm afraid."

Her mother did this shit, too?

He said nothing, staring into her eyes, watching, marveling, at the drama of emotions shaping her features while she replayed the vision in her mind. One of her hands scraped across his thigh as it fell to the sofa and desire sparked in her eyes.

He smothered a groan. *Damn*. Her touch was tinder to his dry wood. His fingers dug into the textured linen sofa to stop himself from touching her. He closed his eyes, needing to hide, feeling desperate and completely out of his element.

She was holding her breath, he realized. They both were. *Powder kegs*. His eyes snapped open. The tip of her tongue darted out to moisten her lips, and his shoulders ached with the effort to hold still.

"Zack?" Her hesitancy calmed him enough so he could slam the door on an erotic visual of easing those teensy shorts down her endless legs. What a dick. As much as he felt like one, he wasn't an animal.

She stood up and laughed shyly. *Cute. As. Hell.*

"That was really something, huh?" She brushed her hands down her hips. An enticing little gesture. "Anchored together in a vision like that is incredibly...intimate. I've never shared one before, so I guess we're sorta bonded. A little. *Maybe*."

Bondage. She wasn't helping to ease his lust haze at all. "Oh great, vision virgins."

"Not anymore." Her laughter bubbled up again. He leaned back against the sofa and laced his fingers behind his head, resigning himself to a permanent hard-on. "So what did you see?"

She bit her lip, and he nearly lost his no-touching resolve at the quiet appeal in her eyes.

So she feels it, too.

Somehow that calmed the beast in him. A paradox, but he was grateful. He smiled at her. She blushed and paced the length of the living room, relaying the details of the vision. By the time she recounted Ann's attack and then her voluntary departure, Zack was wearing his own path in front of the picture window, emotions—different ones this time—running hot and hard through his blood.

The tomcat strolled into the room like he owned it. Sloane bent to stroke him. "So, do you have any idea who the man might be? Someone like him certainly sticks out," she said.

He wanted to pound his fist into the wall. "What type of man is savage enough to knock a woman around like that? I'll find him and kill him. A person like that's a menace to society."

She walked into his personal space. "Let's relax and make a plan, okay? Going ape-shit isn't going to help right now."

"If you think this is going ape-shit, you've led a pretty sheltered life, princess."

"Don't be a jerk, Zack."

They glared at each other until he sat down heavily on the edge of the sofa. "What did he want her to get rid of—"

Oh.

Oh, God. *The baby.* The rushing in his ears, the sick feeling in his gut, told him it *had* to be. He cursed wildly.

Her clapping hands finally got his attention. "Take it easy! Lordy, what is it?" she asked.

"The baby! He was talking about Ann's *baby,* the road kill motherf—" He spun away and pulled on his scalp so hard he was surprised he didn't come away with chunks of hair.

Her eyebrows drew together. "Baby? What baby?"

"Ann's knocked up!"

"Don't be so crass!"

He advanced on her until they were nearly nose to nose. "Fine, fine! Sorry to insult your refined sensibilities, but I'm beyond bent right now, headed full steam toward ape-shit."

"Yep."

He made a sound of disgust and walked away from her to glare out the front window. Ann was having a baby, and the sperm donor not only wanted nothing to do with it, he wanted it *gone*. The man had obviously cut her on so many levels. How could she have gotten tangled up with the likes of someone so heartless? And how could he have been so blind to it all? He turned around to see if Sloane was still there.

Only then did she speak. "I'm sorry. I wish I would have seen more. Seen what is happening *now*, instead of what already happened."

"Did she leave with him later?"

She hesitated. "I don't know. I didn't see out the doorway. I only saw her."

He wanted to start swearing again, but bit the inside of his cheek instead. "Okay, but what's your gut say? I won't hold it against you if you're wrong."

"I don't think she left with him later on."

"Why?"

"She had freshened up, but wasn't wearing any lipstick." At his confused look, she continued. "Her man wears expensive clothes, and his hands and nails look like they've never seen an honest day's work." She looked pointedly at his scraped and callused hands, and he couldn't help but appreciate her comparison. "If she's pregnant with his baby and unsure of his intentions, she's always going to try to look her best for him. That's my guess, anyway." Fear edged into her eyes. She pursed her lips and held out her hand. "Okay. Give me that stupid note."

The woman was a warrior. Truly.

He walked over to the sofa. "You're gonna sit when you do it this time." When she complied, he sat next to her, grabbed her left hand, and put the note in her right one. The minute her fingers clasped the paper, she swayed on the cushions. Zack shot up and knelt between her legs. Her eyes rolled back.

Not knowing what she was experiencing sucked. All he had to go on was her facial expressions and utterances. And that was bad enough. How could she stand it?

"Zack?"

She can talk to me this time? He curled his other hand around her fist holding the paper. "I'm here."

He could feel some of the tension drain out of her fingers. "I can...I'm starting to... I guess, *feel* myself on both sides this time. Oh, wow. Here, with you, and...he...he's writing on a small table. Coffee smells and birds. Feels like morning. Nice, groomed hands. Oh!"

He was probably bruising her, but he couldn't make himself loosen his grip. She moaned. He was ready to burn that fucking paper. Burn it and stomp on the ashes like an Aborigine with face paint and a loin cloth.

"He's tearing off duct tape and affixing the note to a door. He strikes the door with his fist and laughs." Her mouth worked silently as though trying to talk and listen at the same time, but only managing to listen. "His aura is so black. I can't see him. Only his hands. Nice hands. Ann. It's her. The note is about her."

The confirmation was a blow to the solar plexus. He dropped her hands. The note slipped, floating, twirling like a whirligig to the floor. Sloane blinked awake, then sank back against the cushions.

He shouldn't be surprised that the note was indeed about Ann.

People say the *not knowing* is harder.

Not always.

He exhaled so strongly her hair stirred. She smiled weakly, and he shook his head before going to the kitchen and returning with a glass of water. He handed it to her. After a large swallow, she set the glass down and looked at him. He couldn't read her expression, and he wasn't sure his voice wouldn't crack, so he kept silent.

"I'm sorry—so sorry—I couldn't see who it was. I'm…even more afraid for Ann and her baby. And now you. The note writer's malice is…rather overwhelming. Terrifying, actually." She shuddered. He stood, gave in to the emotion driving him, and kissed her hair as he pulled her into his arms.

Who would want to treat Ann that badly?

Or was the hatred for him? *That* he could accept a lot more readily than someone despising Ann.

He leaned back to look at Sloane. "So you saw note-man's hands. And you saw the hands of the cretin who hit Ann. Same guy?"

She pressed her fingertips against her cheekbones. Pressed them so hard her fingers left white marks when they lifted. "Maybe. They seemed very similar."

He was hoping it would be a slam dunk. But life almost never worked that way. He walked to the picture window once more. *Now what?*

"All I can say is they weren't hands like yours…"

He turned back to her. She pressed her fingers over her lips, then let them drop. "I didn't mean that in a bad way."

"I am what I am. I appreciate your efforts."

She bowed her head and didn't say anything as they walked

to the foyer and then outside. She put on a brave smile. He frowned and opened the door of her SUV. She slid into the plush interior, her vanilla scent tempting him to...what?

Ask her to stay?

But she had to go. His head was seriously messed up right now. The note. A baby. ESP. Kidnapping. The day seemed to have ripped a page from one of the thrillers Ann loved so much.

Sloane slid onto the seat. "Have you contacted the police yet? I have a connection in the Fargo PD's intelligence unit who might be able to help."

"Since it's been less than a day, the cops won't do much more than file a report unless there are suspicious circumstances. Adults can go missing if they choose. But...I'll tell them what I can." *Clearly, none of this nutty stuff.*

Her soft smile reached her eyes this time, and he felt like a hero. *Stupid.*

"Then at least we know all the bases are covered. Would you please call me when you hear anything?"

She could have told him to have Ann call her. She didn't. It pleased him. And the fact that it did, *didn't* please him. "Sure."

"The cat?"

"I'll look after the stray until she gets back," he said.

"And if you come across the crystal rhino—"

"I'll hang onto it and let you know. Sorry you didn't find it." He hit the automatic locks on her door and slowly backed away from the vehicle. She started the engine and rolled down the window.

"Well...bye then?" She didn't put the car in gear.

What more did she expect him to say? *I don't really know you, but you're amazing?* She'd think he was a head case. Yet those gray-brown eyes worked to storm his fortress. He moved toward the SUV again and brushed the back his fingers across her cheek before he could think better of it. "You okay? What happened in there..."

Her eyes grew luminous. "I need some time to think about all of it, too. I've never been able to simultaneously stand in both realities—my life and the visions. It...helps. Rather a lot. So thank you for that. Really."

He shrugged. "I'm sure it wasn't me. Maybe you're just growing into your powers or something."

She smiled slightly. "I don't think so. Anyway, I wish I could have been more help, but if anything else comes to me I can call you if you want to give me your number."

Giving her his card felt a lot more personal that it should have.

She tucked it in her purse on the passenger seat and turned back to him. "Be careful, okay?"

Her softness made him ache. He scraped his hands into his front pockets. "I have a lot more to go on than before. I'll stop by a few of the other neighbors around here. Someone else is bound to have seen something. Thanks for everything you've done." Then he backed away from her vehicle and turned toward his truck before his fool self asked her to stay.

Ann was gone and in a hell of a lot of trouble. He'd find her. *He had to.*

Behind him he heard Sloane pull out of Ann's driveway. And suddenly he felt very alone.

NINE

Blinded in the storeroom after the dazzling sunshine outside, Sloane bumped into a ladder, shattering a glass jar. Tori flew into the room, her voluminous turquoise skirts continuing to move for several seconds after she'd come to a standstill. "What the heck, boss?"

"Sorry. Bright outside, dark in here." Sloane grabbed the broom to clean up the glass. Why did she come back here, of all places? She should've gone home after her pit stop at McDonalds. She didn't want to face Tori's questions. But then, if she'd gone home, she'd probably think about the way Zack's eyes had all but stripped her bare. It made her breathless remembering the way he'd—

Tori snapped her fingers in Sloane's face. "Wake up! Benjamin's guy was here hours ago. I tried your phone like twelve times. Where've you been all this time?"

"What?" Sloane set the broom against the wall and dug in her purse for her phone. Sure enough, the sucker was dead. But that didn't make sense. "How the—" It had been fully charged when she'd left her apartment this morning. Then she remembered her mother complaining about technology sometimes acting up when she "worked."

One more 'con' to add to the whole I'm-psychic-and-I'm-pretty-sure-this-blows list.

"Sloane!"

She started, hugging her purse to her chest like she was about to be mugged. "Sorry, what did you say?"

63

"Did you get the rhino?" Tori asked.

Sloane's shoulders fell. She tossed the purse on her desk. "Couldn't find it."

"No!"

Sloane nodded. "What did you tell Benjamin?"

"It wasn't him. He sent a stick-up-the-ass assistant. I told him the rhino was in the safe, but you had a personal emergency and were the only one who knew the code."

"And?"

"His face got all blotchy and gross. He demanded that I call you to get the code. Seriously, the guy's ten pounds of shit in a five pound bag."

Sloane smiled in spite of her churning stomach. "How did it end?"

"He told me Benjamin wants the rhino by tomorrow or he's withdrawing his support for the foundation. God, I'm so sorry!"

Benjamin's ultimatum settled over her. She sank into her desk chair.

Tori spun Sloane's chair around to face her. "Maybe this is for the best. If he was Broken Wing's sponsor, he'd always have first dibs on making you miserable."

"I knew that going in, but I guess I thought it was worth it." This was exactly what she'd been afraid of. No Ann, no crystal rhino. No rhino, no sponsor. No sponsor, no foundation.

Her dream dead in the water.

She hung her head. The gray concrete floor blurred when Tori's fingers touched her shoulder. A ripple of energy flashed diagonally through her torso, scorching her hip. Tori was talking, but Sloane couldn't make sense of the words. A hazy figure rose up in her field of vision, the lower edges wavering like its legs were on fire. Blue flames tinged orange. Scents of burning hair and something else really awful polluted the air.

Melting skin? *Oh.* She was gonna be sick. The figure's arms reached for her.

No!

Contact with her shoulder was gone. She reared away from Tori, tumbling backward in the chair, banging her head on the desk. When she looked up from the floor, her eyes refocused to find Tori staring at her as if she'd sprouted horns and a tail.

"What the devil was that?" Tori knelt beside her. "Seriously. You went somewhere else when I touched you. I've never seen you do that before. Did I bring it on?"

Sloane pressed the heels of her hands to her eyes. This psychic freak show stuff seemed to go hand in hand with the tear factory. "Please, Tori. Can I— I need a moment to myself."

"Forget it, Sloane. I know you're wigging out right now, but I want to help." Her eyes looked concerned, determined. *Excited.* "Here, get up off the floor, you don't want a trip to the doctor's office to remove slivers of glass out of your badonkadonk. Now sit here." She patted the cushy zebra-print chair until Sloane obeyed, then handed her a can of Red Bull. *Extra caffeine might not be such a good idea right now.* But by the time the first sip slid down her throat, she had it a bit more together. Tori sat silently in the swivel chair across from her. Waiting.

Sloane took another drink. "Sorry. Don't know what that was all about."

"Yes you do. Tell me."

"Stop being so pushy."

"I know you've got powers. In all these years, have I ever told another soul?"

Sloane squeezed the blue and silver can. *How to explain?* "When you touched me, I saw a figure...on, well...oh, it was on fire."

65

"On fire? Like *burning?* A person?"

Sloane nodded.

Tori hesitated, blinked. "That's scary stuff. Maybe you're having a breakdown because you've been denying your gift too long."

Sloane pushed back in her chair. "That's ridiculous. I've known how to control it for years. I simply avoid situations that instigate the visions." *Which has worked quite well until a certain tall, dark, and melt-my-panties walking hunk of testosterone stormed into my world this morning.*

Goddamn.

Tori leaned forward in the chair. "Yeah? And how's that working for you? Natural impulses can only be under lock and key for so long before there are repercussions."

Sloane snorted. "There is nothing natural about this."

"You're wrong, Sloane. It's part of who you are, but you refuse to acknowledge it."

She was on the verge of contradicting Tori when Carmen poked her head around the showroom door. "Sorry to interrupt, *chicas,* but I need some help out yonder. Everyone and their gramma's shoppin' today, and one old lady with nothing but sailboat fuel between her ears won't leave me be."

"Be there in a sec." Tori looked at Sloane after Carmen returned to the floor. "I'm not usually superstitious, but I have a bad feeling about all of this. I don't know if it's any help, but Ann keeps a diary. She told me a few weeks ago when I was whining about Teddy."

"Why would she tell you that?"

"She said it was cathartic to write about things you can't tell anyone else. I thought it was sad at the time. She obviously doesn't have any of the if-you're-in-jail-I'm-in-jail type of friends. I didn't say much at the time because I thought maybe we'd become that for her."

A diary? When would she ever find the time to write in it? Maybe she should tell Zack. Maybe they should go back to the condo to look for it.

No. No way. I've fulfilled my obligations. Zack said so himself.

"...and I think your instincts are telling you to be careful, too. Maybe your mom's gone through something like this. You know, when she was your age? Maybe if you talked to her—"

"*Whoa.* Don't even go there. Mom's got the talent to go with the gift. I *don't*. Besides, this is about Ann. Not Zack, and certainly not me." Sloane stood and walked to the mess at her desk where she shuffled a bunch of papers without really seeing them. "Thanks for telling me about the diary. And for your concern. Be sure to let me know if you guys need help. I'll be around till we close." *Figuring out how to plug the holes in my dream.*

She sensed Tori's eyes boring into her back for another moment before the door shut on a soft swish. She collapsed into the chair and dropped her head in her hands.

She was under attack. In the last twenty-four hours she'd experienced more psychic energy than she'd allowed herself in the last six years. Add to that the fact that Benjamin had surely already dropped her like third period French. He'd probably bad-mouth her all over town, too.

Horrors all around.

She should call Benjamin. But what could she say? There was no rhino in her safe.

She caught herself chewing a fingernail, staring blindly at an invoice on the desk. Instead of seeing numbers, she imagined intense green eyes so old with their secrets. What kind of life had Zack led? There was an edge under his practiced nonchalance.

Or was it hurt? Vulnerability disguised by a moody, bad boy veneer. Even without the organ donor thing in the mix, he was one honey of a package. He had a quiet core of strength, a straightforwardness, and down-in-the-trenches humble nature that made you feel like he wouldn't abandon you in stormy weather. And he certainly hadn't. He'd stuck by her through multiple visions when most people would've probably run the other way or else called the psych ward of one of the local hospitals.

She imagined the men who worked at Samuel's respected him. That they gave him their best, along with all their life stories—kids and anniversaries and family dramas. He seemed to draw secrets and personal history from you without even trying.

Even as he, himself, remained a mystery. Because he sure as heck didn't volunteer much about himself. It was another log on her Zack Goldman fire. *Fire.* Maybe that's where that vision had originated. But why? What did it mean?

She walked to the bathroom, brushed her teeth, then gathered her hair into a ponytail. Looking for something to tie it with, she spotted the gauzy blue scarf Zack had wound around his hands this morning. She picked it up, the transparent material sending echoes of his scraped, rugged fingers like whispers across her skin.

Her heart beat uncomfortably faster until she reached for her beat-up cadet hat with the large pink dragonfly. Hats just like it had been among her first purchases for the store, and had become a staple of the boutique since. She put it on and felt more in control. *Smoke and mirrors.*

Well, yeah, but right now she'd take what she could get.

Over the plain white sink of her utilitarian office bathroom, she regarded the gray-brown eyes she'd hated since middle school and told herself that she had nothing more to offer Zack in his search for Ann. She'd tried, but had only come up with more questions.

That was it, then. She'd have to steer clear of emotional attachments to the combustible material that was Zack Goldman.

But damned if he wasn't a fire she hated to put out.

TEN

Twyla Raessler opened the door to the home she shared with her husband, Archie, and smiled at Zack unreservedly. He returned her hug, careful of the growing bump at her waist, and noted the increased pallor of her complexion.

"Where you been so long, sweetheart?" She grabbed his hand to pull him inside, and moments later a powerfully built man roamed into the foyer. His knuckles caressed Twyla's cheek before he shifted his attention to Zack.

"Goldman." Archie Raessler and Zack exchanged a quick handshake and half-hug before Archie's arm settled protectively around his wife's shoulders. A flash of movement on the staircase drew their attention, and Zack extended his arms to catch a flying mass of six-year-old exuberance.

"Uncle Zack! See my cape?" Logan Raessler's arms flapped. "Now I'm a superhero like you!"

Zack looked into Logan's vivid blue eyes and a lump jammed his throat. He squeezed the boy to his chest, catching the brief look between Archie and Twyla before she brushed at her eyes.

This family deserved decades together. He'd give Twyla both damn kidneys if she needed them. No question.

He put his head next to Logan's, inhaled the salty-sweet scent of boyhood, and then tickled the superhero until he wriggled, giggled, and begged to be let down. When Zack set him down, he scurried off to the playroom, his super hero cape billowing out behind him.

Morgan floated down the stairs, examining a light green baby blanket. "Twy, you gotta teach me how to do these bobble stitch borders." When she reached the landing, Zack laughed at the sudden blank look on her face.

"Long time no see, huh, Morgan? Didn't see your car out front. What'd you do, *walk*?" he asked.

Archie snickered. "You know she can't exercise, man, she'd lose a cup size."

"Shut up, loser. You should talk. Married life's making you soft around the middle." Morgan lunged at Archie, but her pinch found nothing but the fabric of his T-shirt. Her cheeks dimpled as she turned to Zack. "Since you're burning to know, I hitched a ride. Wanna know who with?"

Not right now. He had enough to worry about without having to wonder who was carting Morgan around these days.

Twyla grabbed his arm and steered him into the kitchen where he'd spent countless hours talking, laughing, and learning what a healthy marriage looked like.

A safe haven where no one would sell him out.

"This is lovely being together so spontaneously. Are you hungry? Knowing you, you've been too busy to catch some lunch again, right?"

"I stopped at home a little while ago to let the hounds out. I grabbed something then, so don't worry about me."

But within minutes, she'd slid a plate heaped with sweet breads, cold cuts, cheese, and crackers in front of him. He smiled. "This looks great, but not as good as you. You look beautiful like always, Twyla."

Morgan swiped a piece of cheese off Zack's plate. "Brown-noser."

Twyla set a glass of milk in front of Zack, a pretty beam bringing some color to her cheeks. "Hear that, Arch? Six weeks to go, and I'm still beautiful."

Archie pulled her into his lap, his grin softening the scare factor of the jaguar tattoo wrapped around his neck. "I've told you that many times, but do I get the kind of reaction he does?"

Zack felt a curious pang watching them. He took a swig of milk hoping to ease the void in his chest. An image of a leggy blonde sashayed through his mind. He scraped the back of his knuckles against his stubbled cheek and looked up to see Morgan watching him.

Forcing another smile, he dabbed at his mouth with a napkin. "Glad to see you still keep him leashed, Twyla."

Archie rolled his eyes. "Glad to see you up North. Ann all settled into her new condo yet?"

Twyla moved off Archie's lap. "I thought she would've called to keep me posted, but I suppose she was busy between work and packing. I'm dying to see how she set up her new place, especially since she started working at Skinny Dipping. I love that store!"

Zack looked down at his plate, his chest tight. The small hope that either of them might know Ann's current whereabouts flickered and died. But was he really surprised? The note, Sloane's visions, and his gut all told him the same thing.

Someone had taken Ann, and things were bad.

He'd been a jerk. He'd helped Ann move in more than a month ago, and she lived only a few miles from here. He'd meant to stop by. He truly had, but how could he tell these guys that lately their collective happiness made him edgy? How fucked up was that?

He glanced over at Morgan, who was now seemingly engrossed studying the fuzzy blanket. She knew when he'd moved Ann. The hellion had worn out her welcome at Ann's for three miserable hours, mocking how he carried boxes, unwrapped dishes, and arranged furniture until Ann had finally taken pity on him and told Morgan to lay off the wisecracks or she wouldn't get any more designer hand-me-downs.

So, Morgan could have busted him. She normally lived for that kind of thing. Why didn't she say anything? He looked down at his plate again.

"Zack?" Twyla's tone twisted the knife in his chest even moer. "What's wrong?"

Everything. "It's all good. Ann's pretty much settled in her condo now."

"Why've you been such a ghost, then? I thought she lived a stone's throw from here."

He pretended not to notice Archie nudge his wife under the table. *Tell them how it feels like there's a hole the size of a meteor in your chest. How you want John back.*

Ann back.

Her absence hadn't started with the note this morning. They'd been close while John was alive, but that had all changed when the EMTs had pronounced him dead on arrival almost a year ago. Instead of their grief drawing them together, it had isolated them, as though they couldn't stand seeing their own pain reflected in one another's eyes. John would be devastated.

And pissed.

Zack rubbed his palms together, the emptiness inside him expanding until he was sure that if someone yelled in his ear it would echo in his chest cavity. Archie's eyes narrowed.

"Zack?" Twyla laid a hand on his arm, and he almost came out of the chair.

Get a fucking grip, Goldman. "Sorry. I'm sorry. I've been super busy with the mall project. Two days to go until we're done, and in some ways I still wish I hadn't won the bid. The Benjamin Group is a nightmare to work with, not to mention getting them to pay their bills on time."

"Things pretty tight?"

Zack leaned back in the chair, willing his body to relax in spite of Archie's eagle eyes. "Yeah. Ultimately, this project should help us pull out of it, though I need more jobs lined up. None of my people can afford to be laid off."

Another thing that kept him up at night.

One of his foremen had a fifth child on the way. A supervisor's wife had to have a third round of chemo and even though Samuel's provided excellent medical coverage, the family's bills were staggering, especially with two of their kids in college. And on it went with so many of his people.

"I thought John always had good cash flow."

"He did. I don't know what happened. Ross is going over the books to see where the holes are. He's already found a few, so that's promising."

"Someone siphoning?"

"Ross seems to think so, but he doesn't have any proof yet. If anyone can find it, he's the man." *He has to.* "I'm lucky he's stayed with me since John—" He couldn't get the words out. But they knew. Twyla reached over to squeeze his hand. When the ache in his throat eased, he pushed the plate away. "It's my own fault for not taking a more active role in the back office."

Archie sat back. "What, you expect to run the whole business alone?"

"It'd be nice." How was he going to broach the topic of Ann's disappearance? He looked into the eyes of each of his friends. If he couldn't trust these three, everything he'd reconstructed his life on was a sham. "Ann's gone."

"What do you mean gone?" Twyla asked.

He told them about Ann's disappearance and the note, leaving Sloane out of the picture. He wasn't sure how to explain any of that. Nor his growing belief in something that he would have ridiculed only yesterday.

Twyla rubbed her belly. "This is scary. Do you still have the note?"

He pulled it from his pocket and laid it on the table. Archie picked it up, and Zack continued. "I talked to her last night, but she didn't say anything about going out of town or being unavailable. Has she talked to any of you about anyone she's been seeing lately?"

Morgan shook her head and got up to get a pop from the fridge.

"She hasn't said anything to me," Twyla said. "Guys ask her out, but she's just so shy she usually says no. I tease her that she needs a higher power to intercede to make her bold. She always jokes back that it'd be her luck to fall in love with a pastor."

Archie put his elbows on the table. "Have you filed a report with the police?"

"Yeah, right before I stopped at home."

"How were you received at the department?"

Zack interlaced his fingers behind his head. Being around Archie was like living in a Petri dish. Couldn't hide shit even if you grew fur. "Let me put it this way. Barnaba's been promoted to head up the CAPERS unit."

Archie pounded his fist on the table, rattling the silverware. "No way, man."

"A few months ago, I guess. Yay for me." Zack downed the rest of his milk.

"What am I missing? What's CAPERS?"

All three looked at Twyla. Zack tried to remember how

much she already knew. Morgan must have read his mind. "CAPERS is the Crimes Against Persons division within the Criminal Investigations Unit at the Fargo PD. CAPERS scopes out missing persons. And from Zack's information, an old crum bum's now the big dog."

"Crum bum?"

"*Enemy.*" Morgan spit the word out. "Barnaba's the guy who sent Zack to prison."

"That's ridiculous. I know you guys haven't always been model citizens," Twyla said, jabbing Archie when he snorted, "but you've proven to be law abiding for at least ten years now. Isn't a cop supposed to do his or her job, no matter who needs help?"

He and Archie exchanged a smile. He wished everyone could be as forgiving as Twyla, but he knew Detective Tony Barnaba's hatred would follow him to the grave. Thing is, he probably deserved it.

Archie cracked his knuckles. "Zack ever tell you about Barnaba's wife, Kasey?"

"Butter-face bint." They all looked at Morgan, surprised at her vehemence.

Twyla turned back to Zack. "No. But she's the one, isn't she?"

Zack stilled. "The one?"

"Who put that sad look in your eyes," she said.

"You can't read people's feelings in their eyes." *Unless they're she-wolf eyes.*

"You're wrong, Zack. A person's eyes are the proverbial window to their soul."

Archie tucked his hand under Twyla's hair to lightly knead her neck. "Someone said Tony finally threw Kasey out a few years ago. Guess he found her in bed with her karate instructor."

Classic Kasey. "Whatever. Doesn't matter anymore." Zack got up to pace over to one of the windows that faced Archie's large workshop, the river, and their back acreage where three dogs were rolling around like cats in a bed of catnip. He looked back to find Archie watching him, his demeanor calm. "Bart Winters still work in the department? I know he had access to the Motor Vehicle Database," Zack said.

"No. Bart retired a couple years ago. What's up, man? What do you think's going on with Ann?"

"I knocked on a few doors in her neighborhood before I stopped at the station. The police will probably send someone out to do the same, but I...wanted to do something." He paused and Archie nodded. Of course he'd understand. Archie had always been a man of action. "Anyway, one of her neighbors is an old lady on oxygen who does jigsaw puzzles on a card table in front of her picture window. She said she often sees a white Lexus parked in Ann's driveway. She also made sure I knew that the man who drives it is way too old for Ann." He could barely get the words past the ache in his throat.

"There you go. Ann's probably on a weekend tryst." Twyla started clearing the table with Morgan's help. "I sure as heck wouldn't have informed either of my brothers if I was planning a romantic getaway before I was married. They would have been hyper-protective too."

"I wish you were right, honey, but I think Zack should trust his gut and find out who owns the Lexus." Archie looked at Zack. "Winters is out, but I can ask around to see if anyone else has any suggestions. Have you checked the hospitals?"

"Yeah. Nothing."

"The gym, the office, the new store where she works?" After Zack's nod, Archie paused, his eyes steady on Zack. "The morgue?"

Dishes clattered into the sink, but Twyla quickly recovered, her gaze shooting to her husband. Pressure grew in Zack's chest until he felt as though he'd suffocate unless he got outside.

He shouldn't have come. Of course they didn't know anything about Ann. He was on his own.

"Don't need to check the damn morgue. The police would've been more interested in my story if they had an unidentified body floating around." He strode over to kiss Twyla's cheek. "Thanks for lunch. Take care of yourself and those kids." He nodded at the table. "Morgan."

She scrambled up from her chair. "Zack, wait! Do you want me—"

He didn't hear the rest. The door had already slammed behind him like a judge's gavel, sentencing him to stupidity.

Because, for better or for worse, he knew where he was headed. And she might not be too happy about it.

ELEVEN

When the knock came, Sloane knew it was him.

Had to be, otherwise why would her heart be pounding so furiously? Now she knew why she'd felt compelled to stay at the store on a Sunday after they'd closed at six. Glancing at her watch, she crammed the inventory slips to the back of the desk and peeked at the door, wondering what to do. She'd told herself to keep her hormones in line, but that didn't mean she didn't care to know what was happening with Ann. Right?

She nearly knocked a chair over on her way to the door. She slid to a halt beside it, and then took extra slow steps the rest of the way. She pushed it outward so forcefully she nearly clocked him. "Zack?"

A shy smile seemed to form almost against his will. "Hi. Nice hat."

"Thanks. I like dragonflies. They symbolize power, poise, and...living in the moment." His hair was even blacker than the T-shirt that clung to him. And he still hadn't shaved. She wondered how that chiseled, shadowy jaw line would feel against her skin. *How's that for living in the moment?* She rubbed the goose bumps on her arms and drew back to let him in.

He tugged at his shirt collar, avoiding eye contact, and there it was again—vulnerability in a killer package. "I hope I'm not bothering you. I know the mall's not open, but I saw your car in the empty lot..." His comment died away in the silence.

She stuck her hands in her pockets. "It's okay. I'm finishing up some paperwork. Have you heard from Ann?"

"No, but one of her neighbors had some information, and based on that, I'd like to ask a favor. You think your contact at the Fargo PD can help us find out who owns a white Lexus in town?"

She jotted down the information Zack had gleaned from Ann's elderly neighbor and looked up to find him watching her with an expression that made her breath catch.

"Thank you."

His gratitude warmed her from the inside out. She was speechless. Didn't he have anyone to turn to? How could he not? He was intuitive, wildly charming when he wanted to be, not to mention unflappable in the face of scary unknowns. And Lord, he was hot-blooded. The man seethed passion. She sensed it churning under the cool chip-on-his-shoulder surface he presented to the world. She wanted to watch him erupt and stand under the geyser as it rained down.

All over her. Melting her into oblivion.

She touched her neck. "I haven't..." Whatever she'd been about to say was lost when he stepped toward her and laid a finger on her lips.

"'You're welcome' would be an appropriate response. Or better yet..." His warm hands removed her hat, laid it on the desk, and then framed her face. She couldn't look away. Couldn't breathe. His eyes had grown dark. His thumbs traced a lingering brand across her cheekbones while those chiseled lips descended ever so slowly.

***

Zack felt Sloane's body shudder when their lips met. She tasted even better than he'd imagined. And her skin, so fragrant. On his next inhale, she molded her body to his, pouring herself into the kiss until she'd tied him in knots. He reached back to untie the turquoise scarf from her hair, letting it spill over her shoulders in a golden curtain.

He broke the kiss for a moment to drink in the sight of her. Parted lips, perfectly sculpted cheekbones, and heavy-lidded milky brown eyes that burned with more desire than he'd ever seen. This woman drew him—the quiet, hidden part of him. *Why?*

He couldn't think. He brought his lips back to hers, using his tongue to learn the secrets of her mouth until her breathy moans nearly rocked him beyond control. She gasped when he feathered kisses down the exposed column of her throat, his hands slowly exploring her hollows and curves until she trembled against him.

"Please."

Her husky whisper pierced his lust. He stilled.

Please, what? Take her to the cement floor? Holy hell, she made him lose his mind.

His body rebelled while his mind struggled to overrule baser instincts. He buried his face against her neck and wrapped his arms around her body, feeling her tremors echo his own. They remained entwined that way for a few moments, their breathing slowly returning to normal. She shifted first. He didn't want to let go, but he eased away.

She wet her lips. "I'm not sure if I should be grateful or insulted that you stopped." She looked down at his chest. Pink tinged the tops of her cheeks.

How could any woman be so desirable yet doubt herself? He couldn't be any stiffer. "You probably don't want to hear me say I'm sorry, then."

A battle light came into her eyes before she tried to turn

away. He cupped her face, forcing her to look at him. "No. I didn't mean it that way. I meant...I—" He let go of her and grinned. "You made me forget where we are."

Her lips curved into a smile that sent new currents of awareness though his body. "Well, then, what do we do next?"

About twenty different sexual fantasies came to mind, but man, he was such a douche. He was thinking about getting sweaty with Sloane while Ann was God knew where. He prayed John couldn't tap into his thoughts. He cleared his throat. "You ever hear of a Colette O'Neill?"

She stopped fanning herself with her hand. "Colette? Sure. She's the senior pastor's wife at Divine Shepherd Lutheran. I collaborated with her and a few others on the Hope for the Homeless project last year."

"You belong to Divine Shepherd?"

"Heck, no. I'm Catholic. Go to mass every week." She grinned, and he couldn't help his answering smile. This woman had *layers. Damn.*

"What does Colette have to do with Ann?" she asked.

"Not sure, if anything. I reviewed my emails from Ann over the last couple of months and she mentioned Divine Shepherd in several of them. Colette O'Neill in particular. I thought I'd stop by the church to see if I can figure out a new angle."

"It's almost eight. You think anyone'll still be around?"

"Aren't churches always open to sinners?"

One side of her lips lifted. "Not what I meant, wise guy."

"What I gathered from Ann's emails, it sounds like an enterprising congregation. Ann has been on more than one of their committees. I guess I knew that, but I never really asked about her involvement." Another sin to lay at his door.

"Let's check it out. I'll call my contact at the Fargo PD on the way. Who knows, maybe the man in the vision is someone

Ann met through church." She grabbed her purse and thrust it at Zack's midsection. "I need to grab something out front. You ditch me, and you're in trouble." She was gone before he even had a chance to respond.

Left alone in the cavernous room, he tucked Sloane's purple monstrosity under his arm, then realized it was the first time he'd ever held a purse for a female. Shaking his head, he tossed it onto her desk, the draft fluttering several photos attached to the bulletin board at the back of her workspace. He leaned in to look at one of the photos. Sloane stood between two people he assumed were her parents. She was a fascinating blend of both of them. Height and hair color from her father. Eyes and cheekbones from her mother.

For the first time in a long while he wondered what it would've been like to grow up in a loving home. He'd never had any unconditionals.

Except maybe trouble.

Until John.

His index finger traced Sloane's feminine features, lingering on her generous mouth. She was tough, that he'd already witnessed and admired, but she also had a softness—a warm sensitivity that drew him even more than her luscious body. He didn't have a name for the feeling that had settled in his gut since he'd met her. Nothing as simple as lust, though that was there in spades.

Trust? A startling thought.

Archie, Twyla, Morgan, and John were the only ones he'd put his trust in who'd never betrayed him. Even the foster 'parents' the system had tried to force him on had let him down. Most had only wanted the monthly stipend. Or a scapegoat for their own kids' shit.

Whether they'd actually meant to use him or not, he'd run

83

away from every one of those homes until the system thought they had him by packing him off to the Boys Ranch for at-risk teens.

But he'd run away from there, too.

The system had finally left him alone after that. He'd been seventeen, on his own, on the streets.

He'd never considered himself lonely, but looking at Sloane's captivating face in the photo, he wondered what it would be like to come home to someone like her. To hold her every night.

To share their dreams and secrets as they shut the world away.

Suddenly the future stretched before him, the canvas blank. His muscles tensed, and he swung toward the showroom entrance, heart vaulting into his throat. Sloane returned seconds later and froze.

He pivoted toward the exit, putting one foot in front of the other, frustrated that being around her had instigated this restlessness. Then angry with himself for blaming her when she was only trying to help. He white-knuckled the door handle. "Ready, then?"

When she didn't reply, he glanced back. She hadn't moved from the now-darkened showroom doorway, hands on her hips.

"What just happened while I was gone?"

He didn't say anything. Her sandaled foot started tapping. He made himself meet her eyes. *Alpha she-wolf eyes*. Bad idea. He shifted from one foot to the other. "What do you mean?"

"Nice try. You swing from hot to cold faster than a Finn goes from a sauna to a hole in a frozen lake. My great grandparents did that, you know. For real." She grabbed her purse and hat from the desk. "I'll let you get away with it this time. But do it again, and I'll be all over you."

He followed her outside as she adjusted her hat and kept walking until she paused beside his truck. She gingerly opened the door and climbed inside. After her shoulders dropped in apparent relief, she smiled, wiggling onto the seat.

He couldn't help imagining her doing the same thing on his lap.

He readjusted himself in his jeans and made sure the storeroom door latched securely before he strode to his truck, trying to focus on what they might uncover at the church.

And wondering how he was going to keep himself from peeling back layer after layer of Sloane until he found out what was at her core.

TWELVE

Sloane left another message for her friend, Fargo PD intelligence officer Pete Bartley, quickly stating the information they were hoping to find. With any luck, Pete would help them discover if any white Lexuses were registered in town, and if so, who held the titles. When she hung up, she slipped her phone into her purse and took in the scenery as Zack drove.

Lacking the mature elm trees and old character homes of the north side, south Fargo was like an entirely different city with its shiny new buildings and strip malls.

Divine Shepherd Lutheran fronted the new intersection of Twenty-Fifth Street and Ninety-Eighth Avenue, its whitewashed siding gleaming in the late afternoon sun and the domed, multi-colored glass windows drawing the eye up the soaring twin steeples. As one of the largest establishments in this part of town, Sloane thought it stood like a palace amid the ongoing construction around it. She looked at all the signs, but didn't see anything with the Samuel's Construction logo.

"Do you have any projects down here?"

"We finished that taco shop over there a few weeks ago, but nothing else right now. I've had to pull all my guys in for the finish of the mall's new theme park. It opens on Tuesday."

Her hand gripped the passenger armrest. She blinked, then inhaled so hard he looked at her as they turned into the church's property.

Oh Lord. He was doing the amusement park?

He was generaling the mall's amusement park. *Benjamin's*

86

park. He works with Benjamin, and he knows what I can do.

They worked together, but how chummy were they? Did Zack know about Benjamin's granddaughter? If he did, and he thought about her psychic abilities, he might begin to piece it together. The tragedy.

Her secret would come back to destroy her. *God.*

The edges of her vision glimmered. Silver. Red. Narrow prisms of icy color that stabbed at the sides of her eyes. She blinked, trying to focus.

She heard Zack talking, but when they rolled to a stop in the curved driveway, she yanked off her hat and flung open the door, staggering blindly to the curb, seeking a patch of earth. She collapsed on the newly placed sod and burrowed her fingers into the ground. Almost instantly, the wings of panic began to settle back into the shadows of her mind.

Not five seconds later, Zack's boots came into view. "Now I get why you wear blue fingernail polish. FYI, though, Lava soap and the curved file of a clipper work wonders to get the dirt out from underneath your nails."

What? She glanced up to find him smiling, but his eyes…

Made her throat tight.

Why'd he have to be so nice? Made her want to fricking cry all the time. Reluctantly, she drew her hands away from the sod, brushed them on the blue linen shorts she'd changed into at the store, and started to rise. Zack grabbed her upper arms to help her, his touch bringing that now-familiar buzz which flushed out the last of the panic.

"Thank you. I'm sorry, I…" She looked everywhere but at him.

"You don't have to apologize or even tell me what happened if you don't want to. But if you do, I'll listen."

Not this. She filled her lungs with as much air as they could hold, past caring that she looked like a puffer fish when she blew it out. "I guess I'm slightly off kilter today. That had nothing to do with what's going on with Ann. I don't usually have so much...energy exposure. After a good night's sleep, I'm sure I'll be back to normal." She forced a smile.

Zack tilted his head, the sun shining purple on his black hair. The contrast with the vivid green of his eyes was hypnotic. "Okay, but maybe I should take you home. What if you get, I don't know—overwhelmed—by stuff inside? What then?"

Yeah, what then? She'd never pushed the envelope of her exposure like this before. Besides, here was her chance to back off. To protect herself from revealing even more about who she was and how she'd failed the Benjamin family dynasty. Zack was now dangerous by way of his association with the holding company executive. Very few people knew about her abilities. Fewer still knew about her darkest shame.

Her failed attempt to find a little girl the one and only time she'd tried.

Benjamin's granddaughter. Benjamin didn't know. He'd never fund her foundation if he did. But hey, he wasn't going to anyway if she didn't find the rhino, so did it really matter?

She took in Zack's beautiful face, his kind eyes.

Perhaps the rhino would still turn up. "Yeah, I...maybe I should go."

They both turned toward the driveway as a white Lexus jerked to a stop behind Zack's truck. A well-dressed man slipped out and jolted when he noticed them standing on the grass. He recovered, calling out a practiced greeting, the whites of his teeth gleaming, before disappearing through the church's imposing front door.

Trim, dapper, movie-star handsome.

Sloane's blood rushed to her feet. "Oh, my God! That's him.

That's the man who hurt Ann."

***

Zack sprang forward with a sound of rage, his face a mask of fury. Sloane scrambled after him, but tripped, her legs a pile of rubber, scraping her knee and palm on the decorative, stamped concrete. She picked herself up and entered the dimly-lit narthex.

A series of doors lined the right wall, and a long, shadowed hallway lay to the right of the fourth door. Late day sunlight filtered through a stained-glass window, casting an almost unholy glow in the space.

"Zack?" Her ears strained in the expansive silence, but she couldn't hear any yelling or sounds of violence. Why then did her pulse throb so forcefully?

Stay? Or go?

Please don't let Lexus Guy be a man of the cloth.

She could go home, have a nice glass of wine and a bath, and forget this day ever *fucking* happened. She tucked her chin to her chest—genuflecting over thinking the "f" word—and saw a white dove with an olive branch in its beak, immortalized on the beautiful terrazzo floor.

A symbol for peace.

Oh, the irony.

Time. To. Go.

A far-away sound of shattering glass rent the air. She sprinted down the shadowed hallway until her knees jarred before an open door where Zack huddled on the floor near a dark-haired woman in a pink tailored suit. He was picking up chunks of colored glass while the woman held the wastebasket. Sloane put her hand to her chest and shut her eyes.

"I'm really sorry. I'll replace it if you'll tell me where I can find another," he said.

Sloane's eyes snapped open to see the muscles shifting beneath his T-shirt as he stood. He sounded too calm. Where was the rage she'd witnessed mere moments ago? And where was Lexus Guy?

"Don't worry about it." The woman turned the full power of her brown eyes on Zack. With an elegant hand, she pushed at the hair that lay in perfect waves on her shoulders and leered at his chest, then lower. Sloane gasped, feeling her cheeks blaze. Zack swung toward her, completely blocking her view of the woman.

"Ah, there you are. I was just telling Colette that we're looking for Ann." The calm modulation of his voice belied the warning in his eyes. "But, clumsy me, I managed to knock a vase off the desk before she could even respond." His eyes held hers for a pregnant moment before he turned to face Ms. Perfect. "Sloane, I'd like you to meet Colette O'Neill. Colette, this is Sloane Swift."

"Of course, we crossed paths on Hope for the Homeless. What a wonderfully successful project! So nice to see you again, dear." Colette extended a manicured hand.

Sloane coughed into the crook of her elbow. "Sorry, summer cold."

Colette's gaze stayed on Sloane for several seconds though her head was shifting back to Zack.

"Sloane mentioned how you spearheaded the back-to-work program for the homeless. Samuel's Construction offered employment to many of your project applicants. Most are still with us today." Zack's easy smile was devastating, but Sloane was ready to launch with nerves. How could he be so nonchalant? *Where's Lexus Man? Come on, Zack!* She slipped her hand behind him to pinch his butt.

He covered his surprised laugh by clearing his throat. "Ann tells me you and your husband have done a lot for the community in recent years. That was him running down the hall a moment ago, wasn't it?"

Sloane tensed, feeling the stillness in Zack's body beside her. Colette pulled on the hem of her suit coat and moved to stand behind the desk. "Yes, that was *our* Dallan. Always on the run. I swear that man doesn't know how to walk." She laughed lightly, but it was all Sloane could do to remain upright.

Lexus Man was a *pastor!*

A wild squeal of disbelief was working its way up her windpipe. Zack reached out to give her hand a hard double squeeze. Bones grinding together worked pretty well to stifle any revealing response. Her throat burned and, oh, her ticker was going to stop beating one of these minutes from shock. She turned sideways, concentrating on her breathing to forestall hyperventilating, pretending to peruse the shelves of religious books.

Zack squeezed once more before releasing her hand. "Ann really enjoys working on your committees. Like I mentioned before, I thought she told me she'd be here tonight to help out with the Fall Festival. Or do I have my days mixed up?"

Colette frowned. "The planning committee doesn't have a meeting scheduled this evening, but I can pull up the calendar—"

Zack held up a hand. "Don't go to the trouble. I must have the dates confused. But, if she happens to stop by, tell her to turn on her phone for me, would you?" Zack winked, prompting a languid smile from Colette.

"Sure. Dallan does the same thing. What's the point in having a *mobile* phone, right?" She looked out the window briefly before turning back to him. "Now, if you'll excuse me. I need to get home to make sure the kids have all their chores done so they can get to bed on time. Have a nice evening."

As they were leaving, Sloane saw Colette turn to look out the window again. She paused in the doorway and leaned forward enough to see over Colette's shoulder out the window.

The white Lexus peeled out of the driveway.

THIRTEEN

Zack scrutinized Sloane as he held the church door open for her. She looked dazed and exhausted. He surveyed the as-yet undeveloped fields to the southwest where the sinking summer sun was in the throes of being swallowed by a blue-gray mountain of clouds. After the climate-controlled interior of the church, the moist heat wrapped around him like a soggy blanket. Combined with the boiling rage locked tight inside, he wondered how steam didn't shoot out his ears. He practically trembled with it.

Sloane opened her mouth to speak.

"Wait." The strain of the charade made his throat feel like gravel. He unlocked his truck and they climbed inside. Zack peered in his rearview mirror as he exited the church parking lot and pulled onto 25th Street heading north. "Someone can help you get your car later. I'm taking you home."

"Are you crazy? This is crazy! No, I'm not going home. We're going back to Ann's. When you bolted into the church like Rambo on a rampage, I thought you were going to kill him. He's a man of the cloth!" She put her hands on her head. "Senior pastor of one of the largest churches in the state. How can this be? He left a second ago, so he can't be too far ahead of us. Let's find him!"

His fingers gripped the steering wheel so hard the skin over his knuckles paled. "Calm down." *Calm down.* He made himself relax his grip.

"Calm down? This is a nightmare, Zack. How can I be calm?

How can you? If the pastor's not with Ann, who took her? What are we going to do?"

Her hat was gonna be toast if she twisted it any harder. "*We* aren't going to do anything. *I* am. What's your address?"

"Frustrating, *frustrating* man. Why are you always charming with everyone but me?"

"Guess you bring out the best in me." He smiled, but knew it didn't reach his eyes when she shivered and shut up.

For all of five seconds.

"Take me to Ann's," she said.

"No."

"*Yes.*"

He shook his head, praying for patience. "Jesus, Sloane. Can't you see I'm trying to protect you? If something— *Woman.* Okay, home or store?"

"Ann's."

She was going to turn him into a spewing volcano. "Don't you have a business to run? Books to balance, shit to buy or something?"

"Don't *you?*"

"I'm not open Sundays."

She groaned. "Okay, okay. *Okay.*" Her fingernails suddenly raked at her skull. "Lord! I almost forgot. We *have* to go back to Ann's. She has a diary!"

He swerved into an empty parking lot and swiveled to face her, blood pounding in his ears. "What are you talking about?"

"Ann keeps a diary. We have to find it."

"You're just telling me this *now?* You should have goddamn said something right away!"

"Don't you dare curse at me like that, you seismic jackass!"

He had to get *out*. He flung the truck door open and strode across the cracked asphalt. Her door slammed shut moments later, and within seconds she was wagging a finger in his face. "And don't you walk away from me, either!"

"Then don't be such a damn shrew."

Color flooded over her cheekbones seconds before she punched him in the gut. Hard. *What the hell!* An ancient fire lit up his nerve circuits, and adrenaline had him widening his stance. His heart gunned.

His groin tightened.

And she was still shrill. "I'm *not* a shrew! How am I supposed to act in a situation like this? You think I'm enjoying this? I *hate* it! But unfortunately I have a conscience which would haunt me for the rest of my life if I don't follow this through until we have some answers. You came to me and wanted to rule out the church first. Then with everything that happened, I forgot about the diary until right now. That clear enough for you, you—"

Clear enough, honey.

He vised her head between his palms and kissed her. He hadn't meant to, but the moment her mouth opened to his, he was lost. Not breaking contact with her mouth, he wrapped one arm around her, his hand splaying across her ass, locking her hips against him. Her hands were in his hair, her hips grinding, driving him crazy. They feasted on each other's mouth, tongues dueling, daring, seeking. He felt her fingers between their bodies, slipping underneath the waistband of his jeans, pulling at the hem of his shirt. Her fingernail scraped his abs and he groaned. She leaned away from his mouth, her eyes dead sexy. Liquid brown. Fuck, yeah. He was gonna—

A car horn blew, jerking him back to life. Back to the parking lot. He looked over to see a man in a black minivan at a stoplight giving them the thumbs up. He honked twice more, waved, and drove on.

Sloane burst into a fit of laughter that quickly dissolved into tears.

And that clinched it. He'd woken up this morning in some creepy-assed Twilight Zone.

He wiped away her tears and laid his forehead against hers for a few moments to get his brain rewired. Then he guided her over to the passenger side of the truck, opened the door, and nudged her inside. He walked around to the driver's side, then eased into the seat, adjusting this way and that to accommodate the monster in his jeans.

Sloane sniffed loudly. "*Now* can we go to Ann's?"

He banged his head against the steering wheel before glancing at her profile. Her fingers fidgeted in her lap.

Looks. Brains. Compassion. Sense of humor.

Add to that one heaping dose of courage and what do you get?

Zack totally FUBAR.

Definitely time to cut her loose.

She was sitting beside him because she felt obligated to help him find Ann. Their chemistry was a result of the circumstances. Danger always had a way of heightening attraction. God only knew how many brawls Kasey had instigated for him for her viewing pleasure. And she'd only nursed his injuries if he'd been the victor. "What if we're dealing with some psycho here? Doesn't that scare you?"

That dimmed the light in those hellcat eyes. "Well...yeah. But it's too late for me to back out now. Besides, who do you trust with my safety more...you, or the police who don't even know there might be foul play yet?"

Nailed. The woman already knew how to manipulate him. He gave her the scowl he saved for employees who were caught dicking around. "You're really a piece of work." He'd hoped to tick her off, but she actually *smiled* at him. He rubbed his cheek to stop himself from smiling back. "Okay. But before we go to Ann's, you're going to tell me why I feel like I'm hooked up to a navy submarine generator every time I touch you."

Her smile slipped. She shifted on the leather seat, brushing some imaginary lint off her blouse. *Aha.* He *knew* there was something to it.

Seconds ticked by. He purposely turned down the A/C. Then, keeping his eyes between her and the rearview mirror, he laid his right hand on the top of her seat back again, only this time his thumb brushed the bare skin of her neck. Pulses of energy jumped under his skin.

Her gaze flew to his.

Busted, little woman.

"You play mean."

"Not mean, Goldie. *Equal.*"

A few more seconds of silence ticked by while sweat gathered a bead to run between his pecs. He leaned his head against the headrest and narrowed his eyes to slits so he could still use his peripheral vision to keep tabs on her and any activity outside the truck. She brought a hand up to inspect her nails. Then rummaged through her purse until she came out with a nail file, which she promptly tossed on the dash before reaching over to flip the A/C on high.

"Fine! Along with the visions, I sometimes have the ability to be attuned to the energy of others."

Zack studied her, feeling a curious lightness in his chest. She fixed her hat on her head like it was a piece of body armor.

"I don't know why it's so strong with you. Nor why your energy doesn't suck the life out of me like most other people's does if it sneaks past my barriers." She was inspecting her nails again. He brushed the backs of his fingers along her jaw and felt her shiver.

She looked at him with such naked vulnerability it robbed his breath. "And the fact that you also feel this connection is totally unbelievable. It's— I don't share that part of myself with anyone. If I even tried to explain what happens to me... Lord, people would think I was a freak. *Know* I'm a freak."

That she should have to hide parts of herself from the world caused anger to surge through him. His fingers trailed along the exposed column of her neck. "I've met a lot of freaks over the years, and trust me, you don't qualify."

"Must hang with a rough crowd, then," she muttered.

Zack laughed, which finally drew a smile from her. "Back in the day... You have no idea. Last time I checked, though, I wasn't made out of metal."

"Yeah. About that? I'm not sure what's going on. Our energy fields must be highly sensitive to each other."

No shit. "Really," he drawled.

She nodded.

He wanted another smile. "I've been called a lot of things over the years, but *seismic* jackass? That elevates me to a whole new level, I guess."

She smiled. *Bingo.*

"Sorry," she said, but didn't look it. He put his truck into gear, trying not to think about how easily she'd managed to convince him to do what she wanted—go to Ann's—when every cell in his body wanted to call in every favor that every shady character in town owed him to find O'Neill.

He pulled out of the abandoned parking lot, forcing himself not to look at the siren beside him, but doing it anyway. Next stop, Ann's. He had about ten minutes to steel himself for a new round of...who the hell knew.

It was not his damn day.

FOURTEEN

Zack leaned against Ann's bedroom door watching Sloane cautiously inspect a hairbrush. She'd long since ditched her hat, so he could easily see the dark circles under her eyes. He'd obviously put them there because he sure as hell hadn't noticed them earlier. His idea of searching the dresser drawers had been fruitless, so they were back to that hocus pocus thing to find the diary. Which left him feeling worthless.

"What can I do?"

She gave him a shaky smile. "Grab a bucket, and be ready to hold my hair back?"

He straightened to move toward her. "I'm sorry you couldn't find the rhino. I'll pay for a new one."

She held up her hand, concentrating on a pair of diamond studs nesting in a bed of pink velvet on the dresser. A tremor moved through him. Her touch or her gift? He wasn't sure, but he was suddenly hyperaware of the woman next to him. Of the rapid pulse at her neck. The delicate arch of her brows over eyes that changed color with her emotion.

Brown was the color of her passion. Eloquent, dark, complex. The color of disturbed earth at the feet of sequoias.

Her sudden indrawn breath was like a blow because he knew by now what was coming. He almost told her to stop. All those other times had been so hard on her. But she touched the earrings, and her face lost animation. He wrapped his arms around her. Her very essence seemed to quiet, to still in a supernatural concentration.

Zack buried his face in her hair, willing her strength as she faced whatever secrets those earrings might share. When she started, her speech was languorous. "The air is hot, humid. She's laughing at you and John. Catfishing. The three of you are catfishing on the Red River."

The back of Zack's neck crawled. That was four, maybe five years ago now.

"She touches her ear. These earrings. She's happy. Loves you because you're both pretending to enjoy the wilted sandwiches she made. You're nagging about her perfume. It's attracting bugs, you say. She smiles. Dragonflies are everywhere, whizzing around your heads, and she loves the hum of the pontoon's motor. You tease one another and laugh over whose fish has the longest whiskers..."

Zack's vision blurred for the first time since he'd had to explain to the police how he'd found his father's body swinging from a rope. Sloane took him back, resurrecting that day on the river with the family he'd been lucky enough to create later in life.

Good times. A sense of belonging.

All he'd ever wanted.

Sloane's head lolled, then righted itself.

"No, Goldie. *Come back.*"

She blinked, but obviously didn't see him standing in front of her, her voice a mere whisper this time. "Somewhere else now. An office. She knows he's attracted to her, and she's enjoying the attention. The man—I can't see his face—leans against the edge of the counter. His cologne smells expensive. She thinks he has nice teeth, nice hair. Eyes, too, when he isn't trying to intimidate someone...but... He's her father's age. Even older. Oh, Lord, it's Benjamin. Timothy Benj—"

"What? No!" Zack jerked back, his arms breaking the circle

around her. Sloane swayed again, and he grabbed her, sat them both on the bed and scored the small white trash can just in time. Sloane clutched it as she expelled her guts.

Zack held her hair back, murmuring to her until she staggered to the bathroom. His eyeballs burned until he thought his optic nerve had short-circuited. Enough was enough. The woman would need to be hooked up to an IV if she attempted any more readings. And they hadn't even located the diary yet.

He was pretty damn sure he believed in her ESP now.

He went to stand beside the tomcat guarding the bathroom door. He wanted to barge in to make sure she wasn't drowning in all that water he heard running. He listened intently, only turning away when he heard her softly say, "Tori?"

She must've had her phone in her pocket. Why couldn't he remember that she wasn't a loner like him? Their backgrounds probably couldn't be more different. She had people to turn to when things went south.

And what a *poor me* whiner he was becoming.

He walked down the hallway into the kitchen, carefully curbing his urge to knock his fist into the drywall. *Focus on Ann.*

In the vision, Sloane had witnessed Benjamin flirting with Ann. No way could Ann be involved with both the pastor *and* Tim Benjamin. Could she?

He'd obviously left her to the wolves. One who probably walked around his church like a saint. The other who got off on using people for his own gain.

Zack exhaled deeply to tamp down the anger. He walked to Ann's desk, pulled out his cell phone, and dialed Archie.

"What's up, man? You hear from Ann or the police?" Archie yelled at his dogs to stop barking.

"Not Ann, but the police are looking into her phone and bank records to see if anything turns up. So far, nothing." Zack rolled his shoulders. "You still know how to get in touch with Donovan?"

Archie whispered a string of obscenities. "No good reason to get in touch with a low life like that. Not anymore."

"But do you?"

"Of course not."

Liar. Zack tapped a pencil on the desk. "You ever hear of Divine Shepherd Lutheran?"

"Who hasn't?"

"Ann's having an affair with the head pastor."

Archie sputtered on a drink. "No fucking way."

"I need Donovan's number, man."

More obscenities. Then Archie finally rattled off Donovan's number like it was a daily call. "You'd better keep it tight, or you'll have to deal with me."

Zack couldn't reassure him, so he hung up. He slid the phone into his pocket, then leaned against the smooth oak of Ann's pantry door. Archie had kept his nose clean for years now.

Or mostly clean.

Donovan was a mean, morally depraved SOB from Minneapolis who not only ran a wagon show of narcotics and black market weapons, but also a harem of street tarts and computer hackers. So how could Archie spit out his number like that?

Maybe now was a good time to start praying again.

Zack felt her seconds before she entered the kitchen. He shoved the paper with Donovan's number into his pocket. She pulled out a chair at the table and plopped down, stretching those legs that dried the saliva in his mouth. Even her feet with the blue toenail polish made him hot. He turned away and closed his eyes.

"Hey, thanks for holding my hair. I was only kidding, but..."

Zack opened his eyes to look at her when she paused. The thousand watt smile she beamed at him made his pulse hopscotch. "But?"

Her smile broadened impossibly. "It was really sweet of you."

He swallowed. Her normally golden complexion was still ashen. "Sure. It seems..." *Traumatic, overwhelming.* "Pretty rough on you."

She looked down at her hands, engrossed in her nails. "I'm going to find that diary."

"No, I'm taking you home now. You look like you need to sleep for a week."

"Gee, thanks, that's really flattering, but no. The longer Ann's missing..."

Damn her, she didn't need to say it. For a moment he allowed his eyes to trace the contours of her face. The shadows made her cheekbones even more pronounced. "You don't really think she had—*has*—something going on with Benjamin, do you?" he asked.

"I don't know what to think. From the vision, I'd have to say he was certainly interested in her, but at that particular time, I didn't get the sense that she would have been receptive. But who knows what happened later—if there *was* a later. I couldn't tell when that vision took place. Does he—" She clawed at her neck. "Does Benjamin stop by the office a lot?" Her voice cracked on the last word, her hand moving to press against her stomach.

He couldn't stand to see her so affected. "You're going home. Now."

Her pupils dilated even more, and she stood and backed away from him even though she was nodding like that was exactly what she wanted to do. "We need to go over it one more time. Who are all the people who could have picked her up? I mean, she's got to have some other family or friends around. Right? Everyone does."

She hadn't been this agitated even after all those other horrifying episodes. Why now? He edged closer to her—slowly—and pitched his statement as placid as possible. "Ann never knew her mother. John was an only child, and being sixty-eight when he died last year, he'd already lost both his parents."

He reached out to tuck a strand of hair behind her ear when he was sure she wasn't going to either club him or fly to the ceiling. "Before he died, he asked me to look after Ann." She seemed more composed now, but he wasn't sure he wanted to reopen this wound.

"How did you get so close to the family?"

Zack's chest squeezed further, but who was he kidding? The wound had never really healed. Probably never would. "John found me under a bridge eleven years ago and offered me a job. I repaid him by vandalizing one of his job sites. Two years later, he found me under the same bridge. He brought blankets, thermoses of soup and coffee. He told me I had choices—that I could reclaim my self-respect. He said, when I was ready, to find him. He left his business card on the stack of blankets. I still have that card. It's the same story for a lot of the long-timers at the company. Even Ross, my CFO, came to work for John with a felony on his record. All these years later, I finally realize John was building men along with his steel buildings." Zack turned away from her, his face hot and itchy. "Holy Christ, that's melodramatic."

She moved in front of him, holding his upper arms. "I wish I could've met him. He sounds like one of those people you never forget. I'm glad he saw the goodness in you."

He shrugged out of her grip and walked to the sink, where he leaned his backside against the counter. Tomorrow she probably wouldn't even remember his words. No sense worrying about it. "Ann doesn't have any close friends, other than someone who moved to Scotland a while ago. She's real private."

"You must've rubbed off on her." She remained silent for a long moment before she approached him again, the soft sway of her hips so feminine. So arousing. His fingers curled around the lip of the counter when she stopped mere inches away, her scent reaching out to bind his gut in tangles. Her breath on his neck made his abs contract. He ached to touch her.

Everywhere.

Her pupils dilated slightly when his eyes finally burned into hers. "That was mean...I'm...sorry." Her fingertips trailed from her neck down to the tops of her breasts. And *oh,* he watched those fingers as her words came out a breathless whisper. "What should we do now?"

Lay you down in a soft place so I can spend hours learning how your body tastes.

He pushed away from the counter, careful not to touch her. He stopped in front of Ann's desk, staring at her precise arrangement of pencils, feeling Sloane's heated introspection on his back. Her desire and uncertainty were like radio static in his bloodstream. *I'm as confused as you, Goldie.* Even so, he nearly swung back to wrap his arms around her, to lose himself in her warmth.

But then her energy—that pulsing beat of life he'd come to recognize as her essence—disappeared. Like someone had yanked a cord out of a wall socket. He looked back to see her enter the garage, the tomcat on her heels.

Give her some space. As much as he wanted to follow, he needed to get himself under control. They—*he*—had bigger problems right now than his overactive sex drive.

He approached the answering machine. Unable to stop himself, he pressed play. The sound of his own irritation swamped the kitchen. He remembered calling shortly before the storm. Couldn't he have sounded more approachable? He wished he'd come here earlier to find out what was bothering her. Instead, she was gone, and along the way he meets a psychic woman with whom he has an uncontrollable connection. He thought Sloane had layers? A man would have to be a geologist to figure her out.

After his message, the recording played back a second dial tone that supposedly came through at 8:14 p.m. No message. Had Ann already left by the time this second call came in, or was she screening calls?

All he knew was that she had been home around seven-thirty when she'd returned his original call. He looked down at his watch. *10:56 p.m.* Almost twenty-eight hours since they'd talked. Not that much time for an adult to be incommunicado, but then... All the other indicators sucked.

Suddenly, the hairs on the back of his neck stood on end. He pivoted toward the door that led to the garage. Sloane came into view, backlit by the garage lights. He took one step toward her, then stopped, his heart a sledgehammer against his bones.

Sloane held up a cotton candy pink journal. "We found it."

A phone began to ring. "We?" He reached for the journal, but she hugged it to her chest.

"The cat. Remember the garbage? That's what he was trying to tell us all along. The journal was in the trash," she said.

"The cat? That's crazy."

"Is it?" She pointed to his waist. "You'd better see who's calling so late."

What? He felt trapped in a time warp. *Oh, yeah, the phone.* He checked caller ID. Ross. *Great.* His CFO was a *no news is good news* kind of guy. He looked at Sloane when he answered. "What's up, Ross?"

"An officer Janklow from the Fargo Police called here asking for you. Said he'd been at your place too. He needs to talk to you. What's going on?"

Zack frowned. "Where's *here*? You at the office this late again?"

"It's become a habit, I'm afraid. The cops saw lights on in the building, and since the front doors were locked, they called. I'd seen multiple squad cars in the streets, so when the phones rang, I felt like I should answer. Why do they need to see you?"

Maybe they'd found her. But why hadn't they called him directly? He'd given them his number with the report.

"We can't afford any bad PR right now, Zack. This... This is disturbing." Ross paused for a moment. Acid began peeling away the lining of Zack's gut. "Have you had the radio on in the past few minutes?" Ross asked.

Zack froze. What if... *No.* If it was about Ann, Ross would've come right out with it. "No. I've been busy. Benjamin have a cardiac arrest in his sleep?"

"No." Ross's usually calm, modulated delivery betrayed a slight tremor. Zack's eyes found Sloane's as Ross continued. "A few kids found a body along the riverbank less than a half mile from your place. It was... *My God,* the body was on fire."

FIFTEEN

Moody lightning cast a sinister backdrop to the crime scene as Zack pushed through the tall, dewy grasses that lined the banks of the Red River. Though it was nearly midnight, excited members of the media droned like idling planes and an owl swooped from thick branches, startled by the human intrusion, its hunting grounds no longer inviolate.

Zack focused on the boys. Three of them. The untouched six pack at their feet. A cell phone gripped in one of the boys' white-knuckled hands.

Their tear-stained faces and horror-filled eyes.

Their innocence lost.

Zack had listened to the radio on the way. The media had already labeled the boys delinquents, but they were only children testing boundaries, trying on identities. Silently asking for someone to acknowledge their individuality.

They weren't bothering anyone.

Not like the madman who'd savaged the still-smoking figure that lay on the ground not thirty feet away, illuminated by portable lights on rickety poles. The crime scene stretched from the edge of the road down to the riverbank and about a hundred feet on either side of the body, the best Zack could tell.

The native grass had burned to the ground around the body, imbuing the site with a sense of ritualistic offering. A sour fullness backed into his throat. He'd found a body of his own at the age of ten. The overturned chair and his father's lifeless, opaque eyes and free swinging feet remained fixtures in his nightmares all these years later.

But this body... That inhuman form on the ground. That wasn't Ann.

Couldn't be. Or his failure to John would be complete.

He tried to swallow, but his throat was raw. This was someone else's nightmare. He rubbed his chest and fought the urge to leave. To fade into the crowd, get in the car and just keep going. Going until he either ran out of gas or fear.

He looked at the crowd and then back at the uniformed officers who were questioning the boys. They quavered like notes from a wind chime. Why weren't they being comforted? Zack strode forward only to be brought up short when a man cried out, rushing by to scoop all the boys into his arms. Zack felt the impact of their solidarity all the more because it was so genuine. So foreign. The man and three boys clung together, sobbing openly.

The boys were damaged, but they'd be okay. *Eventually.*

"Mr. Goldman, this way please."

His name plate read Officer Miller. The same cop who'd escorted him past the yellow tape when he'd first arrived and identified himself as the one who'd put in a missing person's report mere hours ago.

Felt like eons.

Zack looked up at the stone-colored sky made gauzy by the artificial lighting, then turned to follow the officer, a ruddy cheeked, barrel-chested farm boy whose burly presence kept the media and rubbernecks from straying beyond the secured perimeter.

As they drew near the strangely quiet circle where crime scene technicians scoured the area for evidence, Miller maneuvered in front of Zack, his dark eyes suddenly old. "Brace yourself. Close up is even worse, but maybe you'll be able to recognize the necklace."

Oh, God. It was a woman.

When the officer stepped back, the bursts of light from a technician's digital camera stormed through Zack's sense of the surreal. He ground his teeth together to block a surge of nausea. Surrounded by a scorched circle of earth, the body lay curled on its side, hands pulled into fists, knees drawn in as though for protection. Large patches of blackened skin remained on the skeleton like leather shrink-wrapped to bones. *How fucking long would a body have to burn to turn into that?*

Zack grabbed his chest and turned away, trying to breathe out of his mouth so the stench wouldn't push his stomach into full revolt. This was so wrong. It couldn't be Ann, could it? He thought he'd know instantly, but the thing on the ground didn't resemble anything remotely human, much less a woman he considered a sister. And the necklace he was supposed to identify? Fused to the corpse.

His eyes watered, and he looked up to find himself face to face with an old enemy.

Detective Tony Barnaba, Head of the Crimes Against Persons division at the Fargo PD, addressed his junior officer, but never took his eyes off Zack. "Officer Miller, where in procedure does it say to bring a civilian into the crime scene?"

Miller blanched. "Detective, I thought we could save time by having him try to identify the necklace. Autopsies take time, pictures are never as easy to ID, and with missing persons, every minute—"

Barnaba's head snapped toward Miller. "Are you telling me how to run a missing persons investigation, Officer?"

"No, sir."

"Man your post. We'll continue this discussion later."

"Yes, sir." Miller nodded at Zack before moving toward the

crowd at the edge of the yellow tape.

Zack pressed the fingers of his right hand against his temple again. This was not a good time to appear weak.

Barnaba looked out of place at the grizzly scene with his tailored sport coat, starched blue shirt, and spit-shined badge. Tall and trim, he looked healthy, vigorous, and ready to kick some ass. With the exception of more salt and pepper above his ears, the detective looked the same as he had all those years ago when his courtroom testimony had hammered the nail in Zack's coffin.

Zack made himself meet Barnaba's eyes. "I see you're still Mr. Nice Guy."

Barnaba's eyes darkened, and Zack braced for a punch, but it never came. He wished it would have. He needed to move. Walk, run, fight. Whatever.

"Your opinions don't mean anything to me, Goldman. I need some answers for my vic. You filed a missing persons report. Could this be her?"

What was there to say? Zack couldn't tell by clothing since the corpse had been naked when she was burned. And how the coroner was going to remove that necklace, he had no idea. He prayed the woman—whoever she was—had been dead long before the flames had devoured her flesh.

"Your house isn't too far from here, is it?" Barnaba continued.

"What's your point?"

"What's the nature of your relationship with your missing person?"

"Ann's like my kid sister. We work together at Samuel's. I spelled it out clearly enough in the report."

"You have alibis since she's been missing?"

Zack tamped down the urge to take a swing at the man he'd

unknowingly cuckolded all those years ago. Damned if Kasey didn't stand between them as palpably now as she had back then. Zack had gone to prison because of Kasey's betrayal and her husband's need for revenge. He hadn't been given a fair trial, and Barnaba had been to blame.

"If you want something to do, look into a local pastor. Dallan O'Neill. He's supposed to be a real pillar of the community, but as I learned the hard way, looks can be deceiving." Zack turned away but Barnaba's fingers gouged into his bicep. Zack jerked his arm and squared off, ready for battle, when one of the technicians yelled out from a crouched position next to the corpse.

"Detective, we're gonna have to tarp the body. I need more time to gather evidence, but I don't like the look of these clouds."

Barnaba looked up, muttering under his breath. Moisture hovered in the air as though waiting for permission to fall. After a moment, he leaned into Zack's personal space again. "You better watch every move you make, Goldman. I'll be happy to send you back to your boyfriends at the state lockup if I have even the slightest evidence you're involved here." He paused, and Zack wondered how it would feel to wrap his fingers around the man's neck and squeeze. Hard.

"About your missing person, this Ann... I need every detail. Friends, family, places she frequents, health or medical conditions, DNA samples, photographs. Everything. You have questions about what to bring, ask my staff. I'll be back at my office at oh-seven-hundred. If you're not there by noon with what we need, I'll find you. And you won't like it." Barnaba glared at Zack for another moment before moving on to address members of the investigating team standing in various perimeters of the sealed area.

Zack watched one of the technicians spray dirt hardener to make shoe impressions. Another vanished into a bush to search for God only knew. A plump raindrop spattered against Zack's cheek, and the scene exploded in a flurry of activity to preserve the evidence. He scanned the faces of the snoops lining the county road, looking for Archie. Zack had called him on his way to the river. He should've been here by now. Hopefully Twyla was okay.

Ann, too, because that burnt offering wasn't her.

Zack stepped through the grass toward his truck. He was getting paranoid. But what was worse? Worrying when you didn't have all the information, or pretending everything was all right when your gut bitch slapped you with foreboding?

No more John. Now Ann? What could he do? *What?* And where was Sloane? She'd looked so terrified when he'd told her about the burned body. She'd turned and run from him. Out the door without even saying goodbye.

A sudden helplessness rushed through him, a flaming backdraft of despair that nearly sent him to his knees. John had once remarked that loving is easy, it's the losing that's hard.

Yeah.

Zack wanted to hear Sloane. See her. Touch her.

He was every kind of fool.

"Mr. Goldman." Zack turned to find Officer Miller. "Detective Barnaba wants the name of Ms. Samuel's dentist, as those records will be most expedient to identify the victim. Or at least rule out—"

"Zack!"

Both men looked toward a tall blonde at the edge of the yellow tape. The gentle rain sluiced down her honeyed legs, her arms, molding her shirt to her body. Relief poured through him until he registered her terrorized eyes. He swallowed hard and faced Miller. "Tell Barnaba I'll be at the station later this morning with everything he's requested." Then he moved like a wooden soldier toward Sloane. "You don't belong here."

"Who is it?"

God, the look in her eyes. "Sloane—"

She fisted his T-shirt. "Tell me!"

"They don't know yet—"

"Tori. I can't find her!"

"What? Tori who?"

"My manager. My best friend! It's after midnight, and she's not home. She's *always* home!"

"Shh." He pulled her into his arms. She was shaking. He should probably take her to the ER. Shock was a bitch. He wondered when it was going to lay him low, too.

She clung for a moment before she pushed away and started to duck under the yellow tape. He grabbed her shoulders. "No, *no*. You can't, Sloane."

Lightning flashed, illuminating the hollows under her cheekbones. "I have to know. *Tori*. You don't understand. She was *burning*, Zack. It was her, wasn't it?" She turned, but his fingers held firm.

"What are you talking about?" He was yelling now and vaguely realized people were staring. He pulled her toward his truck, opened the door, and pushed her inside out of the rain, fists on his hips to keep them still. "Start talking."

"I'm sorry! Please don't be mad. I can't stand it." She covered her face with her hands.

"Christ! Sloane...I don't— It's not— Ah, hell!" He grabbed her icy fingers from her face, cupping his much larger ones around them. "I'm not mad at you. Please don't cry. Just tell me why you're so upset."

She pulled her hands from his grasp to place her fingers

against his cheeks, the pads of her thumbs feathering against his lips. The moment she closed her eyes, he felt a low pulse of energy storm through him, bolstering him, warming him from the inside out. When she opened her eyes, she was more composed. She brought her hands to her lap.

"I saw it. I saw *this*." She gestured toward the crime scene. "Someone burning. Earlier—or, I guess it was yesterday afternoon now. I was at the store. Tori touched me, and I saw someone burning. Coming toward me. I thought I was overwhelmed with everything going on with Ann...and you."

"That'd do it, all right."

"No, listen. At Ann's, after seeing her with Mr. Benjamin in the vision, I went into the bathroom and called Tori. I could tell right away she was upset. She saw her boyfriend at a restaurant with someone else when he'd told her he was going to be out of town. She was so beside herself, I told her I was coming over, but she pulled herself together. I tried to get her to talk more about it, but she kept changing the subject. So I let it go. Then when your friend called about the burning..." Her voice caught, and Zack couldn't *not* touch her. He reached for her hands again. She studied their joined fingers before continuing. "I had this awful feeling. I have a key to her place, so I went over there. After knocking with no answer, I let myself in." Her eyes found his. "She wasn't there, but her car was. Just like Ann. Bad things always happen when I try to use my visions."

"You can't possibly think any of this is your fault."

But her subtle shrug told him she did.

"Her car in the garage means nothing. She's probably making nice with her boyfriend."

"*No.*"

"How do you know? Have you met the guy?"

"No. He— Tori said he travels a lot for work."

115

The look in her eye stopped him cold. "Did you read something at her place?"

"Not exactly, but the vibes were the same. First Ann and now Tori." She hugged herself and bent over like she'd been sacked. He pulled her up and gathered her in his arms while his mind spun. *She blames herself. Why?*

If the corpse wasn't Ann, but Tori, the only logical connection between the two was Skinny Dipping. Which left Sloane square in the middle.

Pinpricks of panic needled his extremities. Puddles of water were forming in potholes along the road's shoulder. She shuddered, and he leaned into the truck to grab an old shirt behind the seat to wrap around her.

She looked at him, rain droplets clinging to her lashes. Her haunted expression unleashed every protective instinct in his DNA. Definitely time to start praying. "We'll figure this out, Goldie. We *will*." His arms tightened around her once more, and he pressed her wet head to his chest.

Please, God, help me protect her.

SIXTEEN

MONDAY

In Zack's truck driving back to her apartment complex at Blackhawk Gates, Sloane wondered how the sun continued to rise and the earth continued to turn when grief arrested a person's entire universe.

But this was no bad dream. Tori would never wake up. They'd gotten the call an hour earlier. The corpse's dental patterns had matched her oldest friend's.

Sloane felt small. A puny, insignificant ball in the shell of her body. The few comments Zack had made moments ago seemed to come from far away. Everything seemed so very far away now. Everything but her memories of Tori. Their less-than-carefree adolescence. The fun they'd had at work. Tori's perfectionism. The way she would crack her knuckles. Their fights...

The trust they'd forged over time and shared challenges.

Sloane pressed her lips together to prevent a moan from escaping, but she felt Zack's eyes on her anyway. A giant bomb was waiting to detonate inside her. A vibrating pressure that pounded its way from her stomach to her cranium. She tried to swallow past the razorblades in her throat, but that only made it worse. She squeezed her fists, digging her fingernails into her palms hoping the pain would wake her from this nightmare.

Oh, Tori! What were you hiding? Why couldn't you tell me?

"Why? Why Tori?" Her question hung in the cab for several heartbeats until Zack's hand reached over and cupped her neck.

117

"I wish I had answers for you. I'm so sorry." Emotion made his eyes a jeweled green. Sloane watched his face and knew he believed her. About her visions. About her sanity.

About Tori.

Last night, after she'd told him about her suspicions at the river, the last thing she remembered was his arms closing around her. She awoke hours later to find herself in her own bed. She'd bolted from the room only to be brought up short by Zack. The shadows under his eyes had made her want to weep. He was exhausted, but he'd taken care of everything while she slept. Attended to his dogs. Gathered information and DNA samples from Ann's and delivered them to the police station.

While there, he shared their concerns about Tori so they could do a wellness visit. When the police couldn't track her down, they'd secured a search warrant to enter her home.

That was how they had learned the name of her dentist.

And so the call had come.

Sloane looked down at her lap. Zack had even called Carmen to stay with her while she slept so someone would watch over her. He'd come and gone, and returned once more, and still she'd slept. Now they were in his truck, on the way back to her apartment after the short meeting she'd called for her staff.

He'd said no one should have to be alone after something like that.

She clamped down her eyelids and swallowed hard. He was so protective, but didn't seem to realize it. Didn't seem to know that taking care of others came naturally to him. Didn't know he had every quality she admired in a man.

Everything she ever wanted in the man she would one day love.

Oh.

COME HELL OR HIGH DESIRE

Sloane buried her face in her hands as the grief broke free, forceful sobs that rocked her body. He stopped the truck, hauled her onto his lap in the cramped cab, and wrapped his arms around her. No one had ever just held her and let her cry out her pain. Pain and confusion and vulnerable new feelings.

When the tears finally subsided, her arms were around his neck and he was silently stroking her hair, her back. She brought her face up and realized they were in her parking lot. He swept a matted lock of hair from her eyes.

He filled places she never realized were empty.

And right now she was damned empty. "Can you...can you come up?"

"Yes."

That one word and the intensity in his eyes unsettled her deeply. They stepped into the building entryway, and she had to re-key her pass code three times before she punched in the right series of numbers. As they moved into the elevator, she was acutely aware of the masculine presence of him. His body heat. Why wasn't she numb? Tori was dead. Ann was missing. There was a killer on the loose...

First floor.

Her eyes began to leak again. She wanted to scream from the pressure in her chest. From the longing of her body. It was wrong to want to be with him when her friend was lying on a slab in the morgue.

Say something. She pretended to look for something in her purse just to make some damn noise because she was *this close* to screaming like a crazy woman.

Second floor.

Zack stood perfectly motionless, controlled. How could he be so strong? Ann was probably dead, too.

Dead, dead, dead like Tori.

119

And sweet Abigail, Benjamin's granddaughter.

Sloane choked on another sob and whirled away from Zack. But he pulled her back against his chest, shushing softly into her hair. His body was so warm. She wanted to burrow in that heat. He would shield her from everything dark and ugly.

No, no, no! We'll only end up hurting each other.

He somehow managed to slip past all her barriers. How much longer would she be able to hide her duplicity? She'd be ruined. Her family devastated.

And that was if her visions didn't portend his death first.

I'm sorry, Tori! I should have tried to protect you.

She flinched from Zack's arms, bewildered that he might be her desert and her oasis all at once. When the elevator doors slid open at the third floor, she fled the cramped box and ran to her front door, where she slammed her forearm on the solid wood. She could feel his gaze travel over her.

Her body pulsed like a tuning fork.

She turned to face him, ready to fight, but his eyes—hot, wild—made the words die on her lips.

They came together at the same time. He held onto her face, the coarse calluses on his palms scraping her cheekbones. His teeth nipped, his stubble scoured. She was gasping by the time he seized her keys, unlocked the door, and kicked it shut behind them.

He took her straight to the floor, pulled her blouse down, and ripped open the front clasp of her bra. His eyes glittered.

"So p-perfect."

His hoarse stutter loosened something warm and altogether scary in her chest, but she had no time to think. His dark head replaced his hands at her breasts, and she arched up to meet his mouth, parting her legs so he could settle in closer. *Closer.* His hips rocked into her pelvis, the burning, hard length of him nearly sending her flying. She reached between them to unzip his pants.

"I need—"

"I know, baby." He pulled back to focus on the button-fly on her shorts and in an instant the wood floor was smooth and cool against her buttocks. His head dipped to her belly button, taking his time, tonguing the pink crystal ring there, sending heat rippling low through her abdomen. Made her feel earthy. Beautiful. Idolized. Her fingers curled into his hair, bringing his head up so she could somehow tell him.

But his eyes with their unbanked fire made her words of gratitude fall away.

"Your shirt. Off. Now."

He shifted to his knees in one fluid movement and peeled the black T-shirt still wet with her tears over his head. A black panther tattoo rippled across his pectorals with sinuous grace. Sloane stared at the animal, momentarily transfixed. It looked beautifully dangerous. Like him.

She ached to taste it.

Bare-chested, he paused, looking down at her, his eyes saying everything and then—

A slow smile. It was a promise.

And a threat.

Her bones melted into the floor.

A shaft of sunlight struck his hair when he leaned over her. She reached to touch the shining purple-black strands. He paused for her discovery a moment before taking both of her hands in one of his and stretching her arms over her head. Pinned, exposed, body vibrating, she closed her eyes to give herself up. To no longer think.

Just to feel.

To feel.

And forget.

His lips feathered delicately over her eyelids and time slowed. Nothing else mattered but the sensations he evoked as his mouth discovered the sensitive hairs of her brows, the planes of her cheekbones, the delicate inside of her ear, that small, secret hollow at her throat, on down to her breasts where his tongue traced the shape of her nipples. She arched into him. Lost. Drowning in an ocean of sensation.

Then cool air replaced that wonderful tongue. Her inelegant shiver raised the hairs on her arms, the swift response nearly painful.

She cracked her eyelids open. *What?*

He was watching her.

"Breathe, Goldie. You've got to breathe. It'll make it that much better."

A tremor gathered force at her knees, spiraling up through her pelvis, across her sternum and into her shoulders, finally radiating outward in a fierce pulse at her wrists where he still pinned them against the floor.

And she breathed.

Oh *hell, yeah*, she was breathing.

Restless, she shifted her body in line with his and made a soft cry of protest when he stilled her with a large hand low on her belly.

"*Shh.* Not done memorizing you." He released her hands from over her head and continued his exploration, fanning the curve of her belly, down, down, down her legs and then up the inside flesh of her thighs, rubbing his stubble, his torturous lips against her, until his tongue—Lord, *finally*—found her to assuage the ache.

Sweet Jesus.

Her world erupted in a cascade of blue crystals, hips

bucking off the floor as he clasped her thighs, fingers curling into her muscles to anchor her. The sweet sting of his nails, the bold stroke of his tongue extorted more pleasure from her nerves until she wondered if she could survive the onslaught.

Pulsing blue light fired behind her eyelids. Her fingers crawled through his silky hair. Grasping, pulling, releasing. Flying. She was flying.

Dying.

The little death.

She'd never felt the esoteric blade quite as exquisitely. She couldn't contain the pressure.

Now.

Her eyelids flew open and he moved over her—a dark angel—to swallow her wild cry with his mouth.

***

Zack studied the woman beneath him. Her hair splayed across the floor like a rich wheat field at dusk, her lips parted, her body warm, undulating against his hand, slick, arousing, honest.

He'd never felt so vital, so pulsing with energy. Touching her, experiencing her—the colors, textures, smell, sounds, and taste of her—made every one of his senses seem to awaken for the first time.

He'd been right to come back here with her. He felt awful about Tori, and who knew what was coming next with Ann, but right now they needed this more than anything, or they'd both go crazy. They needed to feel alive. Feel joy.

Love.

Even after everything, he still couldn't help believing in it.

Maybe one day it would kill him.

He continued touching her, his hand moving in rhythm with her hips, his eyes hungrily watching as a new orgasm rolled over and through her body. She clutched at him, arched her back, offering the curve of her throat to his tongue. *So sexy.* Her uninhibited response was a gift. It humbled him.

And made something arcane rise within.

Possession.

God, he wanted to be in her.

Mark her.

She quivered one last time and her lids opened to reveal eyes of molten chocolate. His heart tripped at her tears. "Was I too rough?"

"No, oh, no." Her arms laced around his neck, her legs around his trunk to pull him down into the cradle of her hips. He was gonna explode in these damn jeans any minute now. She lifted her pelvis to grind into him. Beads of sweat rolled down his back, and he shuddered. Her sudden laughter wove around him, husky with spent tears. "Take your clothes off before you hurt yourself," she whispered.

Yes, maybe someday his belief in love would kill him.

But someday wasn't today.

***

This man. He made something effervesce inside her. *Getting too close.* She bit her lip, breathing hard once more as he carried her to the bedroom and laid her gently down. *Don't think. Just don't think about it.*

She eased up on her elbows—damn, her arms were shaking—to watch him quickly shed the rest of his clothes and wrap himself in protection. Butterflies, heat, goose bumps, and greed threaded through her as her legs moved restlessly, twisting the quilt. *Waiting.* All that beautiful, powerful male sinew—that *otherness*—hers to taste. Somehow she knew his taste would linger on her tongue for a long time to come.

She'd never been more aware of her heart beating in her breast. The subtle quavers of her low belly. The fractional tightening of quadriceps, her insides. The swelling of her—

She exhaled heavily. He looked up and smiled. A secret smile, a *knowing* smile that made her nipples contract. *Yes, you* do *know me, don't you?*

She might not like that later. Too late?

Thin ice.

He edged onto the bed, and she shot up on her knees.

He stopped, frowned. "You okay?"

She nodded. *Don't you dare lie to this man.* "I don't know." But she eased toward him anyway, unable to do anything else. She took a deep breath, brushed a lock of hair from his forehead, and looked him in the eye. "Kiss me."

He maintained eye contact as he leaned in and took her bottom lip between his, a torturous massage that drew a moan from the well of her desire. He eased away, still not touching her, to lean back on a pile of pillows against the headboard.

"You drive this, baby."

She bent down to kiss his belly to hide the wetness that sprang to her eyes. His ab wall was firm, hot, and jumpy beneath her lips, and her eyes soon dried. She spread her palms to touch as much of his landscape as she could, her tongue broad and salty with his taste. She turned her head to rub her cheek against the thin trail of hair spearing down to his groin, smiling to see his fist grip the bed covers.

Safe, solid ice? So far he'd proven that his word was good. He'd been inside her head, and nothing bad had happened to him.

Yet.

Stop it.

Okay. Her whole body seemed to sigh. She pressed one last kiss to his belly before sitting up. His eyes were closed, lids fluttering, his whole body taut. She smiled, heart expanding until her smile started to fade.

Don't. Think.

She moved up his body to straddle his legs, easing forward until his erection grazed her, and she gasped at the electrifying contact. His eyes opened, his fingers inching up, curling into her thighs as she rose over him, the wide tip of him pulsing against her heat. His nostrils flared, his mouth opening on a guttural groan to receive her kiss the moment she slid down his length.

She sucked in her breath, neck curving back until strands of her hair brushed the swell of her buttocks. She could feel him, feel him *everywhere*. Hot mouth at her breasts, thumb of one hand beguiling her clit, fingernails of his other hand digging in her ass to enjoy her movement—*her* movement—because, oh yeah, she was driving this thing.

Sssssssafe ice.

Swelling inside. *More.*

He leaned forward, wrapping his arms around her, hands climbing her neck to tangle in her hair and pull.

Her nerve endings sizzled. *Faster.* Open mouths, fingers entwined behind her back. A soul exposed. *Yes.*

She watched their joining. Inhaled the tang of their mating. Impossibly erotic.

The last inhibition fell and with it, incoherent words of...

Love.

Her heart stuttered. *No!*

"Zack!"

Sweat at his temples, his eyes liquid green, so achingly intense. "Let go, baby. I've got you."

That's what I fear.

But the blade cut through the humid air. And untethered like never before, she soared.

SEVENTEEN

Zack cut the A/C and rolled his window down. It was only ten-fourteen p.m., but night had fallen uneasily. The streets remained dry, though lightning bucked restlessly in the clouds. More unsettled weather for the third day in a row.

Suited his state of mind perfectly.

With every mile he put between Sloane and himself, his chest wound tighter. They'd spent the whole day together, going through the motions of monitoring their individual workplaces, feeding Ann's stray cat, checking up on his dogs, reading the alternating anguish and joy in Ann's journal that left them no closer to any answers, and after the five o'clock news, fielding the inevitable phone calls from people expressing their horror over Tori and the now publicly missing Ann.

Less than an hour ago, they'd shared a quiet meal at Sloane's and had fallen asleep on the couch, too exhausted to function any longer. He'd slept maybe thirty minutes before his mind started spinning again. She had murmured when he gently moved away from her, tucking a blanket around her and leaving one last kiss on her lips before he left, double checking the lock behind him.

He would never forget this morning in her arms. It was one of the most generous gifts he'd ever received because he'd never felt closer to another human being. He *felt* her. Felt her down deep where he didn't know if he'd ever get her out.

It was a dangerous path to tread.

She's nothing like Kasey.

No, but he'd only known Sloane for a couple days.

Extraordinary days, though. Christ, he'd practically crawled around in her head.

But still. Two days.

Jesus.

Being with her messed with his mind. Even so, he hadn't wanted to leave her, but one of her questions kept nagging at him.

What if there was a second journal? One that continued where the first one left off? In the first one, Ann hadn't known she was pregnant. At least she hadn't written about it yet.

But...if there was a second journal, why would she have thrown away only the first one? Why *did* she throw it away? Or did someone else?

If there was a second journal, he had to find it.

He stopped a few condos down from Ann's and killed the headlights. Before he even stepped foot on the grass, the back of his neck tingled. A faint light spilled through her picture window, but he hadn't left any lights on this afternoon. He was sure of it. He switched off the truck's dome lights, retrieved a butterfly knife from the glove box, and clipped the sheath to his jeans before slipping into the smothering night.

He crept around to the back of Ann's condo and peered into the darkened window of the guest room. The light was coming from Ann's room. His breathing kicked up another notch. Was she back? He ducked down and shifted in the bushes by the house until he was positioned next to the patio door. The shades were drawn. Something she would surely do. Someone was banging drawers as though putting clean laundry away.

Or looking for something.

He stood upright in front of her patio door, his hand raised in midair to pound on the glass when an icy sensation drifted through him.

Sloane? He felt her presence strongly. He spun, expecting to see her standing there, eyes spitting sparks, but in the next flash of lightning he saw nothing but manicured lawn, the grass spikes silvery.

The banging stopped. Zack stepped away from the door and pressed himself against the cool stucco, straining to hear. The sudden crack of a bullet's report blistered his ears. A scream.

A man's scream.

Zack pulled his knife and dove for the ground as two more shots followed in quick succession. He squeezed the knife's handle in his fist, making himself take large, quiet gulps of air.

Was Ann in there, too? He felt for his cell to dial 911, but it wasn't on him. *Shit.* Must've gotten snagged in the bushes.

He positioned himself next to the guest bedroom window again and used the knife to jimmy the window open wide enough that he could shred the screen. He reached in and turned the lever to fully open the window. Suddenly he heard a dull scraping noise.

Adrenaline kicked through his veins. He'd heard the sound before. Like a body being dragged across the floor. He slid through the window, dropping quietly to the floor in the dark room. He edged toward the door as a ski-masked figure clad in head-to-toe black moved in the hallway. The person was tall, but he had maybe twenty pounds on the guy. Zack lunged, taking them both to the ground. The intruder grunted, his gun skittering across the wood floor to slide under a heavy credenza.

Zack grappled for the ski mask, but the man gave a fierce thrust with powerful legs. Zack flew back, cracking his head against the wall. He didn't have time to catch his breath before his assailant came at him, landing a bruising round house to his ribs and then bending low to charge him.

Zack bent in half at the explosion of pain in his chest and brought his knee up with everything he had. The man grunted and briefly grabbed his midsection before quickly recovering.

Zack reached for his knife but the sheath was empty. He slid to the credenza, fingers sweeping the floor for the gun. Feeling the cool metal in his hands, he rolled away, narrowly missing a bludgeoning by a heavy silver sculpture.

The intruder came at him again, and Zack scrambled to his haunches, sighting the pistol between the bastard's eyes. His finger tightened on the trigger in an agony of indecision. He'd fought so much during his life. Would he never be free of it?

Survive or surrender?

Survive. Sloane's word whispered through his mind as the man's yell tore through the hall. The black-clothed figure lunged and then spun about, flailing his arms to dislodge a gray mass on his back. The cat!

Zack angled the gun down for a non-critical wound and fired. The intruder crumpled against the wall, and Zack ran into the fully lit bedroom, blinking against the sudden brightness.

"Ann! Ann!" Her room was torn asunder. The dresser spewed drawers, the mattress sagged off the box spring, and the bottom half of the closet was ransacked where John had told Ann to store the four gray totes he went to the grave without explaining to either of them. Papers spewed onto the carpeted floor from one of the totes, but he left it lying there and nearly tripped over a body when he came around the other side of the closet island.

A man. Insensate brown eyes gaped at the ceiling, three holes marring his pressed ivory dress shirt.

Distant thunder rumbled through Zack's chest. In death the handsome man looked so young—his smooth, clean nails and callous-free palms so unlike his own. Zack gripped the edge of the island to steady himself. This was the man who'd driven up to Divine Shepherd Lutheran in a Lexus.

The man who'd likely fathered Ann's baby. *Dallan O'Neill.*

What was he doing here? And who was the guy in the hall? What had either of them been looking for?

And where, God, is Ann?

He inhaled deeply, feeling pain in his ribs. He brought his arm up gingerly to test the movement when a sick feeling washed over him. What if he'd hit the femoral artery in the intruder's leg and all the answers bled out with him?

He rushed back into the hallway, finding nothing but a narrow trail of blood leading outside.

He stood at the door, peering out into the darkness. No! *How?*

He needed to call someone. But who? The police? How the hell was he supposed to explain all this?

But the time for thinking was over.

Police cars screamed down the street, sirens blaring, lights spinning, the red and blue an oddly beautiful accompaniment to the pulses of lightning that arced through the sky.

Zack stood in the doorway, backlit from the carnage of Ann's house. Police officers drew their guns behind cover of their car doors and yelled for him to drop his weapon.

Only then did he remember he still held the gun.

A profound stillness gripped him.

The gun clattered to the floor.

He said nothing—did nothing—when they tackled him and yanked his arms behind his back. The metal cuffs that pulled at his wrists were cold. Unyielding. But nothing compared to the fire in his ribs.

In his conscience.

Ann...John...Sloane. I'm sorry.

Somehow he felt Sloane's presence again, but this time, he blocked her, shame burning a wasteland through his hope.

One of the officers, bow-legged and with heavy lines bracketing his mouth, stood watch over him as the others briskly went through the rooms. Zack could hear him radio for the crime scene techs. His mind grasped for options, but he couldn't seem to free himself from a fathomless well of negativity. Why bother trying to explain? It hadn't worked last time.

This time, they'll lock you away forever.

He'd rather die trying to escape than waste away in prison. Feeling cold all over, he looked around the room, assessing his options.

***

Sloane nearly went on two wheels around the corner, but hell if she was going to slow down. If the cops were following her, all the better. Tears ran down her cheeks, and she blinked hard to clear her vision.

She'd woken up alone, a deep, inexplicable fear beating at her. Mindlessly, she'd raced into her bedroom closet and pulled down a carved mahogany chest. Inside was a black tourmaline nestled in red felt. It was supposed to help focus her telepathic energies. She hadn't given it a second look since the day her mother had presented it to her on her twentieth birthday.

Without thinking, she'd grabbed the smooth stone and gasped at the images that suddenly exploded in her mind. Zack going through Ann's window. Struggling for his life. Finding the body. The police coming... Oh God, he'd reached out to her.

Don't be sorry, Zack! Please don't give up!

And then...nothing. Try as she might, she couldn't reach

him. Couldn't *feel* him.

She squinted through the windshield, flew through a red light, and prayed that somehow she'd be able to help in time. Two more blocks. Her heart stuttered when she turned the final corner and saw the circus of police vehicles and nervous neighbors.

She flew out of her SUV without bothering to shut the door and bolted across two lawns to Ann's. They'd already set up the yellow tape with police stationed to keep people away. She ducked under and ran until she was clothes-lined by an officer.

"Zack! Zack!" She scrambled off grass, trying to peel the officer's fingers from her arm. "Let me go! I have information!"

"Don't you fucking touch her!" Zack staggered to his feet, lips twisting in a snarl, triceps bulging as he struggled against the handcuffs behind his back.

Another cop stepped in front of him, addressing the officer who held her. "Giles, bring her here."

Sloane hurried into the living room to stand in front of Zack. She took in the gashes on his face, the empty look in his eyes. How she ached to take him in her arms.

He looked away, a muscle ticking in his jaw. "You shouldn't have come."

Pain in her midsection made her gasp. "You're hurt!"

"Don't cry for me, Goldie."

"Someone has to!"

He hung his head. That scared her more than anything.

"Ready to talk, eh, Goldman?" It was the officer who'd intercepted her.

"He needs a doctor!" She reached out to touch the sleeve of the wiry officer who was clearly in charge of guarding Zack. "Officer...Janklow. Please help him." In her heeled sandals she had about seven inches on him, and by God, she'd send him packing if he didn't help Zack.

The lines around Janklow's mouth deepened. He patted her hand. "Listen, Ms…"

"Sloane."

"Ms. Sloane. Mr. Goldman will receive medical attention soon."

"Not soon enough! Making him sit here and suffer after all he's been through is barbaric."

"Sloane, it's just a bruise. You need to go. Right now."

She swung to face Zack. "You shut up since you can't seem to help yourself." She turned back to Janklow, who was saved a second tongue lashing when another officer came into the room. His assessing blue eyes swept over the scene, lingering on Zack. He turned toward Janklow and jerked his head at Zack. "Take him back to the station."

"Yes, sir." Janklow took Zack's arm. Sloane's heart stuttered and then pounded against her chest like it was ready to burst free of its skin and bone captivity. "No, wait! Sergeant Bradley. I know what happened here. You *must* listen!"

He raised an eyebrow, and Sloane could have sworn he was about to smile, but he only nodded. "Your name?"

"Sloane Swift. I own Ski—ah, I'm a business owner in town. My father is Dr. Henry Swift, and my mother is Veronica Bell Swift. She works with the FBI…as a psychic." Her face heated, but she pressed on. "I can…see things, too, and I'd like to help here." Her tongue felt like fly paper. She noted the swelling around Zack's eyes, the cuts on the lips that had made her body sing, and felt her backbone slide into place. She swallowed hard and met Bradley's eyes. "Please. Hear me out."

A tech came into the living room to take pictures of the blood streaks on the floor. Sergeant Bradley gave Sloane his attention. "How long have you known Mr. Goldman?"

135

She blanched. "Since Sunday morning, sir, but Ann works for me and—"

Bradley held up a hand. "I'm sorry, Ms. Swift, but I have other things to do here. If you'll follow Officer Giles, he'll take your statement."

"No! You aren't *listening*. There's a killer out there. I saw him! He's got to be the same man who killed Tori Daily!"

"Enough, Ms. Swift. Mr. Goldman was holding the gun that took the life of Pastor—" He stopped abruptly, realizing his blunder. "Ah, shit. Take her—"

Sergeant Bradley's lips continued moving, but Sloane didn't hear another word. The room swam in darkness a moment as she fought her way back to coherence.

He'd said pastor. In light of everything, that could only mean Dallan O'Neill.

Murdered? By whom? The same person who killed Tori? There were two different MOs for the kill, though. So did Dallan kill Tori, then meet his own death from the man who'd attacked Zack? And where was Ann?

The only thing Sloane knew for certain was that Zack was innocent. She looked at him and felt her bones hollow. "Zack! Tell them there was another man here when you arrived." She spun toward Sergeant Bradley. "The other man was the one who killed Dallan O'Neill, not Zack!"

"Hold up. I didn't identify the victim. How do you know who—"

"Analyze the blood on the floor. That's the blood of the guy who got away. *He's* the killer. Zack, tell them!" Why wasn't he saying anything?

"Ms. Swift, go with Officer Giles immediately, or we'll let you cool off in the county jail." Bradley's eyes were tired. He turned to respond to a tap on his shoulder from a technician.

"This is crazy. Zack is *innocent*. He was here to retrieve documents to help you in the investigation of Ann's disappearance!" Sloane walked up to Zack as Giles unfastened his handcuffs from his belt. She ignored him, directing all her anger at Zack. "This is *not* okay, dammit. I thought you were a fighter. How are you going to help Ann if you go to jail for something you didn't even do? I was ready to face my demons for you, Zack. Wake the hell up and be the man John thought you could be. The man I know you are."

His clenched jaw let her know she'd hit her mark. She held her wrists out for the cuffs and followed Giles out the front door, every step away from Zack a blow to the heart.

Her highly intellectual father called this sort of thing tough love.

She finally understood.

And hated it.

EIGHTEEN

Zack nearly bit though his cheek watching Officer Giles usher Sloane into the back of the squad car. She didn't belong here surrounded by violence and death. Exposing her to such horror concerned him more than his bruised rib. Almost as much as her blistering censure.

He deserved it.

Somehow, she'd once again cut through all the bullshit. John had been the only other one to do that. John had believed in him.

And so, he finally realized, did Sloane.

By losing Ann, he'd let John down. If he gave up now, he'd do the same to Sloane. How had she known everything that had happened to him since he'd shown up here at Ann's tonight? She'd flown in here like an avenging angel, and he hadn't even backed her up.

He turned to Officer Janklow. "I'll give my statement now."

The cop opened his mouth to say something when another man stepped into view.

"Really? This I'd like to hear, Goldman."

Detective Barnaba. *Perfect.*

Zack forced air through his nose though his chest protested the expansion. He flexed his fingers so they wouldn't ball into fists. He had to rein in his emotions. No way was he going to come out of this if he was as undisciplined as he'd been eleven years ago when he'd had his first encounter with the detective.

"You requested documents of Ann's, and I brought them to

138

the station earlier. Later on, I thought of something else which I came here to get, but someone was already in the condo. I surprised him, we fought, and in defense, I shot him with his own gun. I left him in the hallway to see if Ann was in the house, then I found O'Neill's body. He'd been shot three times and was dead when I found him. I didn't kill him, Barnaba."

"Okay. So where is this 'other' suspect? And who is he? Another lover of Ann's?" Zack started, and Barnaba smiled. "You're surprised I found out about Ann and O'Neill? You underestimate me, Goldman. Like you always have." He paused, placing his hands on his hips. "A theory is sliding around in my mind. A certain love triangle between Ann, O'Neill, and...you."

"You son of a bitch. I could never—"

"Careful, there." Barnaba's teeth flashed, a camera-perfect contrast to his tanned face. "I think Ann chose the esteemed Pastor over you, and you couldn't handle that. Not when you'd been rejected by so many others. Maybe it made you so mad you wanted to get rid of the competition."

Zack strained against his cuffs. "Stop feeling sorry for yourself over Kasey, and do your fucking job. There's a killer out there. That's his blood on the floor. Get your dogs on the scent." The men glared at one another until Barnaba turned to look at one of the officers. "Janklow, send a tech over here to get a sample from this lowlife, then get him out of my face."

"We don't have a warrant on him yet, sir."

Barnaba parted his sport coat to put his hands on his hips and swung around to face Zack. "You gonna sign a release stating we can take a DNA swab off you?"

"My genes should be on record, but what the hell. Sounds like a good time."

A hazmat-suited tech came running from the back room.

"Anybody got a box? We got a feral cat back there."

"*Grab it!*" someone yelled as a streak of gray shot through the house and outside into the night. Barnaba shook his head before he moved off.

Zack's shoulders dropped and he looked at the floor until another tech came over. In no time, he'd signed the release and given his oral swab. What did it really matter? It would either clear him or it wouldn't.

Most likely it wouldn't.

Janklow nudged him toward the door. "Let's go, buddy."

Zack looked around desperately as the warm night air hit his face. Sweat trickled down his back and the sides of his face. The pain in his chest was no more.

Find a way out.

Officer Giles stood talking to one of the other cops. The swirling red lights of the squad cars cast monstrous visages on the faces of the gathered crowd. Sloane was nowhere to be seen. Had she given her statement so quickly? They'd better have let her go.

The closer they got to the waiting police vehicle, the faster the past reared up, flooding him with memories of his beating in that seedy alley so many years ago. He'd held his own with the first three gangbangers Kasey had hired. When four more joined in, he'd gone down in the worst beating of his life. The first responding officers had pulled the thugs off him, clubbing them back with batons, pepper spray, and Tasers.

Then Barnaba had turned up and his luck had hit the road.

History seemed to be repeating itself.

Fuck that.

When Janklow moved ahead of him to open the squad door, Zack brought his right leg up in a jackknife kick that bounced the officer against the car. Janklow went down, momentarily dazed. Zack didn't wait to see if he drew his gun. He ran, weaving through yards, using the element of surprise, mature trees, and the dark to his advantage until his lungs screamed. Behind him he heard men yelling to each other as they spread out in pursuit.

He headed for the river where the trees grew denser, providing more cover. He wanted to go all the way into the water in case they called in the K-9 unit, but with the cuffs, he'd have trouble staying afloat. He continued on, hugging the bank, entering the water where it was shallow enough, putting distance between himself and the officers who didn't have his experience with the terrain. His heart pounded in his throat and mosquitoes swarmed every exposed surface.

If only he could use his hands.

A small branch broke the skin below his eye as he stumbled through thickly tangled underbrush. He managed to right himself at the last instant, but pain shot up his chest through his left arm. He saw stars as he struggled for footing and pressed on toward his destination.

You'd better be home, Raessler.

Like Zack, Archie had always loved the Red River. Zack had never been happier his friend had built his wife's dream house in such a private spot. A few miles later, he climbed the bank toward the Raessler's backyard and sprinted for the patio door. It sucked that he had to involve his friends in any way, but once he got the cuffs off, he'd move on.

Zack heard Archie's dogs barking madly inside the house. Archie had probably grabbed his twelve gauge and posted somewhere strategic. He prayed his buddy wouldn't let the dogs out because they'd bite first and sniff later.

Zack used his foot to pound on the patio door. A light flicked on in the kitchen, and Archie flew outside, his shotgun pointed to the ground. "What the piss, man? Get in here!"

Twyla stood in the kitchen, a navy blue robe belted tightly above her rounded abdomen. Her eyes widened as she took in his swollen, bloody face and handcuffs. Then she turned to the sink to fill a tea kettle.

Zack's torso and legs began to shake. "Don't do that on my account. I'm not sticking around."

Archie slapped a hand on the counter. "Stop that. What's going on?"

"I need these off." He lifted his arms behind his back and winced. "And some ibuprofen. Please."

Twyla hustled to the bathroom and returned with six small pills. Archie lifted a glass of water to Zack's mouth and the pills, then brushed a kiss on his wife's cheek. "Go on back to bed, love. Turn off all the lights. I'll be in soon."

He grabbed a set of keys off the wall and didn't say anything as they neared his workshop behind the house. Once they were inside, he shut the door and pulled the string affixed to the single bulb above the saw table. Then he put on his safety glasses, shoved another pair on Zack, and took an electric angle grinder off a shelf of meticulously arranged power tools. Zack turned around, bent over, and cranked his arms up to lay them on the table. "Hurry."

"I'll cut them apart, then we'll worry about the rest." Archie started the grinder and within seconds, the chain between the cuffs broke apart.

Zack shook out his arms, testing the pain in his chest, and laid his hands on the table. Free arms relieved the pressure in his midsection tremendously.

"I don't know, man," Archie said. "Your wrists are so big, I don't have much leeway to cut."

"I can't leave with these attached. Come on, you're a master with this thing." Zack tried to smile, but failed. Besides, this was Archie. He didn't have to pretend.

For a moment, he thought his buddy would refuse, but then he clamped down on Zack's forearm so tightly he felt his arm tingle. "Lord Almighty, I don't need a tourniquet."

Archie looked up at him and grinned. "Case I nick you, I don't want you to bleed to death on my table."

Great. Zack closed his eyes as the grinder started spinning. The heat of the disc ripping through the metal burned so bad he thought his skin would melt. Archie held his arm in a death grip, the grinder unyielding in his other hand. Bile rose in Zack's throat and he wanted to look away, but couldn't help himself from watching as the disc chewed through the metal, closer and closer until it was almost all the way through.

When mere millimeters held the cuff together, Archie laid the grinder aside and reached for metal clippers to finish the task. The other cuff fell off in quick succession, and Zack was free. He slumped onto his forearms against the work table, and managed the ghost of a smile. "Thanks. I owe you big."

Archie grunted and walked over to his shop fridge and pulled out a water bottle and half a sandwich. "I'm going to clean this up and then lay back down beside my wife where I've been all night. Come tomorrow, if anybody asks, I never moved. What else do you need?"

"Would you check on Kiefer and Kiah and get me a phone? I lost mine somewhere. Either in my truck or on the ground at Ann's. Either way, the cops'll find it."

"No problem. I'll bring your mutts here. You go to ground, then let me know where I can get a phone to you."

When Zack started to thank him, Archie held up his hand. "Shit goes down, we pull together. I saw the news orgy earlier about the poor woman by the river. It's all the media's been talking about all night. And now you find O'Neill dead at Ann's? Leaves a lot more questions, I know." He swept the table with a hand broom, then sprayed it with cleaner. Something spattered on the metal roof of the quonset, and both men froze. But one drop quickly followed another until it became a steady patter. Zack saw Archie's shoulders loosen up and tried to make his do the same. The rain would help cover his tracks.

"I don't know how this has gotten so messed up, but if something happens to me—"

"Shut your damn mouth. This'll be okay. We always land on our feet."

Zack recognized the look on his oldest friend's face. Fear masked by anger. "But if I don't, make them rush me to surgery. Have them take both kidneys—put one on ice or something. Just in case. Hand me some paper. I'll write a note."

Archie slapped the small broom against the table. "Stop it before I turn you in myself." His eyes communicated what he couldn't say. What it meant when someone saw your darkness and fought for you anyway. The unshakable bond born of desperate circumstances and even more desperate despair. The gut-level awareness that your life had meaning beyond death.

Knowing you would leave a hole in someone's life should you go.

It was all there in Archie's expression, so thick with memory Zack nearly choked on it.

"My kids need a goddamn uncle." Archie cleared his throat roughly and emptied the dustpan into a fast-food bag, which he buried at the bottom of a garbage can. He reorganized a few tools that didn't need reorganizing before turning back to Zack. "Friend of mine has a beat up El Camino down behind the Curling Club shack. Keys are under the back fender for emergencies. I guess now qualifies."

144

Zack didn't know how his stomach would be able to handle any food right now, but he held up the sandwich. "Thanks again. I don't know what—"

"Yeah, yeah. I'll call in some IOUs when the baby comes along and Twyla and I need a night out." He smiled, but it didn't reach his eyes. Zack's throat squeezed. The two men stared at each other a moment before Zack grabbed the remains of the handcuffs then quickly slipped out the door and vanished into the night.

It wasn't until a few miles down the river that he chucked the handcuffs into the sluggish water, wondering how Archie already knew the identity of the man who was murdered in Ann's bedroom when there was no way in hell it could have been released to the public yet.

NINETEEN

The world had gone crazy in forty-eight hours. Sloane had just pulled into her parking lot when she'd heard of Zack's escape on the radio. Now, her windshield wipers slapped at the rain, sending it flying as quickly as it landed. The black tourmaline seemed to burn a hole in her jean shorts pocket. Somehow, she'd gone from easygoing business owner to card-carrying psychic freak show whose boyfriend had a price on his head.

Not that said fugitive would consider himself her boyfriend.

Not that Sloane No-Strings-Attached Swift had ever called any other man her boyfriend before.

Awesome. She'd clearly lost touch with reality sometime around seven o'clock Sunday morning.

"Where are you when I need you, Tori?" She gunned it southbound on University Street. Shouldn't need to worry about getting pulled over. All available law enforcement was on a man-hunt for Zack.

The only way to help him was to find out who'd killed Dallan O'Neill. How was she supposed to do that? *CSI* groupie she was not. She was more of a *Modern Family* kind of girl, but she doubted any witty one-liners would score her re-entry to Ann's condo. Especially since the investigators were still on site. No, there was no way she'd get into Ann's.

So, time to see Colette O'Neill. She was willing to bet her livelihood that the put-together society wife knew something

146

about her husband's illicit activities.

The rambling, brick rectory was set so far back from the church proper that Sloane normally wouldn't have seen it at this time of night. Yet, as she approached the five block campus, not only was the rectory ablaze with light, the church was as well. Cars filled the parking lot like it was broad daylight on a Sunday morning.

She parked and ran through the rain into the church. A tall, trim woman in matching green slacks and pumps approached her, her thin lips pursing in a web of vertical lines as she quickly assessed Sloane from head to toe.

Yeah, soaked shorts, frayed sweatshirt, and sexed-up espadrilles weren't exactly proper church attire. *Too bad.*

The woman apparently came to the same conclusion for she continued forward as though she'd never faltered, her arms outstretched. "Come dear. I'll find you a towel. We have sandwiches in the fellowship hall. I'm Betty." The older woman led Sloane down the hallway toward a growing crescendo of noise. "Can you imagine? Dear Lord, it's a sorry world." Betty tucked Sloane in line with the others who'd come to eat, gossip, and offer support amid the scandal.

Sloane turned to find Betty already melting into the crowd. There had to be a least fifty people in the room. Sloane checked her watch, feeling uneasy. *One-thirty-five a.m.* At this time of night, how had all these people found out about a murder that had happened less than three hours ago? It hadn't been on TV. Police scanners? The radio? Seriously, had they organized a phone chain? And why were they all *here?*

The line ahead of Sloane fractured and Colette walked through, a modern day Moses parting the Red Sea, her face a fascinating display of beautiful sorrow. Sloane had never seen anyone's sadness so poignantly lovely. This lass apparently didn't have the ugly-cries in her.

Sloane approached Colette amid her entourage of veteran church ladies. Before they could circle the wagons around her, Sloane reached out and touched Colette's starched white shirt sleeve. Her perfectly made-up eyes tracked slowly to Sloane's face. Something in those brown depths made Sloane snatch her hand away.

"Excuse me, Mrs. O'Neill. I am deeply sorry to hear the news about your husband. Might I have a word with you in private?"

A veteran church lady in beige bounced her apple belly in front of Colette. "Who are you? If you're with the media—"

Colette patted the woman's arm. "It's okay, Edith. This is Miss Swift. She's a friend of the poor, unfortunate Ann Samuel." Edith gasped and looked at Sloane with intermingled horror and interest. Colette brought a hand to her face, her diamond ring glittering under the harsh fluorescent lights. "Oh dear, please tell me the body they discovered at the river isn't hers?"

A knife twisted in Sloane's gut. "No. I'm here because..." She looked at the assembled crowd and wanted to scream. "I know this is a horrendous time for you, but please, I need to talk to you. In private."

Frowning, Edith placed her hand on the ledge of her stomach. "Look here, miss, you should have the good sense not to barge in here in Mrs. O'Neill's time of grieving."

Colette wiped at her tears without smudging her make-up. "It's all right. I need to help if I can. It's what Dallan would want me to do. Please excuse us."

Sloane followed Colette into a darkened room. The door shut with a soft click. In less time than it took for her eyes to adjust, Colette had switched on a delicate swan-shaped lamp.

In the soft light, she stood framed in front of a life-sized oil painting depicting Jesus in The Divine Mercy.

"What do you want with me?" Colette's pretense of sorrow was suddenly gone.

Sloane's stomach turned over. "I am so sorry about your husband."

"So you said. But why are you here?"

Sloane pressed her palms together in front of her body. "I have reason to believe Dallan and Ann were having an affair. I'd like to know if you can give me any information that might help us find her."

"How do you know she wasn't already baked by the side of the river?"

Sloane shivered at her rancor. Colette hadn't even flinched at the admission of her husband's infidelity. Sloane felt the urge to bolt. The black tourmaline in her pocket warmed her. "The victim isn't Ann. How long were they involved?"

"Who knows? Dallan's always had any number of women. I know nothing of Ann."

"But you knew they were involved."

Colette threw her hands up. "Anyone could see how she made such a fool of herself over him. She's a child playing a dangerous game." She moved to stand behind the finely carved mahogany desk. She looked down at its smooth surface, unmarred by even a single stack of papers. With the pink toile parson's chair and voluminous silk curtains, the space looked like a designer showroom.

Sloane's skin crawled, but she waited. Colette's hand clasped a crystal paperweight until her knuckles stretched taut. Sloane's mind started to strum, blue and white lights pulsing in her peripheral vision.

Oh my God, it's the missing Swarovski rhino!

149

How did it get here? Did Ann bring it, or had Dallan? She nearly asked the question out loud—but what if Colette retaliated and destroyed it? *Bide your time.* Maybe she could salvage things with Benjamin, after all.

When Colette finally spoke, she had an edge that cut through the hazy blue in Sloane's mind. "If I were you, I'd keep my nose out of everyone's dirty laundry. Dallan's dead. That selfish son of a bitch has ruined my life!"

Veins stood out in Colette's temples, and she seemed to have forgotten that she wasn't alone as she banged the crystal rhino against the desk. Sloane nearly fainted.

"So much for the big congregation in California. He couldn't keep it in his pants, but I never thought he'd get someone pregnant. He told me he'd fix it. He *told* me."

Sloane's skin felt like it was floating over a stormy sea. "How did you learn about the pregnancy?"

"My trouble-shooter."

Oh Lord, someone else? "Who?"

But Colette only laughed until she burst into tears. Real ones this time.

It wasn't pretty.

Knowing she wouldn't get any more answers from her, Sloane felt in her pocket for the black tourmaline, rubbing her thumb across the smooth surface of the rock. She cast her eyes around the room and edged toward the desk. Colette had collapsed in her chair, lost in a world of stolen dreams and failed aspirations.

Maybe she wouldn't notice.

Now or never. *This is for you, Tori.*

Sloane heaved an exaggerated sigh and clumsily reached toward the tissue box on a small side table, overturning a hand-painted cloche bell jar in the process. Colette lunged toward the glass, but it smashed to pieces. Colette kneeled on the floor, her purple pencil skirt nearly splitting at the seams.

"You idiot! That was an eighteenth century French masterpiece! Get out! And stay away from me!"

Without another word, Sloane slipped from the room, the vision of Colette on the floor gathering the shattered pieces of the cloche in her arms like a mother cradling her child. It was more honest emotion than her performance over her husband's murder for her parishioners.

Something was very wrong here.

Sloane sprinted from the building like it was the seat of evil, the Swarovski crystal heavy and ominous in her pocket.

TWENTY

So this is what prey feels like. Zack's eyes swept the alleyway looking for moving shadows as he killed the El Camino's headlights. Samuel's Construction headquarters was in the building two blocks north, but he didn't dare park and enter through the front doors. There'd be at least one unmarked police vehicle staking out his building.

Thank God there was a hidden underground passageway built a century ago when the company's three-story building had been a hotel.

He'd never forget the first time John had taken him through the tunnel that led from the mechanical room in the Samuel's building to the back of a Chinese restaurant two blocks away. John had won the decrepit hotel in a poker game nearly twenty years ago. He'd purchased the Chinese restaurant only three years later.

And so the passageway belonged to him.

John had crowed like a teenage prankster as they'd descended into the dark bowels of the city, regaling Zack with sordid stories of the tunnel's past. The labyrinth consisted of a main passageway with several offshoots that, once upon a time, had led to nicely-appointed, private rooms used for security, gambling, drinking, and whoring in Prohibition days by thrill-seekers, visiting dignitaries, mob bosses, and upper-class snobs with the right amount of coin. There was a ridiculously small, secret elevator behind John's bookcase paneling as well, but he'd rebuffed all of John's coaxing to stuff himself into that death hole.

John had been so proud to own such a seedy piece of history.

A few years back, a writer had asked to see the tunnel, but John told her it had been destroyed during the building's remodel.

Of course it hadn't.

John had loved the secrecy of it. And though he'd never admit it, the romance of it. He told Zack someday he'd be glad to have it.

Yep.

Zack slipped from the car and unlocked the restaurant's heavy steel door. Inside, sweet and spicy scents made his stomach clench even though he'd eaten the half sandwich Archie had sent with him. He ran through the kitchen toward the cleaning closet. Soft light filtered through the narrow window above a row of hooks that held a broom, mops, and heavy linen tablecloths that hung like teepees in front of the hidden passageway door.

Running his hand along a high ledge searching for a flashlight, he knocked a broom against a tin bucket, the clatter exploding in the small space. He froze, half expecting flood lights and armed officers to jump him from the outer room.

Four seconds.

Nothing but the hum of appliances.

Eight seconds.

Drunken laughter in the alley.

Ten.

The drilling bass of the nightclub half a block away, its door propped open to reduce interior pollution.

Or offer a quick escape for the under-aged.

Twenty.

Flashlight in hand, he pulled back the tablecloths to reveal a wooden pocket door that concealed a small reinforced steel door and vault lock. He slid the wood aside and bent down to shine the flashlight on the lock. *Thirty-eight, thirty-two, thirty-eight.* He smiled, remembering John's ideal woman's curves.

The miniature door squeaked open to expose a dim stairwell barely wide enough for a man's shoulders. With a hiss, he brought an arm across his face to shield the dank basement odor that blitzed him with memories.

He was suddenly eleven years old.

"Please, don't make me stay down there again." His throat ached with a cough that never went away. Sudden heat across his cheek, the force of his mother's slap spinning him toward the opposite wall. He staggered to remain upright, trying to get his eyes to focus, but he slid down the peeling yellow wallpaper with its tiny purple flowers. He focused on the flowers when another fit of coughing rattled his chest and sent an arrow of pain from his jaw to his eye sockets.

The flower petals looked so soft. He wished he could shrink down and wrap himself in them.

Fingernails scraped at his skull, a fist yanking him upright by his hair. "Your momma wants you downstairs, that's where you'll go, you pussy wimp."

His mouth worked as he looked up at his mother, but he couldn't get anything past his lips besides a mortifying squeak.

Save me. Please don't do this. Please love me.

Her gaunt frame turned away. Her boyfriend, who always brought the white powder they snorted, laughed. "You ain't got no daddy, but at least you got me to show you how to be a man."

The boyfriend dragged him by the hair to the downstairs door.

Something in Zack snapped. A volcanic heat surged through his body, throwing off his dogging weakness and ever-present chill. He lashed out at the wiry man, legs kicking, arms swinging. He landed several hits, but the cokehead didn't even seem to feel them. When they got to the doorway, Zack spread-eagled his legs, fingers curling around the sliver-riddled door jam.

Sweat broke out all over his body and his muscles locked as he scrutinized the wet darkness below him. "Don't wanna go down there! Don't make me go. I'll do anything! Please!"

He looked over his shoulder in time to see the fist. As the blow landed he went flying, weightless for an instant above the cinderblock stairs.

He woke, shaking, nauseous, in the darkness, small feet with tiny claws running over an exposed ankle. He swallowed his scream, knowing it would be pointless. He bent over and vomited bitter bile.

Two hunger-filled days later, the gruff, eccentric woman with the wild white hair across the street had finally turned his mother in. As an adult, Zack realized she'd frequently hired him to mow her lawn so she could keep tabs on him. He'd thought she was lonely. His mother thought she was senile, but had been grateful for the cash.

The crazy old woman had been his angel.

After a short stint in the hospital, social workers put him in a foster home where he probably would've been better off, but at the time, he'd wanted nothing to do with any of them. The unknowns lurking in tidy houses were far scarier than life on the streets where he had Archie to keep him company.

Christ, he was cold. Bitter cold straight to his marrow.

Zack now ran a shaking hand over his face and tried to supplant John's grizzled, beloved features across the desolate landscape of what should have been his childhood.

Come on, son. Put one foot right in front t'other. Before you know it, you've come clear across the barren land. But you gotta start with that first step. He could almost feel John's bear paw clap him on the shoulder the way it always had when he needed a bit of encouragement.

John's tunnel. John's tunnel. John's been through here. He'd be okay.

Zack descended two steps and pulled the door shut behind him with a sickening clank. Once he reached the lower landing, there was more room. Yet his torso burned as he sprinted. The flashlight's beam bounced off the muted gray concrete, highlighting cobwebs, rubble, and detritus left behind by industrious rodents. The faster he ran, the more time slowed. The only sound in the tomblike silence...

His heartbeat.

Zack didn't bother wiping the clammy sweat from his face as he rounded the last bend before the passageway drew up into the opposite staircase. *Almost there.* He shuddered as he passed three narrow storage doors inset in the tunnel. Two of them were crisscrossed with cobwebs. Gooseflesh broke out on his body.

Hurry. Gotta find Ann.

And her baby.

He stumbled on the stairs, his breath ragged.

Don't run from your past. We all have our demons. Face 'em with yer God-given grit. How else you gonna get whole? How many times had he heard John's lecture? It hadn't meant much until this moment. *John, help me now.* The flashlight shook as he tried to remember the code for the door. A combination of Ann's birth month and day, plus one other number.

What the hell was it? He sucked air into his nostrils and tried again.

Hurry.

His skin tingled on the back of his neck. He spun the dial forward, back, forward.

No good.

Mother of God. The tunnel was closing in on him.

Chest so tight. Can't breathe.

Hurry.

A sound—a moan—wound around him. His own? His stomach pitched and tumbled. He was going to vomit.

Out. Need out. Help me!

He fist flew up to pound on the door.

Zaaaack...

His arm froze mid-air as her voice whispered through his mind. Her rich vanilla scent as real in his nose as when she'd lain so exquisitely in his arms. He looked behind him, the flashlight's beam illuminating only the time-worn concrete walls. He was still alone.

Yet, not.

Sloane.

Somehow she'd crossed the distance between them. Touched him. His shoulders slumped, his head dipped. The flashlight shone down on his work boots.

He imagined the velvet of her cheek, her parted lips and haunting eyes as she'd made love to him. A new warmth spread through every muscle, every cell of his body. His heartbeat slowed. The awful tightness in his chest unwound.

He raised the flashlight to the dial. *Six, twenty, nine.*

The door swung open. He switched off the flashlight and turned back to face the yawning tunnel. He saw himself as a boy—angry, vulnerable, sad—in the shadows cast by the weak light filtering through the single mechanical room window.

In the next heartbeat, he tasted a burgeoning liberation from all of it. Ironic. But there it was.

The first blush of emancipation from the sting of his childhood while in flight from the local authorities.

Shit.

But they hadn't caught him.

Yet.

TWENTY-ONE

Cool air wrapped around Zack when he stepped into the hallway outside the mechanical room. The hall opened into the comfortable lobby of Samuel's Construction, where hand-blown glass sculptures by local artists graced marble tables. Tables that usually held trays of homemade goodies for the constant flow of laborers, architects, subcontractors, and developers, most of whom were greeted by name by Ann.

Zack skirted around the furniture, staying away from the glass entryway, and ran to the other side of the building and up the stairwell. He shivered when he entered John's spacious office. He'd kept everything intact since the last time his mentor had sat there eleven months and five days ago. Papers still poked out of the token junk drawer John had kept; otherwise the office radiated order and simplicity. Like the man himself.

Zack couldn't help running his hand across the top of the supple chair as he moved toward the vault at the back of the room, the lingering scents of leather and tobacco greeting him like a welcome home. *If only you were still here.*

His head dipped and he pinched the bridge of his nose. *Money. Get the cash and go.* He dialed the third combination John had made him memorize so many years ago. At least this one he'd used before, though not as often as he probably should've.

The vault door opened soundlessly, and he slipped inside, leaving the door open a sliver behind him. The darkness was nearly complete, only this time, the proximity to John's office made him feel cocooned instead of suffocated.

Stepping forward to reach out for the string that turned on the single hanging light bulb, he bumped into a large stack of boxes, upending them to the sound of rushing papers. Cursing, he grasped at air until he found the cord and gave a light tug.

Hell's bells. Take the time to shove all the papers back in the box or leave it? How would he want the cops to find it? It would probably take a cache of dynamite to open the vault, but maybe they had some other way of opening it.

He knelt and began stuffing the papers back into the box. Invoices. He'd never seen them before, but then he'd always spent the least amount of time on the back office side of the business. He enjoyed being in the field with the subcontractors. Couldn't stomach too much desk work.

Which was probably why the business was tanking.

He paused, reading one of the papers. The invoicing company was a bodyguard service. He dug through the pile, discovering security system invoices as well. There had to be a hundred statements dating back two decades.

His stomach rolled over. Ann had had her twentieth birthday two months ago. She would've been a tiny baby when these invoices were prepared. Why would John hire a bodyguard and security services for her? He'd always been super protective of her, but *damn*. This bordered on obsessive. Remarkably out of character for John. Why hadn't he ever told him?

A blue folder marked "IMPORTANT" lay on the bottom of the box. Inside were an unlabeled CD and an old newspaper clipping of an opera singer who'd been recruited by NDSU to teach in its Fine Arts department for a year.

Zack scanned the newsprint for a date, but it had been clipped off. The dark-haired beauty on the page faced the camera as though she knew it loved her. A shudder raced through him. Wide eyes, narrow nose, a tiny cleft in her chin. This woman was Ann all over again except for the wide, full lips. Under her picture was the name *Serena Galasso*.

Then he remembered Agnes's gossip about John and the "high-fallutin' opera singer."

He grabbed the vault phone and dialed Archie. No answer. He prayed he hadn't sent Twyla into early labor with his visit. He left a message asking Archie to probe the bodyguard and security companies to see what he could dig up on them.

"What are you doing here?"

Zack jumped, crumpling the newspaper clipping in his hands and pointed outside the vault. "Turn the lights off!"

Ross quickly moved out of the vault to turn off the lights in John's office. When he came back inside his eyebrows slanted downward. "What the hell, Zack?"

His CFO's face was pale. "Shit, Ross. It's after two in the morning. Why are you still here?" Zack inserted the newspaper, two invoices, and the unlabeled CD into a zippered bank pouch and pushed to his feet.

"In case you forgot, the amusement park is opening later today. I was just making sure everything is in order. Then I thought I heard something fall in here. What's going on?"

Zack spread his arms wide to scoop up the rest of the invoices, then shoved them back into the box and replaced the lid. "John ever talk to you about security for Ann?"

"No, never."

Zack held up the single remaining invoice he clutched. "Twenty years of protection billed to John's personal address, not the business. You know anything about that?"

He saw confusion cross Ross's pale face momentarily before it was replaced by a sort of stunned awareness. "Oh shit, Ann is really missing?"

Ross looked at him with stricken eyes, and Zack felt a blow of pain more than physical this time. Something worse.

Failure. Loss.

We'll find her. Come to me, Zack.

Sloane again. How did she talk in his head like that? On cue. He didn't understand it. But he felt the pull of her, all the same. He wanted to go to her, fill her body and lose himself in her passion. But that would leave him no closer to finding answers about Ann.

And would only drag her further into danger.

He turned away from Ross and moved to the cash box in the back shadows of the vault, mentally picturing a wall to keep Sloane out of his head.

"I've worked for you and John for more than four years now, and you won't trust me? I care about Ann, too."

Zack didn't turn around. "It's not that. I don't want to give you any information that might suck you into this quagmire. I'm *going* to find Ann. And no matter what the media reports, just so you know, I haven't killed anyone."

Both men fell silent. Zack pushed a bundle of bills into the zippered pouch with the other items, then shut the cash box.

"I wish I knew something—anything—that might help you, but—" Ross stopped suddenly, and Zack swung around, his entire body on alert.

"But what?"

Ross rumpled his sandy blond hair. His eyes scanned the room as though looking for a way out. "Last week, Ann was talking on the phone after hours when I was in the conference room preparing for a meeting. She didn't know I was there. And she was upset. She told whomever it was that she loved him and that they could work it out. She asked him to come over for supper. He apparently declined."

Zack scrubbed both hands down his face. "Okay, so what did you do?"

"What could I do? Reveal myself to comfort her? She would have been mortified. So I stayed in the conference room until I knew she'd left for the day. She's been especially unhappy ever since."

"Any idea who she might have been talking to?" Zack asked, though he knew it must have been O'Neill.

"No. But several times in the last couple of weeks, I've seen her in the parking lot after work talking to a man in a white car. I guess I only noticed because she's usually so solitary."

Clearly Zack wasn't the only one in the office to realize Ann wasn't into the dating scene. "How did she seem to you?"

"Giddy mostly, except for once. The last time, I think, she seemed worried," Ross said.

"When was that?"

"Earlier this week. Maybe Tuesday."

"Were they fighting?" Zack asked.

"Well, she wasn't smiling. She was gesturing with her hands, like people do when they're upset. I couldn't see the man's face. He has tinted windows. It looked like a Lexus."

"Why didn't you tell me sooner?"

Ross narrowed his eyes at Zack's sharp tone. "It was none of my business."

"Yeah. Sorry."

He was right, of course. Besides being ultra-professional, Ross was always courteous to a fault. Which only threw Zack's gritty edges into sharp relief. He glanced down one last time at the box of security invoices and knew where he needed to go next. After clicking off the light, he opened the door to the vault and stepped into John's office, holding the door so Ross could pass through.

"I'll do some research on those invoices," Ross said.

"No, that's okay. I'll handle it. Thanks for everything." He turned back to slam the vault door. "Until the authorities confirm that I'm not their prime suspect, I don't want you in their crosshairs because of me. I spoke to my lead foreman a few hours ago and everything is ready to rock on our end, so go get some rest. Looks like you need it."

"How nice of you to say so," Ross said wryly.

Zack smiled at his CFO and felt in the zippered pouch to confirm that both the newspaper clipping featuring Ann's mother and the two invoices were still there, then moved around Ross toward the door.

"Are you sure about not cooperating with the police? With your background—"

"With my background, they were ready to lock me in jail and throw away the fucking key. I didn't kill the monster who was screwing with Ann, but I'll die trying to find out who did—because he's the one...he's the one who took her from us."

Ross nodded. "I hope you have the fortitude to see this through."

Zack grabbed John's Red Hawks baseball cap from the desk and left Ross standing there, a look of concern etched on his face. But Ross's concern had nothing on the wild spew of emotions winging through Zack's veins so fast he was almost dizzy with it. Because if Sloane ended up in the crosshairs next, he'd need more than fortitude.

He'd need a higher power.

Or Donovan.

***

When Zack pulled to the corner two blocks from Sloane's place at Blackhawk Gates, Morgan was lounging against a local heroin dealer's red Camaro. Right where she'd promised she'd be. He'd made a quick call to her before he left the office. A rush of gratitude warmed him as he cut the engine and raised the binoculars, searching the strip for the unmarked police car that was surely staking out Sloane's place.

Waiting for him to show up.

He'd shown up all right, but they weren't going to know thanks to Morgan and a posse of her more adventurous friends.

There. Two men sitting in a generic blue sedan that afforded them views of two sides of Sloane's building, including the parking lot. *Time for action.*

Zack emerged from the El Camino, adjusted the baseball cap in an exaggerated motion, and began walking briskly across the street toward the alley and away from Morgan.

At these signals, a man with more tattoos than naked skin walked by the Camaro with a scantily clad woman on his arm. Morgan pushed away from the car and started screaming at the pair. The plan was for them to take the scene into the middle of the strip on Broadway. By the time he reached the alley, Zack heard cars honking and more people yelling. A few moments later he heard a flash bang—his signal to run.

In the alley behind Sloane's apartment, he peered around a parked Hummer to see if the blue sedan had been dispatched to the disturbance.

Bingo. I owe you one, Morgan.

TWENTY-TWO

It was coming again. Sloane saw Zack gasping, felt his panic as he ran through some sort of tunnel. She cried out, but he couldn't hear her, so embroiled in his own fight to be free of the darkness. There were sounds all around her, so many at once she couldn't make sense of it.

Suddenly it grew so cold her pulse seemed to suffer the effects of hypothermia—the slow pounding of her blood was hypnotic, drowning out the voices until there was only deafening silence between each irregular heartbeat. Silence lengthening until...

There was something crawling over her legs.

Rats! Scrambling all over her, their tiny, hooked claws breaking skin, their teeth sinking deep. *Oh God. Ohgod-ohgod-ohgod.*

She screamed and flailed, scratching and tearing with her nails at the phantom rodents until she finally awoke, pinned to Zack's chest, her body quaking in residual horror.

Incoherent words of comfort spilled from his lips as he sat on the floor with her cradled in his lap. She felt the bunching muscles of his arms as he held her upper body immobile against his solid warmth. She became aware of his heartbeat against her bare arm. Steady. Strong.

Slowly, her gasps subsided into hiccoughs. He brushed his thumb against her cheek. She burrowed into his heat and felt him wince. "Oh! I'm sorry!" She leaned away, but he pulled her back. "How'd you get here? Get *in* here? Cops have gotta be watching my place."

"They don't know I'm here."

"How can you be so sure?"

He didn't say anything for a moment. "An old friend came through for me. She missed her calling as an actress so I'm sure she enjoyed it."

"What's that mean? Wait, don't answer that. I don't want to know." *I'm seriously jealous.*

Another first. *Sucks.*

"It's not what you think. Morgan and I grew up on the same streets. She's like my little sister. Tonight, she created a 'disturbance' in the area, and I slipped into your building when the undercover vehicle moved down the block to check it out."

"You left her alone downtown at three in the morning?"

"Morgan has self-defense down to an art, access to drugs from your worst nightmare, and a wicked way with a knife, so she would have been fine on her own. But, the disturbance was only an act with other friends enjoying their parts. And since we're on the topic of getting in here, you need to buy more foolproof locks."

"You're *not* lecturing me about my locks."

"I'm qualified, believe me." His teeth gleamed in the shadows.

"This isn't funny, Zack."

"*Shhh.* Let me hold you for a minute."

She laid her head back down, the rough pads of his fingertips raising goose bumps as he traced circles down her arms. He was a man on the run, trying to find a missing woman while falsely accused of murder, yet he was comforting *her*.

She'd developed such strong feelings for him in such a short time. It seemed unrealistic, implausible, and uncontrollable.

Kinda like love.

He just can't know about Abigail.

She bit down hard on her lip to keep her drama from erupting. Zack's fingers slowed against her skin, a Braille system translating her emotions.

She inhaled deeply to diffuse the tension. The tinkle of water in her aquarium made a soothing accompaniment to his heartbeat, the glowing tank the only source of light in the apartment, casting mesmerizing blue-green ripples on the wall.

This was crazy. Getting involved with a man who could blow her cover, unravel her dreams, and ruin her family name forever. If exposed, her failure to find Abigail before she was murdered would taint her mother's career. Her father's psychiatry practice, too. She should really box this whole psychic crap up and put it on the shelf. Get back to her life at Skinny Dipping. Spend time with her friends. Date a new, interesting guy every week.

That's what she needed—uncomplicated fun.

More than that, she could move on with her charity foundation now that she had the crystal rhino—

Oh! She bolted upright in Zack's lap. "I found the missing rhino in Colette's office. It's how I know—or feel reasonably certain—that Ann left with Colette Saturday night."

Zack frowned. "Wait. *What?*"

"After I gave my statement at Ann's, I went to the church, thinking I would either try to talk to Colette, or more likely, take something she or Dallan had touched in the church. *If* I could get in there."

"That was foolish."

She was about to place a palm against his chest to rise from his lap when she remembered his injury. "Let me see your chest." She scooted off his lap and would've ripped the shirt out of the waistband of his jeans if he hadn't grabbed her wrists.

"It's just a bruise."

She reached for his shirt again. "Let me see."

He shook his head, fingers tightening around her wrists. "I'm good." The look in his eyes told her she could play nurse in another way however.

She wet her lips, her respiration climbing another notch seeing his pupils expand. "F-fine, suffer, then."

"I didn't say I was a martyr. I'll take some ibuprofen if you have it, but first finish telling me why you think Ann went with Colette."

"I didn't really have a plan, but when I got to the church, they had this—*vigil,* I supposed you'd call it—already in progress. There had to be five dozen people at the church. *At one in the morning.* Seriously, how did they all find out Dallan was dead so soon? It had only been a couple of hours." He shrugged, and she continued. "Anyway, Colette admitted knowing Dallan was a philanderer, but she stayed with him because he was her ticket to prestige. She even knew about Ann's baby."

"Are you kidding me?"

"Nope. And when I asked her how she knew, she said she had a 'troubleshooter.'"

"What's that supposed to mean?"

"I asked, but she started crying. When I knew I wouldn't get any more information from her I fixated on *that*." Sloane pointed at the crystal rhino. She saw the surprise on Zack's face. "It was on her desk. When I took it, she didn't even notice."

"How'd she get it?"

"No freakin' idea, but it showed me Ann sitting in Colette's vehicle. They talked about the Fall Festival and were apparently on their way to a meeting at one of the committee member's houses."

"The meeting wasn't at the church?"

"No, but Ann didn't seem to think anything was amiss until they made an unexpected stop at someone else's house—someone named Patty. I saw Ann's momentary confusion, but when she asked Colette why they were there, Colette said Patty had asked for a ride to the meeting."

"Did Ann know her?"

"Certainly seemed like she did, but it was apparent she'd never been to Patty's house before."

"Did they go in?"

"In the car, Colette's phone rang. She asked Ann if she'd mind letting Patty know they were there and help her start loading the baskets for the bazaar. Colette said she'd finish her call and be in shortly. But she didn't, Zack. Colette *never went into the house*. She didn't talk on the phone either. She watched Ann go inside, and then she backed out of the driveway and went home. *Alone.* After that, the crystal didn't have any other information." Scary stuff.

"How do you know this was even the right time-frame for last Saturday night? It could have been earlier. Days or weeks earlier, knowing how they like to get an early start on that kind of stuff."

"I really don't think so. In this vision with Colette, Ann was wearing the same outfit that she wore in my other vision of her—when she'd freshened up after the attack in her foyer. You know as well as I do that Ann doesn't wear the same outfit too often."

He nodded.

"I *knew* Colette knew something. Whoever's house that was is her troubleshooter. We can find out which church members are named Patty as well as their addresses really quickly, but I

170

doubt that was really her house. It was all a ruse."

He eased up from the floor to the edge of the sofa. Sloane left to get him some pain killers. When she came back into the living room, she gave him a bottle of pills and a glass of water. He took a sip and downed four of them.

"Did you recognize the house Ann went into, or maybe the neighborhood?" he asked.

"It was a newer home, nothing fancy, but nice. Maybe if we drove around—"

"We don't have time. Unless...could you tell how much time had passed between Ann's and Patty's house? Could you see the directions?"

"A psychometric object only reflects thoughts and feelings of the person touching the object, and apparently, when Colette touched the crystal in her office, she was only thinking about keeping Ann talking and getting her to Patty's, not which streets she took to get there. She was nervous, but that's all that was really on her mind. Can we take this to the cops?"

"And say what? That the pastor was having an affair?"

"Colette's involved somehow."

"Of course she is, but we don't know how until we can identify her accomplice." She felt his eyes on her in the distorted shadows from the shifting aquarium water. "I hope the vision wasn't too hard on you."

It had sucked because he hadn't been there to anchor her. "I've had worse. I must've drifted off. When I came home there was a message from the police department. They've sent the blood samples from Ann's hallway to the lab. Detective Barnaba wants you to come in for questioning. He said they won't hold your escape against you if you cooperate this time."

He laughed humorlessly. "Right. Barnaba's more apt to throw me to the piranhas than take any statement from me."

"Why?"

"Too much water under the bridge."

"You can't go on being a fugitive, Zack. You did nothing wrong."

"I wounded a suspect who is now AWOL. He either died holed up somewhere from blood loss or isn't as hurt as I thought he was, and is plotting his next move... Or worse yet, he's the big bad for some other whack job who's got a sick game in progress."

"*Big bad.* As in a hired killer?"

He nodded.

Scary and scarier. She exhaled slowly. "So what's your gut say?"

"That's *my* line."

"Just answer the question. In case you haven't noticed, I'm a bitch when I don't get enough sleep."

Zack smiled for real this time. "You're hot when you're mad." She chucked a sofa pillow at him. "Fine. I think the person I tangled with at Ann's is the heavy for someone else."

"But why? What does this have to do with Ann or Tori?"

He eased down in a stuffed chair. "I'm guessing the diary plays a role—or what certain people might have thought would be incriminating in it."

"Like Ann's involvement with Dallan."

"Exactly," he said. "Tori was the one to tell you about the diary. Who else might Ann or Tori have told?"

Sloane's mind spun for a moment. "You went back looking for a second one, didn't you?" At his nod, she continued. "Do you think that's why Dallan was at Ann's condo? To look for the diary?"

"Probably. In it she admitted to having an affair with him. That kind of information, if leaked, would end his pastoral career."

"How did he found out about it?"

"That's why I asked you who else Ann might have told besides Tori."

Sloane racked her brain. "I really don't think Ann would have told anyone else at the store. Oh shit, what if Tori was somehow involved with Dallan, too, and that's why she was murdered? What if Dallan's the one who killed her?"

She jumped up and reached for her phone, but Zack was quicker. He grasped her shoulders.

"Easy now. Dallan was definitely involved, but I don't think he was the major player. Remember, someone took him out, too. Someone who wanted me to take the fall for killing him. Only, I got there too early for the bad guy to get away unscathed."

She froze. "But who would know you were on your way to Ann's the same time Dallan would be there?"

"On my way there I called my buddy Archie, and my client, Tim Benjamin."

Her gut rolled. "Why would you call Benjamin?"

"Based on your vision of him and Ann, I wanted to see how he'd react to talking about her. So I made up some shit about Ann misfiling documents and other details about the opening of the amusement park later today."

"And?"

"He didn't act contrary to his ordinary pompous self. I don't get the feeling he was involved in...all this. But it really wouldn't matter whether my timing at Ann's was perfect or not because my fingerprints were all over her place already. I'd automatically be a person of interest when the police dusted the scene."

So clearly this wasn't connected to Skinny Dipping as he'd

originally thought. Instead it was definitely something about people associated with Samuel's Construction.

"Wasn't Benjamin surprised you called him so late?"

"Big projects like the amusement park know nothing of the time clock. My employees and their families are counting on me to see this through. Ergo, I even take calls from him in the john. And vice versa."

"Okay, so what do you think about him as a possible suspect in Ann's disappearance? He certainly has the money to hire someone to do his dirty work."

"It'd offend his ego to hold someone against her will. He wants people to kiss his ass of their own accord."

"And if they don't? Then what? Will he try to coerce them?" Lord knew he was a master at controlling the stipulations of his sponsorship. Maybe it wasn't worth putting up with his bullshit, after all. There had to be someone else in the business community who'd believe in her project.

"I don't know what to think. None of this is adding up."

He looked so tired suddenly. She patted the sofa, and he came to sit beside her. "How did you get away from the cops?"

He pulled her legs into his lap, running his palms over her thighs. "Luck? I don't know—timing, riverbank knowledge, and help from an old friend, I suppose."

Sloane leaned her head against the top of the sofa, his touch at once soothing and arousing. An ambulance raced by on the street below. "I want to meet your friends."

"Archie's a good man. He and his wife Twyla are going to have their baby any day now. If they haven't already tonight."

She wanted to ask about his childhood, how he'd met Archie and Morgan, what his favorite foods were, his happiest memories—goodness, so many things—but it would have to wait. They had more pressing things to discuss.

Like survival.

"Barnaba knew you were going to Ann's to get her dental information, right?" He nodded. "Do you think he'd go through the trouble to set you up?"

"I don't think his nose is dirty, but then I haven't run in the same circles in a long time, either. I guess the only thing that matters is that he hates me."

"Tell me." She paused, wondering if she was insane to fall any deeper into his world, but knowing she was helpless to stop herself. "I'm good for secrets, too."

TWENTY-THREE

"It was a long time ago," Zack said.

Sloane ran a fingertip along his shoulder. "Come *on*. You had a front row seat for the airing of my dirty laundry."

He squeezed her leg and sighed. "When I was twenty I started seeing an ER Nurse. She was thirty-two. Then I found out she was married."

"Oh, wow."

"When she sunbathed, she took her wedding ring off so she wouldn't have a tan line. The day I discovered the ring in her nightstand, I told her I couldn't see her again, so she paid some thugs to beat me with pipes in an alley. Then she messed herself up, so it looked like I molested her. After I got out of the hospital, it went to court. I tried to show it was a set up, but she denied even knowing me. The thugs she'd hired—the ones she claimed pulled me off of her and beat me in their own self-defense—were her witnesses at the trial. The thugs did whatever she wanted because they were afraid of her husband."

"But who— Oh, Lord. *Barnaba*?"

He nodded with a small, haunted smile.

"But I can't believe he wouldn't suspect his wife was guilty in some respect. Wasn't it fishy?"

"Sure, but he was only an officer at the time. He had his sights on becoming detective. A scandal like that would've been an ugly blemish on his character. He wouldn't have advanced so easily."

"So what happened to you?"

"Two years in the pen."

She pulled her legs off his lap. "*No*. That's inexcusable!"

"That's life."

"Did anyone believe you? Stand up for you?"

"Archie and Morgan, but Archie's rap sheet was uglier than mine, and Morgan had prostitution on hers. No one was going to believe either one of them over a cop's wife. Kasey has a black belt in karate and manipulation."

"What happened to her?"

"No idea. I haven't seen her in eleven years," he said.

"Are they still together?"

"Barnaba apparently divorced her a few years back."

"I'd think that would make him more sympathetic to you," she said.

"A proud man rarely forgets a wrong."

"But it wasn't your fault."

"He didn't see it that way." He leaned back and waved his hand in the air. "*Whatever*. It's in the past."

Sloane was beginning to piece together a picture of not only a very lonely childhood, but a lost adolescence and early adult years, too. "Where were your parents?"

He began to stand, but she moved up to wrap her arms around his neck, careful of his injury. Softly pressed her lips to his. She felt him stiffen, shoulders tense as though ready for an assault. She tilted her head slightly and pressed tiny kisses against the corners of his mouth, then took his bottom lip gently between her teeth until she felt him shudder and open to her. A soft blue light built behind her eyelids.

His hands grasped the sides of her face so his lips could whisper across her own. When he hauled her onto his lap, she felt a moment's panic at the loss of control. But then he pulled back, eyes a dark, mossy green. "I'm glad I met you, Goldie."

She watched the heavy pulse beating in his neck. Her fingers feathered across it. Somehow, even as tortured as his soul was, she knew she could trust this man. He was kind. Loyal. Compassionate. Generous.

Bruised. "I was with you in that tunnel."

He stilled completely. She rubbed her thumb across his nipple then skipped over his bruised ribs and trailed fingers down his belly until his hips shifted slightly. She felt him hot and full against the cleft of her thighs. She rocked against him.

"Sloane—" A plea.

Oh, she was going to ease him, but first she had to make sure he understood. "Before you found me on the sofa—when I was sleeping—we must have linked up psychically. I was with you—"

"I heard you." It was nearly a growl. "In my head, I've heard you. Several times. How can you do that?"

She didn't understand it herself. She'd never communicated with anyone this way. Didn't remember her mother ever speaking about telepathy, either. "I honestly don't know."

"You scare the hell out of me."

"Well, that makes two of us, because I'm scaring myself," she said.

A shadow of a smile crossed his features before his eyes hardened. "I shouldn't be here endangering you." He stood with her in his arms and lowered her legs to the floor. She was sure he would leave now, yet she clung to him, wanting to say so much.

"I need to talk to Colette again. See if I can make her talk," he said.

Sloane looked at him, really looked this time. Lines bracketed his mouth and the dark circles under his eyes made her heart break. Even his usual swarthy complexion looked pale beneath his black stubble. He was the most virile, stunningly beautiful man she'd ever seen.

"I'm sorry. I shouldn't have come." He gently reached back to disentangle her arms from his neck, but she moved her hands to cup his cheeks. She went on tip toes and pressed her lips to his, feeling a tremor go through him.

"Stop that," she breathed against his lips. "*I* decide who I'm with."

"I picked your locks. I didn't let you choose."

"I called to you in the tunnel. Remember?" Large hands curling around her hips told her he did, but he was still going to leave. She could tell by the way he held his body tense, as though fighting the pull to be near her. "You won't get within twenty feet of Colette without calling down the wrath of her church ladies or the cops. Unless you're planning on turning yourself in now."

"I haven't changed my mind," he said.

The air around them quivered with an acute sense of waiting. He'd made his choice to evade the cops because he was afraid of being trapped by Barnaba again. Whether or not it was a valid position didn't matter. He'd drawn his line. And while she couldn't blame him, she didn't know how to fight his fear of being betrayed by people who got too close.

Because that's what this was really about.

She'd seen and felt it as he'd run through the tunnel. Heard him speak about it regarding his affair with Kasey.

She understood his need to keep people at a distance. It drove her, too. The difference was she kept people away to protect them from the consequences of her gift while he did it to protect himself.

All his life, all his lonely life, the people he'd trusted—those who were supposed to love and care for him—had let him down.

Beat him down.

Goddamn them all. Which fork should she follow? If she let him walk out her door right now, would her life revert to the way it was three days ago? Would she ever see him again?

Regret is a joy thief.

"I want you to stay. Just a while longer," she whispered. When he brought her close, she felt his body pressing below her navel. At her shiver, his eyes flared before his head descended to take her lips with the hunger of a starving man, arching her against his body until she was like a strung bow. She opened her mouth to his demand and his tongue pushed past her teeth, seeking every private place until she was breathless, swept up into his urgency. He broke away suddenly, squeezing her, his lips breathing warm air at her temple. "I'd never hurt you."

On purpose, she thought. But he could so easily devastate her heart. She couldn't help the thought any more than she could help the way his touch made her burn. Any more than she could help wanting him no matter what obstacles stood in their way.

She leaned back to trace the shape of his lips with a fingertip. "I know. You're not like those who've hurt you in the past. I'm not either. But you're hurting me now by stopping."

His slow smile leveled her seconds before he peeled her tank top and flannel bottoms off her body with tender deliberation. She trembled, more aware of her skin than ever before. When her clothes lay on the floor, she stood before him in the shifting aquatic lights feeling virginal and confused. He'd seen her naked before. He'd watched, entranced, as she'd ridden his body and flown apart. So why did it feel like this was her first time? Like now everything was different?

Because I'm falling in love him.

A quaver steamrolled through her nerves—excitement,

wonder, and fear winding her up into a miasma of feeling. He backed up a step, his eyes a brand, scorching their way from her teeth worrying her lips, to the tips of her breasts, across the stubbornly rounded expanse of her stomach and curve of her hips to her sex, down the length of her legs, and back up again until his fevered eyes captured hers and turned her insides to magma.

"God, help me, Sloane. I need you. Every beautiful inch of you."

She could feel his need radiating off his body in waves that threatened to knock her to her knees. Her lips parted, but she couldn't speak. Couldn't move. The intensity of the feelings coursing through her rooted her to the soft rug beneath her feet. She shivered when he finally peeled the shirt over his head.

"What's wrong, baby?" he whispered, frowning, not touching her but near enough that she could feel his body heat. "Cold?"

"No. I—" She closed her eyes and rubbed her arms, trying to find her old, confident self. When she opened them, she was staring at his large purple bruise and the black panther tattooed across his chest. It was so alive, seeming to move with every breath he took. She reached up to touch it and felt his muscles twitch. Her heart throbbed. *So much emotion.*

"I need you, too, Zack." Her words were barely audible. She didn't move. Hesitating, he watched her for a few moments— enough time for her to realize he understood what was happening.

Surrender.

It was her first. A *this is who and what I am* when all the chips were down. A glimpse into her soul. An offering with no expectation of reciprocation. She quivered like a mouse before the lion, knowing she'd never be quite the same when Zack left her arms this time.

He held out his hand and led her into the bedroom. He eased her down on the bed with great care, then stepped away to throw open the curtains.

***

Zack turned back to Sloane, swallowing hard. Soft light from the full moon glowed across her body as though in homage to her loveliness. If not for the demon in his blood, he would have been content to stare at her for hours. She lay against the pillows, her hair a glimmering wave of silk. She watched him remove his jeans and set a condom next to her, two dark blots distressing her cheeks. She wet her lips, shifted on the bed, and his blood boiled.

No matter what, he was going to take her slow this time.

He'd read her struggle to surrender loud and clear, as though she was talking in his mind again.

The last time they'd made love, she'd been in control. He was beginning to realize that she'd built her life around the mantra of control. She was a strong, independent woman. More so than any other woman he'd ever known. For her, losing control was synonymous with failure. And while he didn't understand how she connected the two quite yet, he did comprehend the personal consequences that accompanied a sense of failure. So he was determined to proceed carefully.

He moved to the end of the bed, and she sprang up on her elbows, her worried frown pricking little holes in his heart.

"*Shhh*. I mean to care for you, Goldie."

"But your injury—"

"I'm okay." He placed one knee on the edge of the bed,

leaned toward her, and smiled, and oh, it felt *good.* Even in the midst of this nightmare, he'd smiled more often with her in the last three days than he had in the whole last year.

He slid his palms underneath her calves, then swiveled his thumbs to the undersides of her thighs, pushing her legs slowly apart. When his thumbs reached the swell of her buttocks against the bed, he paused, his hands forming a triangle around her heat. "So lovely. Every part of you."

Her hands fisted in the covers, and her scent—vanilla, woman, *sex*—kindled all manner of outstanding fantasies in his mind. He blew softly across her skin until goose bumps rose up and down her legs and across her belly.

She gasped, and reached down for him. *"Kiss me."*

"Thought you'd never ask," he whispered as his dark head descended.

*** *** ***

Sloane's hips bucked off the bed when his hot mouth and stubbled chin connected with her flesh. *That's not what I meant, you wonderful bastard,* her mind screamed and she grabbed fistfuls of his hair lest he move away.

His head popped up, eyes gleaming at her. "I know."

He'd heard her.

Oh, Lord. Now she'd need to control her thoughts, too.

Her grip loosened on his hair, but he annihilated her next coherent thought with a sweep of his tongue. Pressure was building, coiling, swirling toward one tight spot that seemed to swell ever larger. She writhed against the arms that held her legs in place, but without his restraints she'd feel at sea. His body was her anchor for the energy that expanded, almost painful now, until she finally broke that ceiling, exploded, and then drifted—drifted—in dark waves of pleasure.

Floating down, she felt his body sliding over hers, so hot, his mouth feathering kisses against her hip bone, her navel, the under swells of her breasts. His tongue traced her areola, his erection sliding hot and hard against her legs. He took her nipple all the way in his mouth, and she whimpered. "Give me a second, then I can—"

"Don't be a coward." He rose over her, sheathed himself, then parted her legs wide with his own, his broad tip grazing her skin. She lay beneath him, open, quivering, but not sure she was ready for where he would take her.

"Yes, Sloane, right now, there's no one for you but me." And he breached her with one long, slow stroke that left her breathless, aching, and painfully aware that it was so much more than he'd said.

Because there would probably *never* be anyone else for her but him.

His eyes burned into hers as his body ground deep, then stilled until the only movement was the rhythmic pulsing of him inside her. She bit her lip and moved her hips in an effort to ease the ache that was re-building.

"More?"

She wrapped her legs around his waist in answer. His arms shook as he pulled back slightly, throbbing at her entrance. She tried to push herself up at him, but he held himself back. "Then say it, Sloane. Say the words, and I'll give you anything you need."

Why? You can hear my thoughts, damn you.

"I want to hear you say them out loud."

No.

"Yes," he said.

"No! Yes! *Oh, yes*. I need this. I—" *Love you*, she thought, and his body took hers with wild abandon. Every point of contact between their bodies shimmered with light, a conflagration of energy finding its perfect balance.

Acutely aware of her own heartbeat, she sank her fingernails into the shifting muscles of his back. He grabbed one of her legs, pushing on the back of her thigh and changing his strokes, rocking against her pelvis until she fought for air.

"Look at me, Sloane."

She did and found him watching her, his eyes black, fathomless, as though he'd crawled inside her very soul. So much pleasure. There was no place for her to hide. *What do you see inside me?*

And then all thought vanished.

Her vision grayed and suddenly exploded into a mass of impossible blue light that flashed across her brain, removing inhibition and ambiguity. She gasped his name and felt him spasm. In moments, he collapsed and rolled onto his back, bringing her with him so she was resting halfway across his trunk and legs, her head pillowed on his shoulder. They lay that way for a long time.

Whoa. Just, *whoa.*

For her, sex had always been healthy, fun, recreational. Then she moved on. But now, what she'd lived through with Zack...

How could she move on after an experience like that? He'd gone someplace within her no one else ever had.

Wait! She reared up, alarmed that he might have read her thoughts again. But he was sound asleep, his eyelashes forming jet black crescents against the dark circles under his eyes.

Ah, now you've done it. You've fallen for a complicated, dangerous man.

Earlier, he must not have heard her sudden declaration of

love because he really hadn't reacted. *Thank God.*

So her butt was covered for now. No way was she going to gush any feelings yet. They still had too many horrors to iron out.

She should crawl out of bed and turn on the radio to see if they were saying anything new about the case. But she wanted to savor this time with him.

Softly, she brushed a hand across his bruised midsection and the swarthy skin low on his abdomen. Her eyes tracked back down his body and saw that he was now slightly hard again, but his lips were still parted in slumber. She smiled, nestled more comfortably into the crook of his arm, and tried to go to sleep. Then he shifted and his hand brushed her nipple, making her ache once more.

As she rolled away to take a cold shower, he flattened her on her belly, hooked his arm under her pelvis to raise her hips, and mere seconds after the foil ripped, he entered her from behind. She moaned as he undulated against her, his left hand grasping her hip, the fingers of his right hand massaging her in the most perfect spot.

His breath rasped over her skin, a blanket of sensation. "God, woman. Your need called to me in my sleep."

Oh, how she wanted to deny it. But she was already climaxing.

TWENTY-FOUR

Zack walked into Sloane's kitchen bare-chested, towel-drying his hair, and gave her a grin that would melt a freightliner of ice. She turned to the stove to plate the eggs. She'd managed to get out of the shower first. Or perhaps crawl out would be a more apt description. Her cheeks heated when she recalled how the cool tiles had felt against her back as she'd clung to him, the steam cocooning them in an Eden of erotic sensation.

She took both plates to the table. "Eat, then we talk."

He looked carefully at her. "Okay." He filled her cup with milk, his with coffee, and then slid into a chair beside her. "Amazing what a couple hours of sleep, a decent meal, and...*you* can do."

A trickle of water from his hair streamed down the side of his face, and even as ravished as she was, she wanted to lick it off, climb on top of his wicked body, and find nirvana again.

She got up from her chair, bustling over to the pantry, pretending to look for something until she got her hormones under control. The man was a sexual warrior. He undid her. Completely. As in, *no control.* Her hand stilled on a box of cereal.

Lord, it was glorious.

He burst into delighted laugher behind her. She swiveled, then smacked at the arms that encircled her waist. "Stop that! You can't just jump into my head whenever you feel like it!"

"How can I help it when you think so loud?" He laughed again when she pushed past him to the table and sat down. A smile of her own threatened to break surface at hearing him laugh so freely. He rejoined her at the table. "This psychic business sure gives me an edge. I like it." He winked at her, and her heart turned over.

"*I'm* supposed to be the kook here. I don't understand why you can hear me whenever you want, but I can only hear you when you're under duress."

"You can usually *see* what happens to me."

"Yeah, but I can't *always* hear you—your thoughts—like you can hear mine," she said, puzzled.

He studied his coffee for a moment, then looked up and brushed a strand of her hair back from her eye. "I've heard you bit by bit since yesterday morning. The longer I've been around you, grown to trust you, and I suppose the more you trust me, the more I've been able to hear." He paused. "I guess I'm open to it. And... I'm beginning to listen for you." His lips curved.

Seriously, she wanted to crawl in his lap. His smile grew wider, and he patted his thighs. "Come here, I'm all for it. See? This telepathy's good shit."

She wadded a napkin and threw it at him. "Get over yourself. I'm not sitting in your dang lap. What if you don't always like what you hear?"

He shrugged. "I can take it. As long as you're always honest."

"Can't sensor one's thoughts," she said.

"You'd be surprised." He leaned back, tilting the chair onto its rear legs. She couldn't take her eyes off his magnificent abs and chest. She started to feel warm again. He cleared his throat. When she finally managed to look him in the eyes, he was smirking. "With thoughts like those, however, don't worry about censorship."

"For the love of God, Zack. Give me some privacy. I'd think

you of all people would understand." She grabbed their plates, clinking them together as she set them in the sink. She hadn't meant to snap at him, but it was unsettling to know someone shared your mind. She swung around to return for the mugs only to bump into him. When she tried to grab the cups from his hands, he managed to turn it into an intimate exchange. The teasing light had gone from his eyes.

"You're right. I shouldn't intrude. I'm sorry." She could see that he meant it. She nodded. Things were happening so fast.

She turned back to the sink to busy herself with the dishwasher. She could feel him standing behind her, probably wondering what to do or say next. She wondered the same. Out of her peripheral vision, she saw him reach out a hand to touch her shoulder, but before it got there, he pulled it back and jammed it in his jeans pocket. "As far as you not being able to hear me all the time, maybe you should try trusting your abilities as much as I do."

She turned around. "Okay, maybe I'll try. Thanks."

"Welcome."

Her girly parts tingled when he smiled again. How had she never noticed the tempting hint of dimple in his chin before? That, paired with his sculpted lips...*wow*. Her gaze went back to his, but he gave no indication that he'd heard her that time. Perhaps he was going to honor her request and stay out of her thoughts.

She frowned.

By the time she'd started the dishwasher, he'd left the room and returned with a zippered pouch, a CD, and a notebook. He slid back into a chair. "I'll be out of here before the cops come with a search warrant."

"Oh, stop it. You've only been here three hours. You had to sleep, you know."

When his lips tilted up, she didn't have to read his mind to know they were both remembering—vividly—what had come before and after their sleep.

"Mind if I use your phone? Archie hasn't been able to get one to me yet."

Phone.

Phone!

"Crap! I almost forgot!" She went to the coat closet and pulled Zack's phone out her purse. "On my way back to my car after they released me from the squad car, I spotted this halfway under a bush. It was in the established police perimeter, but they obviously hadn't gotten that far yet."

"Sloane—"

"Don't worry, I took the battery out right away so they couldn't trace it. At least I think that's how it works."

He stood up and a cold wind blew through her. She put a careful hand on his chest. "It's okay. Okay? If you won't go to the police, I want you here." *So I know you're safe.* "I need to go into the store for a bit today. Without Tori—"

For a while, she'd forgotten.

His eyes were intent on hers. "Don't do that to yourself."

"Do what? I told you—"

"I don't have to be in your head to know you're beating yourself up. It's all over your face."

His words released the choke hold on her throat. "But she was *murdered,* and I was—"

"Living." He put his hands on her shoulders. "We're going to find Ann and avenge Tori, but we've got to be tough. Your body—what we shared—was a balm I can't begin to explain. You needed it, too, so stop feeling guilty and let's get to work."

She watched him for a moment. She felt more than saw the torment in him. Subtle waves of energy that brushed against her skin, whisper-soft, as though they were holding back echoes of pain. There was so much to this man. What forces had shaped him to be so guarded, yet so tender? He was so warm when he let down his defenses.

When she realized he was waiting for her to respond, she nodded, and he led her over to the table. He sat down and opened the zippered pouch. Absently, she picked up the CD and immediately dropped it again, her fingers tingling painfully.

Zack looked up from a piece of paper. "What's wrong?"

"What is that?" She pointed at the CD.

"No idea. John never shared any of this stuff with me, though he did say one day he'd fill me in on his past. Guess we both thought we'd have more time."

She squeezed his arm. "I hope someday you'll tell me more about him."

He nodded. "This was in a box I found in the office vault. Twenty years' worth of bodyguard and home security invoices, along with this." He handed her a newspaper clipping.

The resemblance between Ann and the woman in the photo—Serena Galasso—was uncanny. "There's no denying she's her mother, is there? How come Ann never knew her?"

"It's a mystery," he said.

"Maybe she was psychotic and all the security was John's way of protecting Ann from her mother."

He cracked his knuckles. "I don't think so. Even though John wouldn't talk about Ann's mother, I never got the impression he hated her or was afraid of her. Quite the opposite. The only thing he ever told Ann was that her mother was a beautiful woman who could sing like an angel."

"Ann never even knew her name?" It was mind-boggling. Zack nodded. "And she was okay with that?"

"Ann may have tried to press him, but I doubt it. Besides,

there was no moving John once he made up his mind," he said.

Sloane backed away from the table. "Why do you think this stuff is important right now?"

He waited until her eyes met his. "Why do you?" He spoke in hushed tones, almost as if he were talking to a frightened child.

"Apparently you don't need to ask."

He smiled slightly. "You make it so easy for me."

"I don't understand all this." Her arms gestured vaguely.

How could she begin to encompass everything that had happened to and between them in the last couple of days?

He pulled out a chair for her next to his, and she reluctantly sat down. "Don't try so hard," he said. "Your response to the CD only confirms that there's something to be learned from it."

"Like what?"

"John clearly wanted to protect Ann from someone. Why else would he have these?" He looked at the invoices. "Why else would he have made only one request before he died?"

She didn't want to see the guilt spilling shadows in his eyes. "No. You're the one who told me not to—"

"He said, 'Look after her, Zack. She's young and maybe too soft for this world. Not like you and me. After I'm gone, she'll need your guidance.'" Zack got up and walked into the living room.

She followed him. "You can't possibly blame yourself for her disappearance."

His back was to her as he observed the slow moving fish in her aquarium. "Really? He gave me the chance to re-earn my self-respect. He gave so much—*so damn much*—and asked only that one thing in return."

"What were you supposed to do? Live with her? Be her chauffer? Hold her hand when she crossed the street? She's an adult for heaven's sake!"

"When John died she was *so sad*, and I left her to fend for herself. After everything her father had done for me."

"Maybe you didn't know all the gory details of her life, but you still called to check on her the night of the storm. What else were you supposed to do?" She moved to pull on his arm, and he swung around, jaw tight. Her breath caught. This was her Zack.

But different.

More dangerous.

"Yeah, what? Maybe nothing. Maybe I'm good for fucking nothing." He backed her into the wall, sending a framed print swinging on its wire.

An electrifying heat clawed through her. "No pity parties, Zack. You're the one who said we had to be strong."

"I *am* strong." A potent whisper.

Oh, Lord, she felt it. Felt that strength in the coiled power of his thighs, spread to box her in, his jeans lightly abrading her bare skin.

Felt it in the solid wall of his chest that made her simultaneously weak and aware of her own power.

Felt it in the calloused hands that flattened on the wall on either side of her head.

In his eyes.

His eyes.

Her nostrils flared with the effort to keep oxygen pumping to her brain. "You don't scare me."

He leaned in to sniff her neck. "I could."

She shivered, unable to prevent her head from listing to the side. "No." His breath feathered warm torture along her clavicle. Her fingernails curled into the hem of her shorts. "You...you won't win this one. Take it back."

"Take...what...back?" He punctuated each word with a graze of his lips against the line of her jaw.

She was well and truly on fire now. A keen yearning that transcended anything she'd ever known. Her palms came up, dying to touch him, but not. Not yet. "That good-for-nothing BS. Take it back."

"Why does it matter?"

In the green depths of his eyes she saw her future. "Because *you* matter. To me. You're good for *me*."

She felt the stillness in him, the turning over of her words, the weighing, assessing. She swallowed hard.

"Okay. For you, Goldie, *anything*."

His lips were a phantom moving across her skin. She wondered at his restraint.

Passion. Tenderness. So often exclusive.

Not with him.

His gaze dropped to her breasts, and she felt it like a physical caress. Her lips parted in response. When he looked into her eyes, they smoldered with a question.

Yes. Oh, yes.

She thought she'd spoken aloud, but then, it wouldn't have mattered.

This time, he would've heard her either way.

TWENTY-FIVE

Zack watched Sloane as she prepared tea at the stove. Her tousled hair made her seem a mythical forest nymph. Sensual, exotic. The stuff of fantasy. And, *man*. His emotions were getting carried away.

Still, when she set a delicate tea cup in front of him, he pulled her down onto his lap. Her warm laughter tugged at his heart. Tugged at other parts, too.

"Careful or that tea will scorch areas of your body I've come to appreciate," she said.

He pushed the saucer to the far side of the table. "Screw the tea, then. I'll take milk."

She swatted his hands away when he tried to keep her in his lap. "Drink the tea. I'll bring you some milk, too, you big baby." When she returned with another glass, he saw her frown at the CD that sat on the table like a silent elephant. *She's afraid of it.*

He loved her expressive nature, but fear didn't belong in those eyes. He rubbed his knuckles on the softness of her cheek. "I'm going to make a few calls. Any chance you have a CD player?"

"No, but I'll see if my neighbor still has hers. Use my cell phone and save yours for emergencies. Have you received any messages yet?"

"Nothing other than calls from my foreman."

"Okay. I'll try to round up a CD player before I freshen up for work."

"Maybe you should nap first."

195

"The store opens in an hour. I have to be there for the girls." She rubbed the back of her head, tangling her hair even more. He wanted to pick her up, tuck her into bed, and climb in beside her. He'd smooth her hair away from her face and protect her as she drifted away from the ugliness of the world.

Half an hour later, Zack looked up when she walked into the kitchen all gussied up for work. She carried a portable CD player and stopped mid-stride when she looked at him. "What is it?"

He tapped his fingers on this thighs. "I spoke with both the security system and bodyguard companies." And Donovan, but she didn't need to know about that.

"And?"

"They weren't protecting Ann."

"What? Who then?"

"Serena. They were arranged for Ann's mother."

Sloane pulled out a chair across from him and leaned her elbows on the table. "Both companies?"

"Yes," he said.

"But why? Who *is* she?"

"They wouldn't give me a lot of information since I don't have the right passwords. But apparently my name and social security number are on file as an emergency contact so they were at least able to confirm the name of the client." He looked at the clipping of Serena. "They wouldn't tell me where she lives, but one of the customer service reps eventually gave me the name of one of her bodyguards."

"Let me guess. The customer service rep was female, right?" she asked, drolly.

In spite of wanting to pull his hair out, he smiled. "Your point is?"

"Wipe that grin off your face, caveman, your knuckles are

dragging."

His smile widened until he felt his eyes crinkle. "Until I can give the right passwords, I can't get more information from either company. The only other thing the lady told me is that the bodyguard services have been arranged until Serena dies."

"John arranged to have her protected for life?"

"Yep. He even set up a trust for her. I'm guessing the documents are in the office vault. A place I've tried to avoid for the past year. Big mistake in more ways than one."

"Wow. He must've really had a thing for her. So neither of the companies said anything about Ann?"

"No, but thanks to one of my buddies I was able to track down the number for Gunther Smith, Serena's previous bodyguard of about four years. When I told him I'd gotten his name from his previous employer, I suppose he figured it was okay to talk to me. The story he told me rivals anything in the literature books."

"Tell me."

"Ann's neighbor Agnes had the gist of it. John met Serena when she was a guest professor at NDSU in the music department about twenty years ago. A big star, with ardent admirers in many countries. Heaps of fan mail—proposals, sonnets, shit like that. John fell hard, apparently. She preyed on his lavish generosity for a while, then she dumped him and moved on. The end." The more it sank in, the more it pissed him off.

Sloane blinked at him for a second before responding in a flat tone. "If that's your idea of a literary masterpiece, you make a crappy storyteller. Though a secret admirer angle has possibilities."

She made him smile at the worst of times. "Consider me Cliffs Notes," he said. "Besides, did I say secret?"

She rolled her eyes with a faint smile. "No, but I refuse to believe that all of that fan mail had return addresses or people using their real names." She tilted her head. "Maybe Agnes would remember a few other details that might help us understand why John would go to the trouble of arranging security for Serena when she was such a femme fatale."

"I think I already know why. Serena got pregnant. Gunther said John was over the moon because at forty-eight he thought he'd never father a child. But he was also terrified because Serena wanted to have an abortion."

"Really? No wonder John treated Ann like a princess."

"On top of that, one of Serena's long-time *anonymous* admirers started sending hate mail instead of his usual love poems. So yeah, you were right about the secret-thing."

"Sounds like John had probable cause for protecting Serena then." She looked at the picture again. "I wonder why she didn't get the abortion."

Zack felt his face twist into an ugly smile. "According to Gunther, she was getting nervous about the nasty letters. So in exchange for giving birth and handing over the baby, John offered her a fortress in a tropical paradise, bodyguard services for life, and a cool ten million dollars. Pretty small sacrifice."

"*Lord*. No wonder John never talked to Ann about her mother. She would have been devastated. Did they ever find out who was sending Serena the hate mail?" she asked.

"No. Gunther didn't know anything about that since he hadn't been her initial bodyguard. He came on board about six years after she'd left the States. Apparently they'd hidden her well enough that the secret-admirer-turned-hater lost track of her. So no more letters."

"Still. Pretty creepy."

He watched a tremor run through Sloane's body. She

rubbed her hands up and down her arms, and her nipples beckoned him from beneath the silky material of her shirt. This one was black and hugged the tops of her arms, leaving her golden shoulders bare should he want to run his tongue along all that soft skin.

Needing to move, he retrieved a blanket from the living room. A smile lit her eyes when he draped it around her shoulders. Which made him even more agitated. He walked away from her, leaning against the counter with his arms and ankles crossed in front of him.

"So where do all the pieces fit together?" Sloane laid down Serena's picture, and the blanket slipped off one shoulder, exposing her made-for-sucking neck. "If at all."

He bit the inside of his cheek. "I don't know." He pushed away from the counter and picked up the CD. "Let's get this over with."

He held it out to Sloane, but she only pushed the player at him. As the first few stanzas oozed from the speakers, Zack slipped into a chair, the music a siren's song luring the testosterone from his glands, the woman's throaty sound an erotic, auditory delight.

YOU PROTECTED ME,
YOU TOUCHED ME,
AND YOU LEFT ME SO CONFUSED.
MY STRONG MAN IN A RUSH,
YOUR LIPS CARESS MY BLUSH,
YOUR TOUCH SO SOFT AND SWEET.

I'M UP AGAINST A WALL.
NO, I CAN'T TAKE THE FALL.
PLEASE BELIEVE ME, BABY, I TRIED.

THE WORLD'S MY LONELY STAGE,
I NEED A BRAND NEW PAGE,
BUT YOU BROUGHT ME TO THE BRINK.

YOU WANT ME TO STAY,
BUT I'M SURE TO RUN AWAY,
CAUSE I KNOW MY HEART'S A FOOL.
MY FICKLE WAYS DON'T TRUST,
MY LEAVING IS A MUST,
YET I GIFT YOU MY ONE TRUE SONG.

SONG OF SECRETS. OH, MY SONG OF SECRETS.
YOU KNOW MY SECRETS.
MY BURDEN, MY SECRET,
IN MY HEART, IN MY SOUL,
MY SONG, SONG OF SECRETS.

As the music faded, Zack became aware of the drone of vehicles outside. He looked at Sloane. She appeared just as enthralled.

"What a handful," he said.

Sloane's lips curved slightly. "No wonder John was obsessed with her. She was always slightly out of reach. She might have given him her body, but he could never have more."

"Until Ann."

"Her one true song. Her song of secrets."

They stared at each other, letting the significance sink in. The depth of John's love for his only child had never been so poignant. Nor Zack's need to find Ann at any cost. He'd never live with himself if he didn't. "The questions then are, *who* wanted to scare Serena all those years ago, and *why*. And is that person the same one who took Ann?"

"Or *persons*. You said earlier that you think the person you wrestled with at Ann's was a hired heavy, not the actual person behind the scheme," she said.

"Yeah, I know. Square one seems to be finding out who was obsessed with Serena."

"Did Gunther mention any other suspicious activities during the time he was her bodyguard? Or before or after his stint?"

"No, I asked about that, but apparently his employer arranged an elaborate scheme so Serena could vanish. She stopped performing and went underground for a few years. It caused a brief sensation in the States, but since she wasn't as big a star in other countries, and she had plenty of money, she eluded attention by going overseas. According to the reports Gunther received prior to his assignment, the hate mail stopped as soon as she left town, so John's plan was successful."

"Sounds like a lonely life," she said.

Did it? He wasn't sure. Less complications. "Yeah, I guess so."

Sloane opened her mouth to say something, then shut it. Those golden shoulders dropped. He burned to press a kiss in the shadow between her throat and collar bone.

She shivered. "Okay, well, I need to get go—" Her land line rang. She checked caller ID before answering. At his questioning look, she picked up and mouthed *Carmen*. Within moments she gasped, pressing a hand to her stomach. Cold pressure built in Zack's chest.

When she disconnected, he grasped her arms. "What happened?"

She said nothing, and he followed her as she walked mechanically into the living room. She turned on the television and flipped to a local station.

Colette O'Neill stood before the cameras, her eyes bleak, her face pale and tear-streaked as she pled with the public to help the police.

During the night, both of her children had gone missing.

TWENTY-SIX

Snatched out of their beds.

The words played over and over in Sloane's mind until she felt paralyzed with horror for the children. The edges of her vision flickered red, and she reached out to brace herself against the back of a chair. Zack's arms came around her and the red faded away. Silently, he held her until her thudding heart slowed to match the steady rhythm of his.

The world's gone mad.

"Not if I can help it," he said.

Bits of her hair combed against his chin stubble as she leaned back to look at him. "But they're pointing the finger at you. *You*, Zack! You *have* to go to the cops now. The longer you stay underground, the more they'll think you're guilty."

"I can't. How can I find Ann—and now these kids—if I'm locked up? They won't listen to me."

"But if you're in jail when the killer makes another move, they'll know they have the wrong guy."

"Are you really willing to wait for this psycho to fuck with someone else? Think, Sloane. We have to think." He released her and paced to her bookcase. "I have to think."

"Why would he take the O'Neill kids?"

Zack paused. "Yeah, why? Nothing about this has been random. So there must be a reason." He swung to face her, and suddenly she realized it, too.

"He knows we've been to see Colette," she said hoarsely. "He's using her children as collateral so she cooperates. So she doesn't reveal his identity." She wondered how she'd gotten the words past the desert of her throat.

"*Son of a bitch!* She'll be ready to talk now. She has to." He was like a caged animal.

"Wait. We don't know if he's made contact with her, plus I don't think she knows what actually happened to Ann."

"How can she not? She deposited her at the mouth of that monster!"

"But the crystal would've shown that Colette knows more. Colette kept her mind focused on the festival while she was in the car with Ann. When she pulled up to Patty's house, the crystal registered relief and excitement, but no specific thoughts like 'this is what's going to happen to Ann.' She wouldn't have been able to block something that traumatic from her mind. The crystal would've received it. Do you know any Pattys?"

"No. I'm outta here."

She stopped him with both hands curling around his wrist. "If you thought it'd be tough to get to Colette before, you'd be a fool to try it now. There has to be another way. Go to the cops, *please, Zack.*"

"I'm sorry. They'll turn all their attention on me, and meanwhile the killer will strike again. Can't do it."

"I'm an alibi."

"Not for all three days."

She dropped his wrist. She hadn't been with him physically, but she'd been with him psychically for part of the time they were apart. Panic started bubbling in her gut, but she swallowed hard and made herself take a step out onto the ice. "I could...try to see where you were. I could *look*. I could say I was with you. You know, if..." *Just say it!* "If you want me to. And you trust me."

He took her face between his hands and laid his forehead against hers. "God, that you'd even say that..." He cleared his throat. "I'd never, *ever* want you to do that for me. Promise me you'll only ever speak the truth about—and to—me."

She nodded and turned away, waiting for the rending of her heart to tell her he'd departed.

Because he clearly didn't trust her. She shouldn't be surprised. She didn't even trust herself.

Still, it hurt. God, it hurt.

"I can try to get back to Ann's for the metal sculpture that fell on the guy I wrestled," he suggested. "If I can get the sculpture, maybe it can tell us who he's working with. I know you can do it."

I know you can do it.

She looked at him and felt something splinter inside her.

I know you can do it.

It was what the lead detective had told her an hour before they found Abigail's body in the snow. Broken and defiled.

She sank down against the wall as the bottom of her world fell away. She wanted to go to her store and pretend Tori would walk through the showroom door and start grousing about the messiness of the display tables.

She wanted to hide where no one could find her.

A wash of bile rose up in her throat. *Sick.* She was sick. Sick in the head. In spirit. She was a *failure.* She hadn't protected her sister, Megan.

Abigail.

Tori.

She couldn't help Zack either. He had to know the whole, ugly truth. "Abigail Bates was Tim Benjamin's granddaughter."

"What?"

He moved toward her, but she held her hands out to keep

him back. He would leave her now. Hate her. But the words tumbled out anyway. "Abby Bates. The girl who was abducted six years ago in Bismarck? Hers was the only case I ever worked on with the police. I failed. She died before they could find her. She was Benjamin's granddaughter. The police never told his family who I was, and I've never admitted it. And now I'm depending on Benjamin to fund a foundation I'm trying to get off the ground. What a coward, huh? I was going to call it Project Broken Wings. To help families heal after suicide. Benjamin's daughter, Joan, took her own life when they found Abigail. So that family lost not one, but two people because of my failure."

"That's not your fault. Come on, Sloane!"

"She was brutalized. Her precious—" She pressed a hand to her mouth for a moment, swallowing convulsively. "I could hear her cries for help. In my head. I heard her. But I...I couldn't find her in time. Sometimes I still hear her...c-crying."

His face blurred as her hot tears overflowed. Her throat worked as she tried to hold back a moan of agony. He moved toward her, but she scrambled up from the floor away from him.

"Stay back. *Please*."

He stopped, his arm dropping to his side, his eyes shining with...

Pity?

He had to know it all. "My older sister, Megan, committed suicide when I was twelve. I knew she was sad—I *saw* it, *felt* it— but I didn't help mom and dad look after her like they asked. I should have." She couldn't look at him. "And then Tori." Her mouth was dry. Throat, too. Even her eyes were now a dry wasteland, the emptiness inside her too vast for tears. "So you see? I don't help. I *hurt*. People *die* when I see things about them. I'm just...*flawed.*"

He grabbed her shoulders, forcing her to meet his eyes. "That's bullshit, and you know it! You were just a girl when your sister died, Sloane. No parent should ever heap that kind of responsibility on a child. And what happened with the others...no one could change those outcomes."

"My mother could've. She makes happy endings all the time. *She* could have saved Abigail, but I begged the department to let me try. One time. And that one time a child died. And then her mother. I can't help you. Don't you see? I just can't! I'm sorry!"

She twisted out of his grasp as the floodgates of panic opened. A thick, fiery surge of energy that made her reach for her purse and run out the door before he could tackle her. She stumbled down the hall and three flights of stairs, unseeing.

The door. Exit. Outside.

The sun bright. Surreal. She squinted at the nearly empty parking lot. Fingertips across her neck. The breeze? Two men in the unmarked car.

Police.

It's not him, she wanted to scream at them. But they wouldn't listen, would they? They'd haul him away in handcuffs and ask questions later.

She couldn't let that happen. Heavy pressure beat at the backs of her eyeballs.

This much I can do for you, Zack.

She ran to her car, fumbling with the automatic opener as she dug her phone out of her purse. *Pretend there's an emergency. Make them follow.*

Her lips moved in a wild pantomime. She looked over her shoulder for show.

Yes, she was good at putting on a show.

Fraud. I'm a fraud.

She slid behind the wheel, revved the engine, and squealed out of the parking lot. Moisture rose up to blur her field of vision. Only one moment before gravity took over, spilling wetness down her cheeks in sheets. Hot tears that scalded. Such a contrast to the endless cold she felt inside.

When she ran the first stop sign, she scanned the rearview mirror, her fingers tightening on the steering wheel. In this at least she hadn't failed.

The police were in hot pursuit.

Now's your chance. Run, Zack.

TWENTY-SEVEN

Peering out the shuttered window to the parking lot below, Zack saw her performance for the undercover officers.

Run, Zack.

Damn you, you stubborn, impossible woman. He sprinted through her loft, gathering the newspaper clipping, money, invoices, and CD into the zippered pouch, then pulled on John's battered baseball cap and followed the same escape route she'd used moments before.

Two blocks away, he slid behind the wheel of the El Camino, pulled his cell from his jeans pocket, and replaced the battery. After booting up, it indicated a message from an unrecognized number. He entered his password and pressed the phone to his ear.

A woman crying.

Ann? *Ann!* He couldn't understand what she was saying. Sobbing.

"Damn it!" His fingers curled around the phone. What was she saying? Then, "How c-could you do this to us? You monst—" Her yell caved in upon itself, her body clearly absorbing a physical blow of some sort.

Zack's skin prickled as hot fury quickly replaced the chill that had flooded his system. A pause in the message, then a ghostly whisper, "Tiiime'sss almossst up. *Boom*!"

And that was it.

The phone indicated the call had come through three hours earlier. *What?* He'd checked messages two hours ago. No way could he have missed this one. His hand trembled as he listened to the message twice more. The person could be male or female for all he could tell.

He pounded the steering wheel, furious because Ann was still missing.

Giddy because she was still alive as of two or three hours ago.

Hope could be a terrible thing.

Time's almost up. What was that supposed to mean? Time for what? To find her? She'd said, *How could you do this to us?* So, she obviously knew her captor. Did she mean *us*, as in her and him, or her and the baby? Whoever was holding her was obviously enjoying this, the rank puss-bucket piece of shit.

And what the hell did *boom* mean?

He swallowed hard. *Don't go there. Not now.*

He started the car and pulled onto the street. Should he turn himself in? Give them his phone? The cops had to have ways to track incoming calls like that.

The phone rang in his hand, and he swerved, nearly offing a pedestrian. When he glanced back at the phone, he didn't recognize the number. "Ann?"

"I've been trying to reach you for hours, Zack! I do you a huge favor and you don't have the gooch ass decency to say thank you?"

"Morgan, I don't have time for drama."

"Where are you?"

"I gotta go."

"Oh sure! Use me and then toss me aside, mother felching douche bag! You're just like all the others, you selfish—"

He disconnected, the sudden silence in the car an amplification of his guilt. He powered off the phone and removed the battery again before slipping both into his pocket.

He couldn't fix this with Morgan right now. But he would.

Just as he'd fix it with Sloane.

After he fixed about a million other things. Ann and her baby were still out there.

Somewhere.

He pressed down on the accelerator.

***

Zack cursed when the El Camino sputtered and died four blocks north of Divine Shepherd Lutheran campus. He'd known it would be a long shot to find Colette alone, but what else could he do? She knew something. He'd have to get her alone and convince her to tell him.

And he wanted her to know he didn't take her kids. Made him sick to think anyone could do such a thing.

He slipped out the passenger door, the zippered pouch tucked into the waistband of his jeans. He walked as casually as possible over to two cars parked by the curb, pretending to scrape something off the tire walls, all the while scanning the two-block vicinity. A dog was barking behind a west-facing house and someone was baking, the heavy chocolate scent wafting through the air. It was all so...normal.

Only it wasn't.

Sure enough, there was a nondescript white van about a hundred feet from the rectory's driveway on the opposite side of the road. Cops most likely.

Of course Colette wasn't alone. He turned and jogged a few blocks away. Walking on the boulevards, he looked into all the parked cars until he found an old Pontiac Grand Am with the keys in the ignition. Ignoring a shaft of guilt, he climbed in and took off.

He spent the first ten miles watching the rearview mirror. He crossed the North Dakota border into Minnesota and wondered if this was how some people ended up losing their minds.

Backed into a corner with nowhere to go and no friendly faces.

He was being a fool. A crazy, reckless fool.

He could've turned himself in back there, but he wasn't sure he believed in the whole martyr thing, especially when it didn't guarantee Ann's recovery.

This wasn't how his life was supposed to spin out. As much as he'd resisted, John had changed him, he realized. Made him want more than guarded isolation.

He wanted a life. Even when it hurt. A few friends, an honest career, his dogs, a chance to pay it forward. A family someday.

Sloane.

He just had to think.

With all the police around, Colette wasn't a productive avenue. The bodyguard and security companies were also a lost cause until he could give them the codes so he had to find them. John wasn't one to write a lot of things down, but if he did, where would he have put the passwords?

The more Zack thought about it, if John had written the passwords anywhere, they were either in the office vault or in the totes in Ann's closet he'd seen when he'd found Dallan. When Zack had moved Ann in, she'd told him they were her father's.

That would certainly be John's style. Keep something hidden right under your nose until he thought you were good and ready to handle it.

Zack turned the stolen car around, put his phone back

together and tried Archie's number. This time it went to voicemail. Where was he? Twyla trouble? *Let their baby be okay.*

A few miles from Ann's, he reached into his pocket for a crumpled piece of paper. Donovan had nothing to report yet on Barnaba, but he'd excavated the shit out of Benjamin's backstory. Apparently Benjamin had not only had sex with Serena the same night she went home with John following one of her sold-out performances, but Donovan had also found out that the holding company executive had a private investigator on his payroll.

No final word yet on how long Benjamin had engaged the services, but Donovan had said it was at least the last ten years. Sloane would die if she knew. Benji had probably known all along she'd been the one working his granddaughter's case. The old goat was probably setting her up for something ugly.

Or maybe it was all part of a subversive plot to bring John down. But why? To win the fickle Serena?

Every question answered only seemed to conjure more questions.

Zack's lips tightened. As he turned the final corner onto Ann's block he saw what looked like a blue Ford Explorer vanish down the opposite street. *Archie?*

His imagination was on overdrive. Besides, blue SUVs were a dime a dozen.

Where should he park to get into Ann's? The cops were long gone, but the neighbors would still be on alert. He froze when the phone rang. Twyla's number lit up his display. "Twyla?"

"Please tell me Archie's with you. I'm having contractions, and this stupid media terrorism's got me scared. Now there's a building on fire downtown—"

"Whoa, *whoa.* What building? Not Samuel's—"

"No. Some ritzy joint."

His heart stopped. "Blackhawk Gates?"

"That's it."

Sloane. "Are they—did they make sure everyone was out of the building?" He gunned it down the street, passing Ann's condo. When he turned the corner, he didn't see any sign of the blue vehicle.

"I think so. I'm nervous for you, Zack. Is Archie there?"

Wings battered his gut. "No, but I'm sure everything's okay. He's probably helping one of his buddies and left his phone in the truck again." The Blue Explorer? Zack had a feeling Archie was scoping out more than he'd let on. If that had been his truck, what was he up to? "Maybe you should go to the clinic to make sure you and the baby are okay. Call Morgan. She'll take you and help watch Logan."

"But—"

"Take care of your family, Twyla. I'll find Archie and be in touch." He hung up. What else could he say? He didn't know anything anymore, and he didn't want to frighten her. He looked at the speedometer and forced himself to ease up on the gas. He'd need to ditch this vehicle soon.

But first he had to know Sloane was safe.

He dialed her cell number. When she picked up, his back slumped against the seat in relief. "Sloane—"

"That murdering bastard burned my home! It had to have been him!"

"Where are you?"

"Watching the flames. All the black smoke. Nothing left."

"Can you leave without the police or firefighters knowing?"

"No."

"You gotta try, Goldie."

"Who hates us so much?"

214

"I'm going to find out. But you have to get away, okay?" Silence on the other end. He could feel his pulse in the hand holding the phone. "Do you trust me?"

"Yes." No hesitation.

He released his breath. "Meet me in the hospital parking ramp. Top level. I'll take you somewhere safe."

"I don't want—"

"I'll be there in less than five minutes."

"Zack—"

"Your parents are out of the country, right?"

"Yes."

"I need to keep you safe, Sloane. *Please*."

Finally, she whispered, "Top level?"

"Top level in five." He disconnected quickly. As much as he wanted to stay on the line until he could see the whites of her eyes, he had one more call to make.

Ross picked up on the second ring. "I hope you're sitting on an island far, far away because the shit has officially hit the fan, Zack. How in the *hell* are you going to dig out of this?"

"I need a favor, buddy."

***

Zack pulled into the YMCA parking lot where Ross had agreed to meet him to pick up Sloane.

"I want to stay with you." She laid a hand on his thigh. "Look at me."

He did. *Big mistake*. Her eyes turned his rational faculties to mush. "Sloane—"

"I feel safer with you."

"I've got a target on my back," he said.

She blanched and looked down at her lap. "I'm so sorry."

215

"Jesus, it's not your fault." He brought her chin up so she could see it in his eyes. "None of this is. I believe in you, Goldie. Your gift, too. I know you can help, but I can't let you right now. Someone has it in for people connected to Samuel's, and anyone associated with us is in jeopardy. Tori knew about Ann's diary. She's dead. You've been seen with me, and look at your building. God, Sloane, what if you'd been in there?" The horror of it had replayed over and over in his mind.

"I wish I could help." Her tone told him she didn't believe that would ever happen. But there was no time to make her see. To help her trust.

Ross had opened his car door and stepped outside to wait. From his look of unease, Zack could tell he hated it, was scared to do it—didn't *want* to do it—but Zack felt more relieved than ever that his right hand man had agreed to safeguard Sloane until the bulk of this disaster was over.

He pressed a hard kiss to Sloane's lips and a piece of paper into her hand. "Ross is going to take you back to Samuel's. John has a fold-out bed in the wall of his office and a full bathroom next door. The number on this paper is the combination for the vault behind his desk. The vault is fireproof and indestructible. No one alive has the combination besides me. If you have the slightest feeling of trouble, get in. There's a small stash of food, water, and a phone inside, and a handle so you can get out again. For now, Ross will bring you clothes, toiletries, food, whatever you need."

"Why can't the police protect me?"

"They've got their hands full. Even if they would assign one or two officers to watch over you—which they won't—flesh and blood can't protect you as well as the four-foot concrete walls of that vault."

She stopped him before he could unbuckle her seatbelt.

"This is ridiculous. I don't *want* to hide out while you're hunting down the bad guys!"

"Are you willing to shoot someone to save your own life?" When she didn't reply, he brushed his fingers against her cheek. "We are in survival mode. Promise me you'll stay there."

"What about my shop?"

"Won't matter if you're dead. Promise me, Goldie."

"Promise to call me."

"If I'm able to," he said.

"Promise."

He gripped the steering wheel hard in one hand. "Okay, yes. I promise. Okay?"

"Okay," she whispered.

He reached across her lap to open her door. She hesitated. His fingers reached up to slide into the hair at her temple. She leaned her head into his hand and closed her eyes. His throat tightened. Arms went around her. Too soon, he gave her a nudge out the door toward Ross, who stood sideways, offering them a modicum of privacy.

At the door of Ross's car, she turned back to face him. She raised a hand to her lips and blew him a kiss before climbing inside.

I love you.

Had she really projected the words? Or was he only hearing what he wanted to hear?

He sprinted across the parking lot, slipped into the company truck Ross had one of their workers bring for him, and pulled out of the parking lot prepared to face a thousand monsters. What the landscape would look like at the end of this battle, he had no idea, but at least he could count on having Sloane protected.

TWENTY-EIGHT

Zack was en route to Ann's when Archie finally called. "You've got a lot of explaining to do."

Archie chuckled. "Yeah, I see you called like ten times. Where'd you get a phone?"

"Tell you later."

"*Uh, huh.* Thought so."

"You know squat."

"I know the cops are pissed you're AWOL."

"Thanks, I wasn't aware of that. They probably already have a bead on me since my phone's been on for the last hour. You talk to Twyla?" Zack spotted a police cruiser dead ahead and made a quick right turn, pulled to the curb, and sank in his seat. Sweat rolled down his back as he adjusted the side mirror to watch behind him.

"Yeah, I made it to her appointment. Her mom's with her now. She's jumpy, but fine."

Makes two of us. "Whatcha got?" The police vehicle passed his block. He exhaled.

"Ann use a cleaning service?" Archie asked.

"I don't think so. Why?"

"Some dude had a key to her place, got in, then came out like twenty five minutes later. Truck sign said *Presto Perfect Cleaners*. Thing is...this was at six a.m. this morning. And there's no Presto Perfect Cleaners in the phone book," Archie said.

"Why were you at Ann's?"

"Cops aren't the only ones who use surveillance. Since the guy you shot got away, there's a missing piece here. A big one. My gut tells me someone's still sniffing around her place."

"I didn't call any cleaners. And even if Ann used someone regularly, she'd never have them there that early. You trail 'em?"

"Straight to Benji's fancy new mall project," Archie said.

"The cleaner went to the mall? That doesn't make any sense. We use a different company for clean—"

It had to be the guy he'd surprised at Ann's. Zack smacked the seat beside him. "Did he get inside?"

"At the mall? Yeah. I tried to follow, but the door locked behind him. I stuck around for almost an hour, but then had to go with Twy for her appointment. When I went back later, the truck was gone."

"What'd he look like?" Zack asked.

"Average to solid build. Average height. I couldn't tell a lot because I was pretty far away and he wore a crap-load of white and a cap pulled low with sunglasses. Looked like he had sandy blond hair, but it also could have been gray for all I could tell under his hat. Wasn't dark-skinned or dark-haired, that much I know."

"Or he was in disguise. Dammit, I have nothing. You hear about the kidnapping?"

"Yeah, he's one twisted loser. Twyla's pretty freaked out."

"To cover so many places at once, he can't be working alone," Zack said.

"Whoever it is, he wants to mess with you, man. Pick you apart until you bleed. Go through it all again. Connect the dots. Ann. Sloane's girl at the store. Now Sloane's building. There's got to be a pattern. Figure it out, then tell me what I can do next."

Zack's entire frame had tensed. "How do you know about Sloane?"

"I have another angle to work. I'll be in touch."

"No! Wait!" The line went dead. Zack gritted his teeth and turned the car around.

No more running. Time for a come-to-Jesus with Benjamin. The holding company exec been a slightly younger contemporary of John's, but they'd hungered for the same woman. And John had been the one to have her. Temporarily and publicly anyway.

Something must have happened to scare John enough to think she needed lifetime protection. Even though she was an epic bitch.

In her vision, Sloane had seen Benjamin fawning over Ann. And of course he'd shown up at Ann's intending to ask her to model for the charity event, so he obviously liked her. But he had almost four decades on her. He couldn't possibly think she'd fall for him, especially when she had her own trust fund. Was he trying to recreate a fantasy about Serena? The thought was disturbing.

And Colette. How did she figure in? What about Tori's and Dallan's murders? Was there something in the diary they'd missed? Was Barnaba somehow involved?

Ann was the only solid piece tying everything together.

Definitely time to find out what Benjamin knew.

It had been roughly four hours since the call from Ann's abductor. *Time's almost up,* the voice had said. But how much time was left? Or had he meant the fire at Sloane's?

Ten minutes later, he grabbed his gun and a narrow rope from the truck's glove box—*thank you, Ross*—and slammed the door in Benjamin's circular driveway. The early afternoon sun reflected off the multi-faceted glass on the massive double doors, shining rainbows on the brass handles. Three stories, six garages, and a reported twenty thousand square feet, the house was a gray brick monstrosity.

Zack rang the bell, gripping the rope like a lifeline.

The door opened and Zack pushed a lanky, hook-nosed man—*a butler? Really?*—inside, the gun snug against his back. "Where's Benjamin?" The man nearly fainted, but Zack grabbed him by the arm. "You don't need to be afraid if you cooperate."

The man half-stumbled, half-leaned against Zack as they made their way toward a nine-foot door. "He's in th-th-there."

The guy's lips were blue. Looked like he was about to pass out, too. Zack felt bad about it, but lives were at stake. He opened what turned out to be the library door and pushed the butler inside. Benjamin stood up behind his desk, a look of outrage adding vigor to his normally sallow features.

"What the hell is going on? I'm calling the police!"

Zack raised the pistol. "Wanna bet my bullet travels faster than your fingers?"

Benjamin sent him a look of raw hatred, but he lowered the handset. "You're out of your mind."

Zack threw the rope on the desk. "Tie the good butler to the chair. Make it tight. If I have to redo it, you'll be the one with regrets."

The employee voluntarily took a seat and Benjamin leaned one knee on the floor to tie the man's hands behind his back. "You'll pay for this, Goldman." A faint sheen glistened over his upper lip.

"Where's Ann?"

Benjamin shot to his feet. "Her name shouldn't even cross your filthy mouth!"

"Where is she?"

"You tell me! You're the lowlife John resurrected from the

221

riverb—" Zack's fist connected with Benjamin's middle, bending him in half. Then Zack grabbed him by the hair and hauled him backward against the heavy bookcases lining the far wall.

He pressed close enough to see the gold flecks in Benjamin's muddy green eyes. "Me? What about *you*? You *like* her. Her looks. Always have, haven't you? You wanted her so much you gave your enemy your business, hoping to get near her. Your taste of the mother was so sweet, might as well sample the daughter, too, right?"

"P-pond scum!" Benjamin's eyes widened and in the next instant his face crumpled. "She's nearly Serena's doppelganger."

Zack jerked back to avoid knocking heads with him as Benjamin's anger deflated like a leaky balloon. "You have one last chance to tell me where she is."

"Or what?" Benjamin's head flew up, his eyes bloodshot. "I don't know! I would move heaven and earth to find her. I've had a PI on it, but she's just gone. Gone! Just like Abby. Joan. *Serena.*"

Zack let him sag in a heap to the floor. The guy was a case. Seriously. But then, he was probably allowed, after what had happened to his granddaughter. And then his daughter, Joan, who'd taken her own life after the tragedy, according to Sloane.

And somehow, Zack believed him. "Tell me about Serena. Why did she disappear?"

Benjamin shakily climbed into his desk chair. After a moment he almost looked like his arrogant self again. "Put your infernal weapon away. You know it wasn't me."

Zack stuck the gun in the waistband of his jeans. "If you care about Ann, you'd better tell me why Serena had to leave. This is somehow connected, and we don't have a lot of time."

"Serena was a goddess. Her voice, her beauty. She made

you feel like the only person in the world when she talked to you." He looked down at his perfectly groomed hands like they were a stranger's. "Why someone would try to scare her…"

"Who was it?"

"We never found out."

"We?"

Benjamin smiled sadly. "I've had private investigators on this for more than twenty years now."

"A tad obsessive, don't you think? Maybe it was *you* sending the letters," Zack said.

A hard look came into Benjamin's eyes. "Women like Serena—like Ann—are meant to be cherished."

"You mean *kept*."

Benjamin waved a hand in the air. "Men of your generation don't understand. All this stupid equality of the sexes nonsense. Men are stronger. We make the money, then we take care of the women."

Zack thought of Sloane's fear that Benjamin would find out about her role in Abigail's tragic story. That Benjamin couldn't protect his granddaughter must have been horrific on so many levels, especially given his patriarchal slant. Had he been as calculating and cold before Abigail's death and his daughter's suicide? Could he have been the one to send Serena the letters, hoping fear would drive a wedge between her and John?

"What did John do when he found out you were having an affair with her, too?"

Benjamin snorted. "John was oblivious to anything—anyone—but her. He didn't know. At least not at first… But your man Ross did."

The air stopped midway in Zack's throat. "What?" He stepped toward Benjamin, who rolled backwards in his chair. "What does Ross have to do with any of this?"

223

Benjamin stood up. "Get out! You've threatened me at gunpoint, and I've had enough!"

Zack moved fast. He had him up against the bookcase once more, his arm tight across Benjamin's windpipe. "And I'll do it again and again until I have the information I need to find Ann and stop a killer. Did you know she's pregnant?" The old man flinched. "Yeah, Ann's more vulnerable than ever. You thought she needed protection before? Guess what, the ante's up. Are you in?"

Benjamin pulled at Zack's arm and managed a nod. Zack released the pressure against his throat. "Then tell me what I need to know, starting with Ross." *Sloane?* He tried reaching out, but she didn't answer. The back of his neck prickled. "Hurry up, man!"

Benjamin wet his lips, then cleared his throat, rubbing at it with his hand. "Ross was an undergrad at the time, but it seems he had a thing for Serena, too. More than once I'd stop by her office at the university, and he'd be sitting in the hallway outside. When I started working with your outfit, I didn't recognize him because as a college student he'd been a long-haired slob. It wasn't until recently—probably about a month ago when I got a good look at his unusual eyes—that I realized your impeccably groomed CFO was the new, improved version of the undergrad who'd pined for Serena."

Zack sucked air through his nose to try to calm his heartbeat, but it only made it worse. "How'd you make the connection?"

"I walked into the office one afternoon and saw Ross staring at Ann with those pale green eyes of his. It was déjà vu, only I couldn't reconcile the feeling until later on."

"Déjà vu meaning you'd seen Ross looking at Serena that way a couple decades ago?"

Benjamin nodded, and a key turned in the lock.

Now he knew why his attacker at Ann's had seemed so familiar. Zack's world tilted as an uncharted feeling swamped him. He clenched his fists, but he couldn't feel them. Cold. *Cold.* The bite crawled into his chest, pierced his throat. *Can't breathe.*

Ross. *My God.* No.

No.

Sloane.

Panic razored through him.

He'd led her right to the slaughter.

TWENTY-NINE

Sloane's fingers felt brittle as they curled around the railing for support. Perhaps one tap against the warm metal and they would shatter. Maybe her whole body would shatter. Fall to a million pieces on the stairs where Zack had doubtless climbed hundreds of times.

Though the temperature sweltered in the back stairwell, she shuddered, wondering when she'd ever feel warm again. She looked up at the man preceding her. From the short-clipped hairs on his head to the polished shoes that made merely a whisper on the steps, Ross was attractive in an older, clean-cut sort of fashion. So very different from Zack, who was rough-around-the-edges. Raw, elemental and...

Comforting.

She wanted to be with him. Should have made him take her with him.

When he called, she was going to demand he come back for her.

No. She was going to call him the minute she reached John's office and make him turn around.

Damn, how long does it take to climb three flights, anyway? She regarded Ross again. He'd been so silent. Would he turn them in? Zack seemed to trust him. She should really try to talk to him. After all, he was helping her out. "Uh...I know this is really...awkward, but I appreciate your help."

Ross paused on the stairs and looked over his shoulder at her, one hand going to a white gauze patch on his neck. The unexpected humor in his eyes was a surprise after his earlier tension when Zack was still around. "It's okay. Sometimes you have to draw outside the lines. Not everything is black or white."

Huh. She supposed he was right. Rules and laws don't take everything into account. Still, what an odd comment. "What should I tell the staff if they see me in John's office?"

"We'll just say you're a temp." He turned around and continued up the stairs, his footfalls softly swishing in the stairwell.

When they reached the third floor, he stepped aside to hold open the metal door. In the back draft, his cologne washed over her. She shivered again, hesitating on the landing. Her gaze shot to his. She'd never seen such a pale shade of green. Did he even have pupils? It wasn't *that* bright in here that they should be so constricted. Looked like those eyes belonged to a unicorn or some other mythical being. A dragon maybe?

I'm losing it. She put a hand to her temple. Fingerlike fringes of red began seeping into her peripheral vision.

He smiled tentatively. "Something wrong?"

Only everything. "Oh, no. Sorry." But as she passed him, a sudden blast of energy surged through her. *Black, black, it's black!* The energy scalded, excruciating pain, boiling alive— *acid, acid!*—skin peeling back. Nothing left but a bloody pulp.

Red eyes gleamed from black shadows. Blood demon eyes. Mesmerizing.

Perfectly, beautifully evil.

In her head she was screaming. Screaming at those eyes that would do so much worse than destroy her body. They'd pillage her soul, and she'd scream forever.

A violent wind swirled between her and the glowing orbs.

Then the vision was over.

She stumbled against the door jamb, then shuffled into the hallway. She leaned her hands against her knees for support, gasping for air.

"Please say you're not going to be sick."

She looked up at Zack's dragon-eyed CFO. She eased herself upright but couldn't muster the energy to glare at him. Her heart rate refused to settle, though. "Gosh...just...*whew!*... All those stairs. Just trying to catch my breath. That's...that's all."

"*Good.* John's office is this way."

Lord, she felt ill. What the hell was going on with her? And that stupid furrow between his brows just cranked her anxiety up another notch. She bent over again, feeling his glower on the crown of her head. The carpet had come alive with its busy geometric pattern. Her stomach pitched, her cheeks and ears suddenly on fire. "On second thought, can you direct me...to the nearest bathroom?"

She glanced up to see his jaw clench. A trickle of sweat rolled down the side of his face even though it was probably twenty degrees cooler in the hall than it had been in the stairwell. He pointed to a door on the left.

Inside the small, square bathroom, she locked the door and leaned her butt against the dark wood, pushing the heels of her hands into her eye sockets.

Breathe in. Out.

At the faucet she splashed cool water on her face, feeling the nausea abate slightly.

What the devil had gotten into her? At this point, she wasn't ultra-concerned with giving Ross a good impression, but this was ridiculous. *Red eyes.* Where had *that* come from? It was as if the gates of Hell had opened for that brief instant as she'd passed in front of him. Why?

I learned to trust my gut at a young age, Zack had said.

228

And given his sad upbringing, look how wonderful he'd turned out. Maybe she needed to start trusting her own shadow side.

But where did that leave her right now? Clearly, her gut was telling her to be on guard, yet she didn't want to sell Ross short since Zack obviously trusted him.

He wouldn't have left her with Ross if he didn't.

She turned off the faucet, dried her face and hands, and opened the door. Down the hall, a woman was reading Ross the riot act, her arms flailing near his face. Snatches of her impassioned speech floated toward Sloane.

"—gave you what you wanted, you'd better not flake out on my part—"

"Enough, Morgan!" When he raised his arm, she quieted. And spotted Sloane. She rapidly composed her face.

But not her eyes.

A shiver shot from Sloane's feet to her shoulders, leaving gooseflesh in its wake. Ross moved to stand in front of the petite younger woman. Sloane felt unaccountably drawn to her, as if she should know her or had met her before. She came toward the pair, angling her head to try to look at the woman behind Ross.

Then she saw it. Blood seeping through his bandaged neck.

Two stripes of blood.

Time slowed. Her vision narrowed. She heard the rush of her own blood zinging through her veins.

Zack's words coming back to her. *I learned to trust my gut at a young age.*

Sloane reached out to tear the bandage from Ross's neck. Two parallel, severe scratches sliced diagonally across his neck, the pattern too narrow to be human.

Had to be an animal.

Claws.

229

Two.

Cat.

Two-clawed cat.

Tomcat.

Ann.

She gaped at him. *Dear God.* "You?"

Lunging away from him, she tripped on a snag in the carpet and went down hard. Her elbow exploded like an IED, searing pain radiating up her arm. She scrambled to her feet, cradling her elbow. She looked around, but the woman was gone. Her only option was the staircase they'd climbed, but she was afraid to turn her back on him again.

"Help! *Help!*" She inched backward toward the exit stairwell.

He smiled, his perfect white teeth gleaming as he strolled toward her. "Save your lungs. No one can hear you. We got rid of everybody, and this cracker barrel's built like fucking Fort Knox."

She cradled her arm and eased up from the carpet. "What have you done with Ann?"

He stopped, put his hands on his hips. "Ah yes, *Ann...* Would you believe I actually thought she was mine until last month?"

He actually looked *sad*. It took a moment for his comment to register. "*Yours?* You mean like, *your daughter?*"

"Your surprise is not very flattering, I'm afraid." His voice was soft.

"But...Serena was so much...*older.*"

His laughter made her heart pound.

Oh, man, that sounded naïve. But just, wow.

His full-bodied laugh was an honest sound you might hear anywhere on the street. *This can't be happening.* How could he

230

be so crazy, yet seem so normal?

He's an honest to God sociopath. The man was a walking terror in his calm derangement. And she needed to get *the hell* away.

She took a subtle side step toward the exit.

His laughter stopped abruptly, and she froze. "Serena was actually my professor. And as such, she gave me twenty glorious nights between her alabaster thighs. Told me she loved me, and that if she ever had a child, she'd want it to be mine. And then she was just...*gone*. All because of *John*."

A fresh wave of goose bumps flashed across Sloane's skin at his hoarse delivery. "But you started sending her hate mail."

"To make her turn to me, you idiot. I told her I'd keep her safe, but—"

"But she turned to John instead."

His nostrils flared and he took an awkward diagonal step, moving closer to the exit, too. *Shit!* Warning bells sounded a five alarm fire in her head. *Keep him talking to distract him.* "Did you kill Dallan because you thought Ann was your daughter?"

He wiped at the sweat that had started oozing down his face like he'd finished an extended race. His other hand fluttered at his thigh. "I was ready to tell her. I would have made her so happy! But then I found some of John's old medical records. At first I couldn't believe he had the same rare blood type that Ann does. But when I used one of her office cups for a DNA paternity test..."

His words trailed off, his eyes so *haunted* she knew she'd have to reconsider her old mental illness stereotypes.

If she made it out alive.

Less than twelve feet to the stairway.

Between his pale, sweaty face, bloody neck, and distraction

231

with his leg, he looked quite sick. *Or coming off a high.* One of her cousins had looked like that when he'd been forced to dry out. Maybe with the element of surprise she could knock him over on her way to the exit. "Serena's been gone for twenty years. Why didn't you claim Ann sooner?"

Eight feet to the exit.

"This is how much time it's taken! *Fuck!*" His arms flailed in an arc, and something metallic flashed on his wrist. *A watch.* "When John brainwashed Serena and sent her away, I was young and undisciplined. My rage spilled over onto a worthless piece of humanity no one would ever miss, but they caught me and locked me up for six goddamn years! All those years, all those years *wasted,* I thought. Until I began to see that it was my time to strategize."

She stretched her leg to the side, trying to put more space between them without his notice, every shift a knife jab to her elbow. "You mean time to find Serena?"

"*No.* My plan to destroy—piece by deliberate piece—everything John ever cared about. I didn't know about Ann until after I got out. At that point, I had three goals—take John out, find Serena, and make my daughter proud. Making Ann proud meant going to school. I received both a law degree and a CPA to make enough money to rescue Serena, provide for Ann, and infiltrate John. It was going to be *perfect!* Then he had to go and have a fucking heart attack!"

The pasty white of his face filled with explosive color. *Oh, God.* It was all falling into place. He was truly mad. But this was his time on stage. Mother had said sociopaths enjoyed having an audience when they eventually unveiled their brilliant plots. It was part of the payoff for their patience. But his carefully cultivated composure was eroding bit by bit. Ferocity struggling against civility for dominance.

And he was going to kill her unless she thought of something fast. "Where's Ann?" Maybe she was still okay since he'd obviously had feelings for her for so long.

"The trust fund waif will be fresh meat when the bomb explodes in…" He glanced over her shoulder at the wall clock. "Less than two hours now." He made a mock explosion sound, gesturing expressively with his hands.

Bomb? The word wrapped around her consciousness slowly, like weeds choking out a stagnant pond. She slumped against the wall. Where? Where would he have taken her?

Touch him.

She gasped. *Can't! I'd rather die than see inside his mind.*

But *Ann.*

Bile backed up her throat. She looked at her watch and confirmed the time on the wall clock. Eleven-thirty-four. *Two hours.* The bomb was going to detonate around one-thirty if what Ross said was true. "Why *Tori*? She had nothing to do—"

"Wrong again! Tori was a mildly entertaining pastime whenever I 'happened to be in town.'" His fingers came away from his thigh for a moment to curl in the air for quotation, his sing-song voice trailing off as he paused for effect.

When it hit her, her vision crashed and rebooted. "Oh *my God! You're* Teddy?"

"When Zack found Dallan's dead body didn't you fools wonder why he was there? Tori told me about Ann's diary, and Morgan fed me information on Zack's whereabouts, so the set-up at Ann's worked out better than I had even planned." His TV anchor smile made her shiver. "Dallan flipped when we told him about the diary. He rushed right over there. Too early, but it worked out."

"But why frame Zack?"

His eyes narrowed. "You really are slow, aren't you? Zack

233

will suffer more than anyone because John loved him. He's done nothing to deserve what he has."

"You're wrong!"

"Zack is a nauseating blot on humanity. Now I see you're stupid *and* blind!"

Her heartbeat pounded in her injured elbow. It was so hard not to bolt. But he'd be like a wolf on its prey, his predatory instinct activated. *One more minute.* Three more side steps, and she'd probably be able to make it to the stairs before he pulled her down. She blinked to refocus on his words.

"—you're gonna die because he has feelings for you. I'm guessing he's figured all this out by now and is on his way back here. But by then it'll be too late. He'll be *so sad.*"

"You sick creep!" She sprinted toward the back stairwell, but he lunged, catching her by a fistful of hair. Her chin flew up as her head whiplashed back. Turning, she swung with her injured arm, crying out when she connected with his shoulder. Her head cracked against the clock with his line drive into the wall. The cloying scent of his cologne and the damage to her body made her gorge rise again. She panted through the pain, the fingers of her good arm curling around his forearm to try to dislodge him. "Zack's going to...hunt you...like the animal you are!"

He leaned into her, the pressure on her neck excruciating, the warm metal of his watch cutting into her skin. The edges of her vision flickered. He clicked his tongue like a parent reprimanding a child, his ragged breath hot on her face. "Such blind faith. It's rather admirable. I'm not quite sure how he manages it, but people do seem to like him." His voice became hypnotic, like the taint of blood on his starched white shirt collar. Her free arm fell to her side. She wanted to sleep. Her eyes fluttered. Snapped open.

Then shut.

It's coming.

Suddenly she was moving through a dead landscape. Barren, but for a solitary tree, a gnarled silhouette on a distant hill. No sounds of birds here. No fragrance of flowers or odor of decay. Not even the shifting wind to lift tendrils of her hair.

A place of shadows.

She swayed but remained upright, slowly trudging forward in the vision, letting the gray palette envelop her, sapping the vigor from her legs as though lumbering through increasingly compacted snow drifts. Past the lone tree. Over another hill.

Then she saw it.

A large, round metal structure.

Her heart knocked against her ribs, fingernails cut into her palms. *Hurry.* She struggled to make her legs move faster.

A Ferris wheel. She looked up and the air arrested in her lungs. A pale arm hung lifelessly over the edge of the uppermost seat. As Sloane stood below it, the fist jerked opened, and a sparkling light floated down to the leaden earth.

She didn't want to see it. Didn't want to look.

Because she already knew.

Beneath the shadow of the joyless Ferris wheel, she crouched to pick up the glittering cat brooch. The brooch from her first vision only days ago. It singed her skin.

Only then did she hear the ticking. A relentless beat, a herald of death that crept across her flesh, shrouding her with its horror.

My God, the bomb.

Ann!

Sloane threw her head back to yell into the endless sea of gray, aware that her logic was beginning to slip.

Hurts. Too much. Loss. Don't want to do it anymore.

235

Soon, she was floating toward a blanket of darkness. *Feels good. No more pain. Leave it behind...*

Sloane!

The deep sound pierced through her psyche like a million finger pricks. She fought against the pull, wanting to sleep—*sleep*—but the noise wrapped around her, grew louder, an arrow of golden light ever brighter until the darkness was no more.

From far away, she heard another's harsh voice. "...a broken man with no choice but to give me the vault keys. Then I'll learn where John has hidden Serena. And she will be mine at last."

Broken? Who?

Zack! No!

Her eyes opened, and she was momentarily blinded. She blinked to focus. *Killing me. Need air. Weapon.* A gilt-framed oil painting hung less than ten inches away.

I love you, Zack.

She sagged like a rag doll, her full weight shifting unexpectedly, knocking Ross off balance. As he tried to follow her down the wall, she lunged at him, teeth tearing into the soft flesh of his neck above his injury. He screamed, bringing both hands to his mangled skin. She dodged away, gagging and spitting, and ripped the painting from the wall with her good arm. She swung for all she was worth, connecting solidly with his neck. He went down with a sound she'd never forget. She kicked his midsection before she turned and bolted for the emergency exit.

Make it to the stairs. She could do stairs fast.

She was going to make it.

Two steps to the door, it swung open. "Stop!" The petite blonde aimed a pistol at Sloane.

"K-kill her!"

236

Feverish, Sloane watched Ross, panting, struggling to pull himself upright, bloody fingers leaving gruesome red tracks on the beige walls.

"Do it! Shoot her now, you s-stupid whore!" he roared.

Sloane prayed. *Lord, send me an angel!*

The woman swung the pistol toward Ross. "You rotten motherfucker." And fired.

Once to the head.

Once to the chest.

Once to the groin.

Precise. Cold. Deadly.

In the echoing silence of the hall, she remembered Ross saying the woman's name.

Morgan.

Sloane swung away from the carnage that had been Ross when she felt a biting sting in her neck. *Jesus!* Her hand went to her neck as a syringe thumped softly on the carpet. She met the blonde's blazing blue eyes and her stone cold pistol. This ferocious woman couldn't be Zack's friend. "What *the hell* are you doing? What was in that syringe?"

"Ten...nine...*eight—*"

Morgan suddenly had four eyes. Then six. Sloane's vision swam. *So fuzzy. What's...happening...* "Zack?" she whispered.

A smile teased the edges of Morgan's lips. "*Mine.*"

Sloane's stomach rose to meet her throat.

Oh fu—

Then nothing.

THIRTY

One way or another, the flames of Hell were coming for him. Zack hung up with Archie and felt the fire because he was going to murder Ross Julik with his bare hands if he so much as sneezed on Sloane. Archie's stunned disbelief had only made Zack's anger burn that much hotter.

Rage like a tidal wave moving across acres of water—building, rising, consuming—flowed through him. A line of cars waited at a red light so he jumped the curb and took the bike path, turning right at the intersection, cutting off oncoming traffic. Horns blared, but he stepped on the accelerator and mentally charted a less congested route to the office.

Until he got behind a line of cars in a funeral procession.

Dammit! He turned at the next corner, but it was slow going because he was afraid of hitting a little kid in this residential part of town.

All the devastation...

Ross. Did everything come back to him?

The inexplicable financial trouble Samuel's was experiencing. Ann's disappearance. Dallan O'Neill's death. Tori's horrific ordeal. Sloane's building fire. The O'Neill kids...

While he couldn't connect the dots yet, in a way, some things were starting to make sense now that he knew Ross's obsession with Serena was what had forced John to hide her all those years ago. It was irony of the worst sort because John *hadn't known* Ross was the culprit, and instead had brought him into the fold.

John had mentioned a long time ago how Ross had all but bullied him to be hired. John had admired Ross's self-confidence, and was flattered that such an intelligent, accomplished man insisted on working for him. The part that Zack didn't understand was why Ross had pressed on with his diabolical scheme after John's death.

And why the hell did he wait so long to unleash it in the first place?

What was the point? Who was supposed to suffer? Ann? Him?

His fingers tightened around the steering wheel. Ross obviously planned to destroy the business John had spent a lifetime building. The business that had grown to mean as much to Zack.

But even more important than the business...Ann. The one person John loved more than life.

And now Ross had Sloane. The one person Zack—

In that moment he felt her. *Sloane!*

Or rather, her departure. Like a ripping of his soul. Her essence. *Leaving.* Panic spurted through his veins. He yelled her name. Praying for her to live. To stay. *She had to stay.* No one like her. Even if he couldn't have her. The world needed her goodness and light.

He pressed the pedal to the floorboards and laid on the horn before every intersection to forewarn pedestrians. Eight blocks from Samuel's, blaring sirens edged into his consciousness. He looked at the rearview mirror to see patrol car lights flashing. Another squad car was oncoming from the left.

He prayed through red lights.

Prayed.

The rubber of his tires flying ahead of the sirens.

Prayed.

For the chance to save Sloane.

To kill Ross.

The flames of Hell would have to wait.

***

Sloane was floating through a dim tunnel. *Light.* Yes, there was a murky glow far ahead. If she could just—

A sharp thorn of pain brought her back. Her eyes snapped open to a blurry gray. She blinked repeatedly, struggling against the urge to sleep, somehow knowing she shouldn't. After a moment her eyes finally focused to see a small black spider crawling sideways on a rough concrete wall. She gasped and bumped into something behind her.

"Don't move."

A woman? All at once, Sloane remembered.

Morgan. Ross.

Ann!

She must have passed out. No, she'd been drugged. How much time had gone by? Panic warred with the nauseating pain in her elbow and the disorientation of the drug still circulating in her system.

"I said, don't move."

Have to get away. Couldn't do it if she was freaking out or vomiting. Lord, though, what was that smell? Like opening a Tupperware container filled with raw hamburger that had been left in the sun for a week. She gagged, and Morgan chuckled quietly.

There was a brief tearing noise, and she felt warm fingers a few inches below her wrists. Her eyes reopened. The spider wasn't really crawling sideways. She was lying on her side on the floor of a dank and rancid room, her limbs so heavy it was as though her veins ran with lead instead of blood. She twisted her neck as far as she could to look behind her at the woman adding another layer of duct tape to her already well-secured wrists.

Morgan was attractive in an edgy way with her short blond mop and pert nose. What was she to Zack? She'd blown Ross to bits, and she'd certainly had time to kill Sloane, too, but she hadn't. Maybe there was still hope. "Please don't do this. We need to get to Ann. It's not too late. She's at the mall, isn't she? On top of one of the rides? We can save her. I'll tell the police you were defending me."

Another hunk of tape peeled from the roll, Morgan's bow-shaped lips pursed, eyes squinting as she focused on wrapping the tape tightly around Sloane's legs.

You're lying here just letting her tie you up. Get up!

Her heart accelerated. She must outweigh the petite woman by at least thirty-five pounds. If she could catch her unaware, she might be able to overpower her.

She scanned the wall and floor as far as her prone position allowed. Even a sharp fragment of concrete could do some damage. When she looked up, the single exposed light bulb illuminated pockmarks on the rough concrete wall and ceiling.

Concrete ceiling?

She forced herself to look at Morgan again and saw a pair of scissors next to her knee.

"How'd you get me down here?"

Morgan didn't respond, continuing to wrap layer after layer down her legs.

"Where am I?" This time she didn't even expect an answer. *I'm a mummy in a concrete coffin. This can't be happening.* "Zack wouldn't want you to—"

"Don't you dare tell me what Zack wants!" Morgan scooted up to glare at her, the sudden fury in her eyes making Sloane's stomach turn over. "No one knows him like I do!"

"You made a deal with Ross, didn't you?" Sloane's mind spun with possibilities. "With Ann out of the way, you get Zack all to yourself. That's it, isn't it? But you're wrong, you know. He doesn't love her like—"

Morgan slapped a length of tape across Sloane's mouth. "He's been burned so many ways by so many people, and now it's my turn to punish the haters. I'll make sure he's never hurt again." Morgan whipped her head to the side as though addressing someone else in the room. "Stop crying! Stop it!"

Now.

Sloane rolled onto her back and thrust her legs out in an explosive rush. The blow came sideways at Morgan's shoulders, her head whiplashing, then bouncing against the concrete wall. She brought her hand toward her temple, but before she could recover, Sloane jabbed her with her bound legs again. This time a direct hit to the side of the head.

Morgan collapsed to her side, her mouth slack.

Sloane lay silently for a moment, shaking, wanting to scream but couldn't for the tape. She scrunched her eyes for a second to gather her wits. *The scissors.* She needed to use the scissors.

A whimper behind her.

She scooted her body around, trying to avoid jarring her injured elbow. But the pain faded away as a new horror revealed itself in the shadows some fifteen feet away.

Oh. My. God.

Two children. Glassy-eyed. Pale-faced. The younger boy curled as closely around his sister as their gray bondage would allow.

242

The O'Neill kids.

Still alive! *Thank you, Lord. Help me keep them that way.*

She pushed her bound hands into the floor for leverage until she was sitting upright. She waited for the lightheadedness to pass, then scooted toward them until they recoiled, their muffled screams making her want to die. She looked at the ground helplessly, and then saw what had been making her gag.

A darkened pool of what looked like blood clots on a once gauzy, white skirt. A one-of-a-kind skirt with rosettes embroidered around the border.

Purchased at Skinny Dipping. *By Ann.*

Sloane scrambled away from the mess of Ann's skirt, her breath coming fast. Oh, sweet Jesus, had she lost the baby in this Godforsaken hole? *No time to think about the horror.*

Have to get the kids out. If what Ross said was true and he wanted her dead, too, there must be a bomb around here somewhere. Sloane turned back toward the scissors when she caught a movement from the corner of her eye. A second later, a gust of air pushed through the room.

Morgan stood framed in the doorway, her eyes glowing. "I don't hold that kick against you, Amazon. Woulda done it myself. I like girls who know how to take care of themselves." She frowned at the O'Neills. "Stupid Ross, getting kids involved. But then, that wasn't his only mistake. He was going to renege on his promise to help me. I just know it." Then her eyes met Sloane's once more, and she smiled. "But that's lucky for you, I guess. You would've suffered worse at his hands. Don't worry about Zack. I'll take good care of him."

Sloane threw herself toward the door, screaming behind the tape. But it was too late. The light flicked off a heartbeat before the door slammed shut in her face.

243

THIRTY-ONE

Zack's boots hit the pavement before the cops screeched into the Samuel's Construction parking lot. He flew out the door and jerked on the glass back door. *Locked.* He spun around to look for something to smash the door in.

"Stop! Put your hands up." Three cruisers lined up, car doors shielding the officers with their Glocks aimed at his torso. A wild current raced through him. *Run!* His hands clenched. A large cargo truck roared up behind the squad cars. Men in camouflage poured out.

SWAT.

Zack's legs itched. There was enough firepower aimed on him to guarantee a closed casket. He wanted to squirm. He looked down. A piece of rebar was only inches from his right boot.

No more running.

He cupped his hands around his mouth. "Sloane Swift is being held hostage inside by Ross Julik. I'm going in!"

He thought he heard a man yell, but the rebar connected with the glass, fragmenting the Samuel's Construction logo into a thousand blue and green shards. He crouched between the glass and took the back stairs three at a time.

"Sloane! *Sloane!*" He rounded the corner on the top floor and bumped into Morgan as she was stepping off the elevator. His fingers bit into the skin of her upper arms, and her eyes grew round.

"Jesus, Morgan! What the hell are you doing here, and what

happened to you?"

When she looked over his shoulder and started to cry, he was floored. He'd only seen her cry once before. Not the time he'd found her in an alleyway, battered and raped. And not when she'd been slashed by an ex-boyfriend. But rather, the night *he'd* been beaten senseless by Kasey's thugs.

He loosened his hold and brushed the hair from her swelling forehead. "Take it easy. Have you seen Sloane or Ross?"

She plowed into him, wrapping her arms around him in a death grip. He wanted to shake the information out of her, but his head was growing foggy. He squinted, trying to get his eyes to focus, but Morgan's face swam before him. He could see her lips moving, but he couldn't quite understand her. What was happening? He tasted blood on his tongue. Then he heard it.

Zack!

A river of ice poured through him. *Sloane?*

Help me!

A sensation of damp, cool air drifted through his mind. *Where are you?* He held his breath, listening for her, but heard only his own heartbeat. His vision cleared, and he looked down to see Morgan's face plastered to his chest. He leaned away from her, his fingers shaking on her arms. "Right now, Morgan. *Tell me where they are.*"

She lifted her tear-streaked face, then leaned to the side and pointed behind him. Zack twisted around and nearly staggered to see what was left of his CFO. He tore away from Morgan and hunkered down beside Ross. He thought he'd feel sadness and regret, but there was only urgency. He looked back at Morgan. "Where's the gun?"

"I...threw it in the dumpster. Outside."

That must have been where she was coming from when he

ran into her. "Where's Sloane?"

"He was going to kill her, and I couldn't let him! You know how I feel about men assaulting women."

"Where the fuck is she?"

She backed up slightly. "He...uh, he'd...someone else took her. To hide her. For Ross. She was so scared, Zack! She hasn't had the experiences we have—"

Bad experiences.

All of a sudden, he knew. *Cold and damp.*

Hell, yeah, he knew. *The tunnel.*

Abruptly, he pressed Morgan against the wall, a hand covering her mouth. He shushed her silently while he listened. There it was again.

A slight shifting of leather.

Someone was in the stairwell.

He motioned for her to hurry with him down the hall, past Ross's lifeless body, into John's office. Inside, he shut the door soundlessly, grabbed a flashlight from the desk, then led her to the bookshelf.

"Aren't we going to—"

Again, he shushed her, and felt with his hands along the paneling until the bookshelf slid away to reveal a small, secret elevator. He'd never used it. Had never been able to make himself, though John had told him it'd be good to know where it let out in the tunnel.

Just in case.

He used to laugh at many of John's just-in-cases. *Pretty damn unwise.*

When he joined Morgan inside, he had to put his arms up to make room for both of them to fit. He waited for a stir of panic in the cramped space, but it didn't come. The door closed, the light dimmed, and she leaned against him.

SWAT officers had to be spreading through the building like a marauding virus by now. He ignored the blinking elevator light. *Hold on, Goldie.*

"Who was working with Ross? Who took Sloane just now?"

She hesitated for a moment. "Colette O'Neill."

"*What?*"

"I swear it's true. Once Ross learned of Dallan's involvement with Ann, he blackmailed Colette into helping him. He told her he'd help fix her problem, but after she took Ann to his house, she refused to help him anymore. Until he took her kids, the evil bastard."

Zack slammed the elevator ceiling with his fist and looked at Morgan's feverish eyes. "Where is she?"

"Colette? How am I supposed to know?" She hooked her fingers in the waistband of his jeans. He tried to angle his body away from Morgan but the space was too cramped.

Hold on, Goldie, I'm coming for you.

None of this seemed to make any sense. "Why are *you* here?"

"I promise I'll tell you everything, but please, let's just get out of here," Morgan said.

The elevator door opened, and he pushed back an iron gate to step into the dark passageway. Relieved to put some distance between Morgan and himself, he turned on the flashlight, its weak beam projecting onto rough-hewn concrete.

Sloane was down here. He'd bet his life on it. "What do you mean you'll tell me *everything*?"

"I...I have a theory. But I won't— What are we doing down here? I thought we were going to leave the building—"

A low clang came from the passageway. He started jogging down the long tunnel, praying he'd know which turns to make to find Sloane.

"Wait!" Morgan ran after him and grabbed his arm. "We have to leave! Please, Zack, I...I love you! Please, let's go. I think Ross put a bomb down here."

"*What* did you say?"

"I love you. I always have." Her bottom lip trembled.

"Not that. A bomb? Ross knew how to make a *bomb*? How could you know that?"

"When he and Sloane were fighting, he said that's how she was gonna go. It's too late for her, but we can still make it. *Please*. We have to hurry." She pulled on his arm, but he brushed her off.

"I'm not leaving Sloane down here to die."

"You don't have to be anybody's damn hero!"

He didn't understand the look in her eyes. "I'm sorry. You'll have to deal with the police, but they'll realize you're innocent." He pushed her back inside the cramped elevator and slid the gate's lock in place to prevent her from returning to the passageway. This might be their final goodbye.

At least she would be safe. "Take care, Morgan."

Her pale fingers gripped the gate and rattled the metal until the sound reverberated up his spine. "You'll regret this!"

"Only if I die." Then he sprinted away, hearing her cries and feeling her eyes on him until the elevator doors slid shut, enveloping him in a woolen darkness pierced only by the thin beam of his flashlight.

Help me find you, Goldie.

Again, a low clang. But farther away this time. Zack shucked his shirt, tore strips of fabric with his teeth, and changed directions, running through the maze, leaving pieces of his shirt to find his way out, until the clanging grew louder. He set the flashlight down before one of the doors and pressed his cupped his hands to the metal to project through the door. "Sloane?"

"Zack!"

He nearly dropped to his knees in relief. He stooped to grab the flashlight, panning for something to break the padlock. He ran down the passageway where he'd noticed a concrete block set on its side, overlaid by a small piece of wood in a makeshift stool. He grabbed the block and carried it back to the door.

He hefted the concrete block over his head and crashed the corner edge against the lock. The sound was unbelievably loud in the soul-sucking shaft. *Screw it.* He could live without eardrums. But not without Sloane.

He did it again.

And again.

Sweat stung his eyes as he raised the cinder block once more. This time the lock gave way. He put his lips near the spot the lock had been. "Stand back from the door, Goldie!"

He backed up and kicked, heel first, extending his leg until the muscles jarred like a sledgehammer connecting with a locomotive. The door sprang open on the third try, and he had her in his arms in a heartbeat, his hands covering as much of her body as possible, searching for signs of injury. "My God, woman, you have no idea—"

She wrenched back, nodding, and turned away to gather...

Children.

The girl had wide brown eyes in a face so expressionless his throat burned. "O'Neill's?"

Sloane nodded again, her arms tightening briefly around them before shuffling them toward the door. "They're dehydrated. We have to hurry! Ann's at the mall. I think on top of the Ferris wheel."

"The Ferris wheel?"

"No time to explain. I know from the vision I had when Ross...he..."

When she gasped, he examined the arm she was favoring. "I know. I know everything now," he said. Satisfied her arm didn't seem to be broken, he looked at her. "I left you with him. Sloane, I didn't know. If he would have—"

"But he didn't." She checked her watch and blanched. "We really have to hurry. If Ross wasn't lying, Ann's bomb is gonna blow at one-thirty."

He couldn't have heard her right. "Wait. The bomb is on *Ann*?" But Morgan had said the bomb was down here...

"In the vision she was on top of a Ferris Wheel. I heard the ticking of a bomb. I saw the brooch from before, too. Let's go!"

His gut plummeted. Less than ninety minutes before they'd have to scrape Ann's remains off the mall's eight story skylights. During business hours.

When the amusement park was set to open.

There'd be a huge line waiting at the entrance. *Son of a bitch.*

He stepped back to hurry them out of the room when he saw pieces of duct tape scattered around. And what looked like old blood. "Colette tied you up?"

Sloane had taken the flashlight and was already following his ripped shirt trail. When she looked back, her face was set in fierce lines. "No, Morgan did. She wanted you all to herself so she helped Ross get Ann out of the way! I thought you said you knew everything."

"*Whoa.* Whoa, whoa, *wait!*" He grabbed her by the shoulders. "You're lying." She had to be.

"No, Zack. Your beloved Morgan's in on the whole thing. She made hambu—" She glanced at the children cowering in the shadows and spoke softer. "She took care of Ross, then injected me with some drug and tied me up. She left me to die. *With these children.*"

Morgan? *No!*

The world shuddered. Literally. The ground and the walls around them. Shook so hard they stumbled into one another. He reached for Sloane after breaking the little girl's fall. Sloane's pupils dilated in the shadows. "Oh, Lord, was that what I think it was?"

He nodded and saw a ripple of panic flow over her features. "We're going to make it." He squeezed her arm, watching her struggle to master her fear. She managed it as the little boy began to cry, his tears leaving a soft peach trail on his otherwise grimy face. Zack fought back fury as he hugged the boy and looked at Sloane over the child's head. "Their names?"

"Derek and Kate."

He set the boy in front of him, still holding his hand. "It's going to be all right, Derek. We're going to get you and your sister out of here, but we have to hurry. I need you to be brave for a while longer, okay?"

Derek nodded, and Zack could see he was weak with hunger, so he scooped him into his arms and reached for the flashlight, wishing Ross was still breathing so he could skin him alive. They were nearly back at the elevator when Zack began seeing dust and small chunks of concrete on the shirt strips he'd left on the ground. A bad feeling rolled through his gut, but he didn't want to believe it. Until he saw the rubble in front of them.

The bomb had sealed the tunnel back to the elevator.

THIRTY-TWO

If she made it out of this alive, she was never—*ever*—going into a basement again. Sloane's lungs, legs, and arm burned from piggybacking Kate the last few minutes, but they were almost there. Wherever *there* was in this labrynth. "We're almost out of here, right?"

"Yes." Zack wasn't even breathing hard, and he'd carried Derek the whole way.

She knew he'd come to get her out. A bone-deep sort of knowledge. He'd demonstrated he was kind, loving, strong—so many qualities. Actions speak louder than words, and his had shouted. But...

He'd worked with Ross. And did *what* with Morgan? Were they lovers? How had he not known they were conspiring against him? Could he really be so oblivious?

Don't judge until you have not only all the information, but knowledge of the situation as well. Another of mother's pithy little sayings.

Her head was gonna explode right along with her limbs any minute now. "Dammit!"

When Zack turned to face her, she saw strain written on every contour of his face. He shifted Derek to one arm and reached for Kate with the other. "Here, let me take her. I can carry both."

"No. I'm fine. Just get us out of here," she snapped.

When they finally reached a narrow wooden staircase, Zack set Derek down and looked at Sloane. "You need to stay here for a minute while I make sure the area's safe. I'll be back."

"No! I don't want to stay down here—"

"I can't risk you and the kids getting shot if SWAT's waiting for me beyond that door." He stepped closer and looked like he wanted to touch her. Her muscles jumped in anticipation.

"Trust me?" he asked.

She nodded, but her stomach churned. If he'd only touch her, she would feel so much better.

But he didn't. He turned away, taking the flashlight from Kate to shine it on the combination lock to put in the series of numbers. A shaft of white light poured onto the stairs when he opened the door a crack. He peeked through it, then turned around to hand Sloane the flashlight. She couldn't read his expression. *Please don't leave us.*

His fingers came up to feather over her cheekbone. "Trust, Goldie."

"Ann lost her baby in that *tomb,* you know. Morgan and Ross are gonna burn in Hell."

His jaw tightened, and he nodded, then slipped outside and shut the door, leaving her and the children behind in the silent darkness.

***

Zack arranged the large tablecloth over the hidden door, grateful none of the Chinese restaurant staff was in the supply room when he'd made his entrance. He nudged a stepstool to the wall to peer out a high window facing the alley. *So far so good.* No police that he could see. He exhaled, grabbed a Shanghai Surprise T-shirt from a stack on the shelves, and slipped it on since the one he'd had was now in shreds in the tunnel.

Morgan. She had a mean streak, but never in a million years did he think she'd be vicious enough to kill an innocent adult, much less children. *Why?* He curled his sweaty palm around the supply room doorknob and twisted ever so slowly. Peered out. A slim, bent cook stood by the industrial sized dishwasher while two tiny waitresses bustled about, unloading bowls of food from a cart.

He jammed the doorstop under the door, grabbed his phone out of his pocket, and speed dialed Archie, who picked up before Zack even heard it ring. "Wherein the Sam Hell are you, man? Did you find Ross?"

"*Shhh.* I found Sloane and the O'Neill kids."

"They okay?"

"Yeah." Zack pinched the bridge of his nose. "Christ, Arch. Morgan's part of this."

"What?"

"Long story, but Morgan offed Ross, then drugged and tied up Sloane in the underground with the kids." Silence on the line. "She was going to leave them there to die." More silence. "Did you hear?"

"I can't— *You sure?*"

Archie's disbelief nearly did him in. "It's killing me, too."

"Where is she?"

"I don't know. She took off when I wouldn't leave the building with her. I need you to pick up Sloane and the O'Neill kids at the corner of Broadway and Second Avenue North. ASAP. Take them to the hospital. Phone the cops on the way, tell them to get a bead on Morgan."

"She packin'?"

"When isn't she?"

"Right. What else do you need?"

Zack pressed his ear to the door, listening. "A bomb squad

at the mall."

"What?"

"Ann's in the top car of the mall's Ferris wheel wired with a bomb that's set to go off at one-thirty." He ground the phone's speaker into his thigh to muffle Archie's response. When it sounded quiet again, he put the phone back to his ear. "They'll need a heavy law enforcement presence because the mall's bound to be packed with the opening of the amusement park."Archie exhaled loudly. "*Fucking A.* Someone in the universe hates you, brother."

"One last thing. I need you to have our buddy Peter cause a disturbance on the south side of the mall by the theater so I can get in Skinny Dipping's back door unseen."

"Ah, shit, you oughtta let the police handle this, man."

"I can't sit back and not help Ann. Besides, I have a bad feeling about Morgan showing up there. You know how she hates uniforms. But she might listen to me. I've gotta be there. Let's just hope my gut isn't right this time."

Archie's heavy silence reinforced his instincts.

Finally, "I've got you covered, buddy. I'm out."

Zack pushed the phone back in his pocket and opened the passage door again. He put his finger to his mouth to keep them silent, then reached out to Sloane. He brought his other hand on top of hers to chafe it while she looked around, obviously trying to figure out where they were.

"Shanghai Surprise on First and Broadway," he said quietly.

She nodded, bringing the children in front of her. Almost like a shield between them. He frowned, grabbing two water bottles from the shelf for the children, and looked at Sloane. "I'm going to get everyone out onto the restaurant floor while you and the kids sneak out the back door into the alley. If anyone's on break, ignore them and keep running north up the

255

alley toward Toscana's. My buddy Archie will pick you up in a blue Explorer. He's bald and has a jaguar tattoo on his neck."

"Like yours," Sloane said. Their eyes held for a moment. God, he wanted to hold her.

Derek's lips started quivering, and the sight of the beautiful children pressing close to Sloane put a lump in his throat. He wondered not for the first time why bad things happened to innocents. He smiled to give them confidence. "Archie's kind of scary looking, but he'll protect you and get you to the hospital."

"What about you?"

He understood what she was asking. "You need to go with them. They need you right now."

She opened her mouth, but shut it again. It had been a safe gamble. She'd never leave the children alone. He needed her, too, but he wouldn't tell her that. Besides, he couldn't let her go to the mall with him. "I suppose you don't have a key for the back door of your shop, do you?"

"No, my purse is in the hallway of your office, but I keep a key duct taped to the underside of the dumpster nearby. If Carmen's still there tell her I'll let her have the Salvador Dali oil if she helps you." She smiled slightly, then looked down at her hands. "I had to have a backup plan because Tori was notorious for losing keys, and I didn't want to have to run to the store on my mornings off."

So much had happened. So much still *had* to happen before this nightmare was over. What if he never had another chance?

Fuck this distance shit. He crushed Sloane in his arms, careful of her injury, and whispered in her hair. "You make me want to believe in happily ever after, Goldie."

He squeezed her reflexively, then turned and slipped out the door.

THIRTY-THREE

Drop that thing about happily ever after, then leave us again, why don't you.

Sloane squeezed the hands of the children on either side of her. Their terrified eyes would haunt her for a long time. She couldn't carry both of them, so she slowed her pace as much as she dared. How was Colette taking their abduction? She'd faked her grief over Dallan. Could she be as heartless with her own children?

They turned out of the alley onto the blister-hot sidewalk on Broadway. Clouds hugged the tops of the buildings, their gray underbellies a portent of yet more rain. A scrolling digital display proclaimed ninety-five degrees and ninety percent humidity. *Suffocating.* Suddenly she didn't want to live downtown anymore.

Then she remembered she no longer had a home there, anyway.

A slow rumble of thunder ricocheted around them, reverberating off the faded brick façades. Kate looked up blankly, and a new urgency lit up Sloane's nerves. "Take another sip of water, sweetheart."

One more block to meet Archie. One block to decide if she was going to trust that he was who Zack thought he was.

And not another whack job.

So far Zack had a pretty terrible record. Kasey. Ross. Morgan. They'd been in his life for years. He'd trusted them, and look what they'd done to him.

Her pulse skittered when she spotted the blue SUV. She squinted, trying to feel something. *Good guy or bad?* Nothing. If she touched the truck, would *that* tell her what she needed to know? Her stomach somersaulted along with another roll of thunder.

When the last two hundred feet separated them, a man got out of the SUV. He was bald.

And intimidating as hell.

Beads of sweat at her hairline slid down the side of her face. The man began weaving between a group of people who'd exited a shop when a police car turned the corner onto the strip.

"Come!" She pulled the children off the sidewalk and hid them between two parked cars. "Kate, hang on to your brother. Stay down, I'll be right back." She dashed out into the street, waving her arms until the squad car stopped in the middle of the street.

A salt and pepper-haired officer rolled down the window with a frown. "Ma'am, what—"

"Sir! Those children over there are the missing O'Neill kids. They need immediate medical attention!" She raced over to the children, glancing to see where Archie was, but he'd hung back when he saw her interacting with the cop. She took the children by the hand and rushed back to the cruiser. People on the sidewalk were staring. The officer stood outside his vehicle. After halting traffic, he opened the back door for them. "I need your name and how you came by these children."

"Sloane Swift. I was tied up in an underground passageway with these children until Zack Goldman freed us. Ross Julik and a woman named Morgan are the guilty ones."

"All right, I'll take your statement at the hospital. I need you to get in the car, ma'am."

Sloane attempted to locate Archie, but there was no sign of

him. Had he left, or was he hiding somewhere? She squeezed Kate and Derek before gently pushing them toward the back seat. "It'll be all right now. In you go."

"You, too, Ms. Swift."

The officer was moving his body to block her. *Now or never*. She twisted away from the open door and ran toward the opposite sidewalk. She heard the officer yelling, but didn't stop. She needed to put as much distance between them as possible.

And between her and Archie. Lord, she hoped he'd decided to leave.

She ran hard for three blocks, ignoring the jarring pain in her arm and people's looks as she dashed by. *What the hell am I doing running from the police?* She hadn't done anything wrong. But she wouldn't be able to help Zack if she was detained.

Three blocks later, out of breath and adrenaline, she stopped in front of her favorite antique shop, looking behind her. No sign of Archie.

She put a hand to her chest and entered the building. A confused look quickly replaced a wave from the shop owner, but fortunately she was occupied with another customer. As casually as possible, Sloane made her way to the exit near the rear of the store, glancing at a narrow grandfather clock, its heavy pendulum a sickening reminder that there was only so much time left. *Twelve-thirty-three.*

The storefront bell jingled again, and she knew without looking.

Archie.

Forgetting caution, she sprinted toward the back door, hearing Archie swear, cracking baskets and shattering glass as he tore after her. By the time they were both in the alley he was gaining on her.

"Stop, dammit! Why are you running?"

Because you can't be who Zack thinks you are. She swerved to upend a large stack of freight that had been unloaded but not brought inside yet. It slowed him down, but not nearly enough. If she could make it to the end of the alley, maybe he'd hang back again.

"If you care about Zack, stop!" But he didn't let her decide. Her head snapped forward the instant he tackled her around the knees, and they both went down hard. The air whooshed out of her lungs, and she must've hit her head and passed out for few seconds because she woke up face down in the gravel with Archie sitting on top of her, breathing heavily.

"*Jesus H Christ*, woman. Don't know what he's thinking, hooking up with you."

She gagged. Her arm was surely dislocated—if not broken—this time. The nausea nearly did her in, but dying would be worse. She thrashed to unseat him.

He cursed viciously. "All right! You've been enough damn trouble. I'll help Zack by myself since you obviously don't give a fuck about him the way he hopes you do."

Wait, what?

Archie got off of her and started jogging down the alley away from her.

A trick?

"Wait!" she called after him, but he didn't slow down. Didn't even look back.

She staggered to her feet, cradling her arm. "Archie, please!" He finally stopped, but didn't turn around. Her throat ached with the need to cry. "I thought you were...like the others. Kasey, Ross, Morgan. They all betrayed him. I...I love Zack. *God, I do.* I need to help him, but I don't know how to...trust you."

He turned around, jaw rigid. He reached for something in his waistband, and she tensed. He withdrew a small but wicked looking blade. He tossed it on the ground a few feet in front of her seconds before the first fat raindrops began pelting the alley.

"How's that for insurance? Now get moving. I'm driving."

THIRTY-FOUR

Zack adjusted the wig and hat combo that Sloane's employee, Carmen, had outfitted for him. He tried to modulate his breathing as he made his way upstream through the throngs of people at the mall, getting steadily closer to the epicenter of the coming drama. Local law enforcement was in the process of evacuating the building, but he'd still never seen so many people there at once.

He was twenty feet away from the expansive, eight story pavilion that housed the new amusement park when the power surged and went down amid screams of panic. The emergency generators immediately kicked on, powering only about a quarter of the lights that had been on previously.

Great. Morgan, or the weather?

The storm had moved in fast, sucking light from the sky and reducing the mall's spectacular skylights to shadow-casters in the park, which was set up like an ancient forest complete with dinosaurs, tall trees, rock waterfalls, and bushy plant life. Shades of gray slid across the lose-your-lunch roller coaster that looped around the whole mess.

Watching for police, Zack broke through the crowd to run toward a much tamer carousel where he crouched in the shadows, focusing on the motionless Ferris wheel about fifty yards ahead.

According to Sloane's vision, Ann was in one of those buckets.

She'd even predicted the gray desolation bathing this place.

He hoped she and the kids were at the hospital by now. He noted the time—*forty minutes to detonation*—then panned the vicinity around him while shucking off the light-colored wig and hat.

More officers were arriving by the minute, and the crowds were rapidly thinning, but where the hell was the SWAT bomb squad? A trickle of sweat ran between his pecs, and he quietly filled his lungs before sprinting to the base of Drop Tower. Lightning briefly illuminated the grotesque faces painted on the seats of the Flying Condor, and for a moment he thought a sound had come from the ride.

He moved farther into the shadow of the hundred foot steel tower, gauging how he might use the park's forest features to get to the Ferris wheel unseen. The ride manufacturers had tested the machines last week, so he knew it was operable. If he could get to the power box, he could figure out how to operate it and hopefully get Ann down before they cuffed him. *Or at least get the wheel turning before they shoot me.*

Comforting thought.

Then it was up to the bomb squad...if they ever got here.

Thirty-five minutes.

 Faint, feminine strains of Pearl Jam's *Black* floated underneath the military-style orders issuing from an officer's megaphone. Zack's muscles clenched from his shoulders to his fists as the last of the crowd filed down the hallway and out of sight. The large space made it difficult to determine where the voice had originated.

But it was definitely Morgan.

Pearl Jam had been one of her favorite bands since forever. As various law enforcement officers spread out to investigate, he grasped the cool metal bars, scaling up the side of Drop Tower. And up. And *up* even higher, until he didn't dare look

263

down. The best he could guess, Morgan might be near Screamin' Swing, but he couldn't tell how high she was. He didn't think she was on the ground level, but it didn't sound like she was on the balcony that overlooked the park either.

The problem was, if she *was* on the balcony, she'd have a clear view of him running toward the Ferris wheel. Unless he could make it to the roller coaster and cover some distance in the enclosed, special effects section...

He *had* to stay hidden. She'd shoot him no matter how much she imagined she loved him. Her situation was too desperate.

He climbed higher still.

"It didn't have to turn out this way, you know."

His gut somersaulted, but he didn't dare respond. The police didn't either.

Yet.

Sounded like she was somewhere in the vicinity of the massive Tree of Life, some fifty feet to his left.

"I can't believe you're surprised." Her laughter erupted, brittle and empty, leaving a sense of desolation as it faded.

Though they'd proceed carefully, the police were surely closing in on her location by now. *Don't let her kill anyone.*

His fingers began to cramp on the reinforced steel side of the amusement ride. He was as high as he could go, but it would probably be enough. The rollercoaster was eye-level about five feet away. He looked down, stomach in his throat. He was six stories up, though the cold concrete below didn't bother him as much as what Morgan might have up her sleeve.

And how much time Ann had left.

He looked at the rollercoaster again. If he could get enough leverage to jump over to it, he could make his way inside the special effects tunnel that looped between Drop Tower and the

Ferris wheel, and remain hidden for about forty feet. From there, he'd have to wing it in plain sight. Hopefully the shadows would be to his advantage.

If Morgan was actually where he thought she might be.

And she didn't move again.

Another bolt of lightning shining through the skylights helped illuminate the crisscrossing bars of the roller coaster track. *Just like monkey bars.* He'd always hated playing on those.

He bent his knees and lunged from the metal tower, one sweaty hand slipping off the rollercoaster track. His body dangled, swinging sixty feet off the ground, the fingers of his other hand beginning to slide. Forearm and bicep flexing in a one-armed pull-up, he grasped the railing with his free hand, then swung his legs up toward the open triangle of the track's underbelly. Once his legs were wedged into the opening, he saw movement below him. He scanned the floor until he saw a camo-garbed, helmeted man slip behind the ticket booth.

Quick. Silent. Predatory.

SWAT was in the house. They'd better have brought the bomb team.

A rumble of thunder rolled through the now quiet space, vibrating the metal like an oncoming train. He pushed his legs through the opening on the bottom of the rollercoaster track, then pulled himself the rest of the way through. He moved on hands and knees toward the special effects tunnel, careful not to fall through the large holes, hoping Morgan or SWAT wouldn't gut him from below. As he made it around a curve six feet from the tunnel, he was finally able to see into the top seat of the Ferris wheel.

His hands plowed through his hair. Slumped back in the chair, the luminescence of Ann's exposed throat stood out in sharp relief against the black box on her chest. *Jesus.* It was actually strapped to her body! *Fuck.*

He watched the bomb, hoping to notice a slight rise and fall that would indicate she was still alive. She looked much too pale, but then, she'd always avoided the sun.

And after losing all that blood in the miscarriage...

Can't think about that now. Maybe he'd be able to cut the straps tying the bomb to her. It didn't look very sophisticated. Now if a pair of scissors would magically appear, things would be looking up.

Bang!

He flattened himself to the rails as a bullet flew by way too close for comfort, shattering a window high above him. Not many handguns carried that kind of power.

Which meant Morgan had a rifle.

"Cease fire! This is lieutenant Rod Carver with Red River Valley SWAT. Toss your weapons in the open and come out with your hands up."

Only wind and rain splatter against the skylights greeted Lt. Carver's ear-splitting, megaphoned demand. Zack inched forward, the FX tunnel's entrance still seeming miles away. He stopped when a strange feeling passed through him. He looked down toward the west side of the park, his body going numb.

A shadowy figure ducked behind the rock waterfall near the Scorpion. And then a moment later... Another.

More SWAT? Surely they had the place locked down by now. No one else should be able to get in. Unless someone had gotten inside before the evacuation was complete.

Or had successfully hidden. There were a crazy lot of nooks, crannies, plants, and caves in the park.

Zack eased forward on the track again when the Scorpion blared to life, its four arms lifting in a frenzied display of colors and music. With the rest of the park mostly encased in shadows, the circles of empty cars looked possessed, the heavy metal music a sinister accompaniment to the wicked twirling of the Scorpion's limbs.

He crouched to race toward the tunnel when a barrage of bullets sprayed the Scorpion, busting lights, zinging off the metal cars, and likely plugging the life-sized plaster dinosaurs lined up behind the ride, until the cars stopped mid-air, the music fading on a discordant, sickening note.

He scrambled for the tunnel. *Thank God.* He made it. He rested for a moment to take stock and re-pump oxygen to his brain. Morgan had some serious firepower. An UZI maybe? She could get her hands on anything. Weapons, drugs, you name it.

But who'd turned on the Scorpion? Didn't seem like a SWAT maneuver, yet distraction or intimidation was clearly the intent.

Run, Zack. Hurry!

His heart kicked as a fresh wave of panic floored his system. *Sloane? You'd better be at the hospital with the children, woman.*

Her answering silence said it all.

Holy hell. She was *here*. It had probably been her and Archie who'd ducked behind the waterfall. He gritted his teeth. *You can actually hear everything I'm projecting now?*

Yes, came her response.

Hot damn. *Progress.* He'd better make it out of here alive. *Are you injured?*

No.

But she'd hesitated for the briefest moment. *Don't get yourself killed or I'll kill you myself.*

I love you, too, Zack.

Ah, Goldie... He closed his eyes. *Did you start the ride?*

267

Where are you?

Go to Ann, she's fading.

I saw two people. Archie with you?

Go, Zack! Time's almost up.

Yeah, they were all gonna be pulverized if they kept up this cat and mouse game with Morgan. Now he had to worry about Sloane, too. As he neared the end of the tunnel closest to Ann, he heard three things simultaneously.

The SWAT lieutenant resuming negotiations.

The *fifteen minutes left* alarm on his watch.

And John's voice... *Don't ever give up on something or someone you can't go a full day without thinking about.*

Zack carefully stood in the tunnel opening, panning the area below, hoping Morgan would reveal her location. A flood of warmth entered his body seconds before his vision grayed. His hands rose to grip the sides of the tunnel. He had the sensation of movement, a forward motion. It made his stomach pitch, his head spin. He suddenly heard two heartbeats.

Shhh. I've got her. Stay with me so you know where she is. Okay? Sloane's instructions sounded like they were coming through water. And she sounded weak.

Don't do this, Sloane. I can't help Ann and worry about you, too.

Let me do this. Please, Zack. I can't bring Abigail, Joan, Tori, or my sister back, but...maybe...

He understood. She was beginning to believe in herself—in her gift—again. That's why she could hear him the way he could hear her. *Okay, baby, but please—please—be careful.*

She didn't respond. When he blinked, he had the sensation of looking through a third party's eyes. Someone who was on one of the rides. Where it was especially dark. Another heartbeat.

That made three. *What the hell?*

Zack felt nausea rise up, and he pressed the heels of his hands to his head.

Stay with me, so you know where she is.

He was obviously remote viewing through Sloane's eyes, but who were they looking at? *Morgan.*

If a bomb wasn't set to explode in ten minutes he'd have laughed at the absurdity of the situation. Hearing others' thoughts? Remote viewing? *Riiight.*

Sloane, stay away from her.

He breathed deep to dispel the gray, then moved to the edge of the track to line up with one of the spokes on the big wheel. He'd made the right decision to climb. It had bought him some time.

If he could grip one of those spokes and slide down, he'd be on the ground in seconds. Surely the Ferris wheel would be easy to operate once he got to the control box. The wild card was SWAT. How much did they know about what was happening and who was to blame? Would they shoot him first thinking he was trying to hurt Ann? They had to have a sniper poised somewhere. Morgan would realize it, too.

Which was why everyone was hanging back and this whole clusterfuck was moving too slow and Ann was probably *dying* in that goddamn bucket.

Time to roll.

He tensed the muscles of his thighs, swung his arms back...and jumped.

Zack!

He lost his breath, the bruised and battered portion of his chest compressing on impact and the metal spoke slicing his palms as he tried to slow his fall. He used his hands, elbows, knees, and feet to snag the outside of the beam to slow the pull of gravity. He grunted when his foot finally jammed in a wedge of the spoke's center. From his position on the outer hub of the wheel, he was better able to choose the rest of his path downward. After his feet hit the concrete, he quickly found the Ferris wheel motor and tripped the red switch.

Suddenly bright green, purple, and yellow lights flooded the interior with an eerie glow. He pushed the gear shaft forward and a series of belts and pulleys began to turn the wheel.

Rapid footfalls sounded behind him.

The lieutenant yelled over the megaphone again, and he swung around to find himself in a Mexican standoff with Morgan's UZI aimed at his chest and the red dots of the SWAT tactical team sights clustered on hers.

He looked into the barrel of Morgan's gun, then up at her eyes.

She'd been crying.

And using.

Even in the darkened space around them, the haggard lines and pallor of her face told the story of her pain and how she'd chosen to dull it. Regret and sadness pulled at him. But he couldn't take responsibility for her bad choices any more. "Put the gun down, Morgan."

The four SWAT officers were standing perpendicular to her under the second story overhang, the aim of their semiautomatics steady. Another team had staged beyond them in the shadows, motionless. Alert.

Please be the bomb techs.

Behind him, the Ferris wheel slowly turned.

The skin on his palms itched. "You really don't want another death on your conscience, do you?"

Her lips tipped up for a moment, something wavering in her eyes. "We're both warriors who live best on the fringes. I wanted to protect you from all who would hurt you, Zack."

"That's too much responsibility for one person." He edged backward toward the wheel's controls. He had to stop it when Ann's car was at the bottom.

"You're worth it."

"Yet you have an UZI on me?"

"If I can't have you, she can't either!" She gestured to Ann, whose car now dangled ten feet above them, inching closer.

"You think I'm in love with *Ann*?"

"I think you feel guilty. You're confused because John was so nice. You think you need to be her man because of that."

"I promise we'll talk about this when she's down. Okay? That bomb's gonna go off and kill us all."

The light snuffed from her eyes. "Always goes back to her, doesn't it. Fine then. See you on the other side." She raised the gun to look through the scope, and his blood ran cold.

Time slowed. A pop exploded in his eardrums. Someone screamed. A flash of blue clothing blurred as he was tackled sideways.

More pops.

Gunfire.

The inertia of his fall barreled him to the ground, where his head bounced off the concrete in an eruption of pain. His eyes opened to register Morgan crumpling to the concrete with horrible, wet gurgling sounds. Nausea roiled through his gut, the floor like ice against his stomach.

Something warm on his back. Metallic-tasting in his mouth. He gagged and spit blood.

Sloane, where are you?

C-cold. His teeth clacked together. SWAT boots swam double, then triple, in his vision, swarming Morgan's inert form on the floor. More men in camouflage rushing the scene, surrounding the Ferris wheel bucket that held Ann.

Someone yelled, "Clear the area!"

A liquid warmth seeped onto his back. Someone grabbed his boots, began dragging him. His head swam. He blinked again and a ghastly apparition of Ross rose up, blood and gore sliding down his face.

Zack struggled against the hands around his boots, twisting and bucking to get free until he couldn't breathe anymore through the fire in his chest and the jackhammer splintering his skull.

"Easy, brother. Take it easy." Then quieter, "I've got his arms."

The panther had said it. *Panther?* Goddamn, his head hurt. He struggled again until his shirt rode up, leaving his stomach bare to suffer the concrete friction. He wanted to howl. Needed to clear his head. Get his muscles to move.

Someone shifted near his line of vision.

"Don't move her yet. We don't know where she was hit."

I'm not shot. He tried to tell them. Tell the panther. But he couldn't get the words to come out right. *Hit my head. Must've.*

The voice had said *her.*

What?

The blue flash before the tackle.

The heap beside him with the golden head wasn't moving. *Golden head.*

"*Sloane!*" A spurt of adrenaline fired his blood, and his senses came back online. He kicked once more at the hands that held his ankles and twisted an arm to grab her, lifting her as he rolled over to accept her weight on the front of his body. Her mouth opened slightly, and she blinked down at him, but didn't recognize him. Hot fear lit up his circuits. He hurried to sit up with her in his lap.

"Hold still! She's been shot, you could make it worse. We need to move you as a unit because that shit's gonna blow."

"Archie! Look at her. Look what she did!" He was babbling. He knew it, but the panic over Sloane was gonna kill him. How bad was she hurt? Jesus, if she died... *Please, God, no.*

Two more SWAT medics ran over to grab him under the arms, and together they got him and Sloane behind a thick concrete wall on the mall's first floor thoroughfare. Placing him on the carpet, they set to work on her injury. Rolling to his feet, Zack staggered slightly until Archie slipped an arm around his waist to support him.

Zack watched the medics apply pressure to the bullet entrance wound with multiple layers of gauze. *Can you die from a shot in the arm?* He pushed Archie away, moving toward Sloane. "You need to get her to the hospital. *Please.*"

The SWAT medics closed ranks around her, their broad shoulders and helmets shutting him out. Another came up to him and shined a light in his eyes. "Local paramedics are standing by outside." He motioned to an officer just entering the scene and turned to Archie. "The sergeant will have some questions for you so you need to go along, too. No funny shit." He glanced at Officer Blake and jerked his head at Archie. "Pat 'em down and get 'em outside." Zack followed the medic's gaze to Sloane. "She's gotta go *now*, fellas."

He wanted to go with Sloane. Needed to reassure himself that she'd be okay. But how could he leave John's daughter here to die?

I can't.

If Ann died here, how could he look himself in the mirror knowing the man who'd done this to her had been under their roof for years?

He had promised to protect her.

273

"Ninety seconds! Fuller, clear out!" the commander snarled at one of the bomb techs.

The medics shifted into high gear, raising Sloane in the stretcher, running toward the east mall entrance. As Zack broke away, he heard the medic yelling at him and someone giving chase, but he kept going.

As he rounded the corner near the park entrance, his gaze went to the focused, bearded tech.

"Cut the damn straps!"

One of the other techs passed a tool to Fuller. "Can't. They're booby trapped all over her."

"Ten more seconds is all you've got! Then I'm coming in to drag you out!"

"Yes, sir!" Fuller barked at his commander. Then, "Fuck, she's waking up!"

Everyone froze.

Sweet Jesus.

Ann's sudden scream echoed through the amusement park down into Zack's soul where he thought it would live forever.

He sprinted past one SWAT officer only to be cut short by two others. He pushed back, a wild panic beating in his chest, a fountain of magma melting him from the inside out.

Archie rushed him from behind to put him in a standing full nelson. Zack bent in half to try to throw him over his head, but Archie planted his feet and counter-shifted back.

Helpless rage pulsed through Zack. "Sonofa—! She's terrified! Sedate...her!"

Lt. Carver got in his face and glared, the veins in his forehead standing out. "No time!"

The bomb started beeping loud, continuous chirps. Archie released Zack and sprinted toward cover.

"Fifteen seconds!" Blake or Jones yelled.

Carver swiped at the sweat running down his face. "Fuller, Blake, Jones, clear out right now! Everybody! Move, move, *move!*"

Everyone cleared out except the techs.

Zack, come to me! Please.

He nearly stumbled to hear her voice, strong and passionate, in his head. *Goldie, I trust you. I believe in your gift. You can help us.*

His feet tore across the concrete he'd helped pour, laughing and joking with one of his crews as they'd smoothed and buffed the surface.The bomb bleeps shortened, their piercing sound pouring through Zack as he looked at the wires coming out of the box.

The two techs tried to pull him along as they ran for cover. He shoved them away, bolted toward Fuller, and pressed his palms to Ann's icy cheeks, calling her name until her eyes finally focused, and she blinked at him in stunned silence.

"Hold still, Ann. *Don't. Move.*"

He looked at the bomb. Touched it. *Which wire, Goldie? Try to feel it!*

The bomb bleeps faded into the background. Zack heard only his heartbeat as he looked up to see the perfect concentration on Fuller's grizzled face. In that quiet space, John came to him. *Come hell or high water, hold tight to your beliefs. For every mountain there is a miracle.*

Zack's pulse slowed, his vision tunneled. John had never lied to him before.

The bleeps became one steady, unrelenting pitch. The bomb's final warning.

Five, four, three…

Sloane!

Fuller's fingers reached forward.

275

The green one! her voice cried in his mind.

"Green! The green!" Zack yelled above the bomb's blare.

Fuller jerked the green wire free.

The abrupt silence in the vacuous space was almost more terrifying than the bomb's imminent alarm. Fuller sat back on his heels and hung his head, shoulders slumped as though all the air had spontaneously left his body.

A roll of thunder echoed the mottled emotion moving through Zack. Through his belly and up his chest to lodge in his throat, a tight mass of feeling too big for words. He squeezed Ann's arm and laid a palm on Fuller's back, who looked up to hoarsely yell the all clear.

Then reality broke through, fast and loud.

SWAT flooded the area around Ann. The bomb unit cleared the device before the medics attended her. Zack backed a few feet away, turning when he felt her.

Ah, Goldie.

He felt her tears bathing him in a communion of minds, hearts, souls.

He couldn't wait to hold her. To lose himself in the fathomless brown of her eyes, the exquisite touch of her fingertips reminding him how good it felt to *feel*.

She wasn't speaking in his head, but it was all right.

Knowing she was safe was enough for now.

Words were for tomorrow.

THIRTY-FIVE

ONE WEEK LATER

Sloane was watching Zack uncork a bottle of cabernet when the dogs bolted from their spots on either side of her on the couch. They ran for the door, barking so relentlessly that he threw a soft, mangled chew toy at them.

He came around the small kitchen island and handed her a wine glass before nudging the dogs aside to turn on the outside light. She smiled at the trio until she saw Zack's shoulders tense.

Now what? She couldn't stop the negative thought, even though the past week had been a beautiful, unexpected dream. Her arm was healing nicely since the bullet had only damaged muscle, and she didn't even care that she'd lost Benjamin's support for her foundation. She and Zack had a truckload of baggage, but they'd loved each other enough these past seven days to help hasten the healing process.

Maybe they'd even loved enough to last a lifetime.

Don't think like that.

Zack ordered the dogs to sit before opening the door. She set her glass on the pile of drafting books, then moved toward him, looking out into the night. When she touched his back, his muscles relaxed a fraction.

"Who is—" The words died on her lips, and she ran out into the meager light cast by the light fixture, straight into Ann's open arms. Deep emotion put a choke hold on her throat to feel

Zack's arms come around the two of them.

Ann brushed at her eyes and laughed shyly when Sloane's mouth dropped open and her fingers slid through Ann's newly-shortened, glossy black strands.

"Dear Lord, I didn't think you could get any more beautiful, but *look* at you. This style suits you perfectly." She hugged Ann to her again, crying and laughing at once. "You must have just cut it. Here, come in, come in!"

Zack held the door open for them, then closed it, stationing himself in front of it like a guardian. *For goodness' sake, stop glowering at her.* He glanced at Sloane quickly and his shoulders loosened up, but he didn't move away from the door. He looked back at Ann. "Why didn't you call? I would have picked you up from the hospital."

Ann set her purse on the floor, sat down, and exhaled quietly. "I was actually released yesterday, shortly after you guys left." She shrugged when Zack opened his mouth to speak. "It's okay. I...I wanted time alone. To think." The female dog laid her head across Ann's thighs. Her fingers stroked through the deep pile of her fur. "Anyway, I've learned a lot...about myself." She rubbed a hand against her belly, and Sloane's throat closed up again, thinking of all Ann had lost. Her father, a lover, a baby.

A silent communication passed between the two women before Ann nodded and closed her eyes. When she opened them again, Sloane saw a strength that wasn't there before. "Detective Barnaba came to see me at home this morning."

Zack's arms dropped to his sides as he bit out, "Haven't they bothered you enough this week?"

Ann's gaze met Zack's directly. "They tracked down Serena."

Sloane pressed a hand to her chest. "Where is she?"

"He couldn't say. She wants to remain hidden."

Zack cursed and pushed away from the door.

A ghost of a smile played around Ann's lips, and she shrugged. "It's okay. *Really.* She would only be a disappointment after having a parent like Dad anyway."

"Damn right. Barnaba tell you anything else about the case?" Zack asked.

"I can't believe how Ross had it all planned out. He was just so…normal. And smart. Barnaba said he had shrines to Serena all over his house. Part of his payoff was stringing this out. He chose a career in tax law based on how he wanted to infiltrate Dad's life. The excitement of building his plan, evading detection, and putting each new phase into play was what kept him going for more than two decades. We're lucky his goal wasn't as well-executed as it was well-planned. He used a lot of people along the way."

Sloane's eyes blurred. "Like Tori." Zack sat down beside her and pulled her into the crook of his shoulder. "He used Tori to keep tabs on you," he said, looking at Ann. "And she told him about your involvement with Dallan. Then he used Colette's anger against Dallan to deliver you to his front door."

Ann frowned. "How do you know all that?"

Heat rushed up Sloane's neck to her cheeks. She looked down at her hands in her lap. Pressed them flat against the tops of her thighs. What could she say? *Well, see now, I'm your regular psychic mutant.*

You're perfect.

Her eyes widened, her gaze darting to Zack's face. He was doing that soft smile thing that made her insides go all shy and amazed and happy.

He squeezed her thigh, then looked back at Ann. "Morgan was a part of this."

"It's not your fault," Ann said. "Ross was hell bent on

279

destroying Dad because of Serena, and then you and me due to his disappointment that I wasn't his daughter. It wouldn't have made any difference if you weren't involved. He tapped into a lot of people's motivations in order to achieve his goal."

Zack stood and paced to the window, the darkness a profound backdrop against his body's strong lines.

Ann took a deep breath. "Look, I know there's so much upheaval at Samuel's Construction right now with the building damage and the audits, but… I'm sorry, Zack, I won't be coming back to the office. I hope you're not upset, but I'm going to go back to school."

Zack turned back to face her and smiled. "Good."

"That's wonderful, Ann!" But a thread of sadness drifted through Sloane. "Does this mean you won't be at Skinny Dipping anymore?"

Ann rolled her eyes. "Goodness no! I don't think you'll ever get me away from that store."

"Oh, thank heavens! This calls for a celebration! I'll get you a glass."

Ann stopped her before she could leave the room. "Thanks, but I'll take a rain check on that, okay? I need to get home. Surry's waiting for supper." She smiled.

Zack frowned. "Who the hell's Surry?"

"The tomcat. I named him Surry for survivor. We both are."

Maybe we all are. Sloane rubbed her arms, feeling chilled.

Ann put her purse over her shoulder, twisting the straps. "I don't know how to thank you both for…not giving up on me. I'd be dead if not for you."

"I don't want you to think about it anymore," Zack said.

"Too bad." Ann winked at Sloane and smiled at Zack's raised eyebrow. "From now on I'm going to be doing a lot of thinking."

She's really going to be okay.

One side of Zack's mouth lifted. He indicated the door with his head. "I'll walk you out."

And that opened the floodgates.

Sloane was still wiping her eyes when Zack re-entered the house alone, the dogs bouncing up and down like they hadn't seen him in a year. He gave each a fierce pat, then moved toward her, his gaze traveling over her face, down her neck, breasts, belly...*lower.*

So possessive.

She sniffed and became aware of her skin beneath her clothes. The slide of her tank top as she shifted on the sofa. Her toes curling into the rug at her feet. When his eyes returned to hers, they burned with an emerald fire that sucked the moisture from her mouth. She reached for her wine, toppling the glass. "Oh, darn it! I'm sorry! Here let me—"

"Leave it."

His secret smile, masculine bass, and sexy eyes jacked her pulse. Lord, why was she so nervous? "No, really. I should clean this up before it ruins your lovely books." She tried to stand up from the sofa without touching him, but the way he braced his legs apart made it pretty much impossible. She tried to move away to retrieve a towel, catch her breath, pitch her head under a cold shower—*anything*—but he grasped her hand, led her through the house, grabbing a heavy blanket on his way out the back door.

She pulled him back inside for a moment. "Kiefer! Kiah!" The dogs' toenails *scritched* across the hardwood as they sprinted from the living room.

Zack squeezed her hand with a warm smile. "I'm glad you enjoy them, but I think we'll leave them in. Tonight I don't want anyone licking you but me."

Oh.

Oh.

The cool night air helped settle her nerves. He walked her near the river's edge to the fire pit—where he'd obviously planned to be much earlier, by the looks of the mature embers.

Spreading the blanket on the grass, he sat first, then motioned her to sit between his outstretched legs. When she did, he brought her back against his chest, folding his arms and the blanket around her, cocooning them in the quiet symphony of the night.

It took a moment for her eyes to adjust to the darkness, then she looked up at the thousands of stars that twinkled in their midnight palette. She inhaled slowly, the crisp, clean scent of flowers and river vegetation flowing into her, a steadying influence. But nothing would ever settle her, bring her peace, the way Zack did.

"I love being out here with you," she said.

"You do?"

She also loved the way his voice rumbled against her back, his breath warm against her ear. "*Mmm.* I could stay this way forever."

He remained silent, but she could almost feel the synapses in his brain leaping. She smiled, knowing he was open enough that she'd be able to read his thoughts, but also knowing she wouldn't do that.

"Then why don't you?" he finally whispered.

Her smile slipped. A bell rang, the gates opened, and her heart was on the racetrack. She crossed her legs and scooted around to face him. Firelight flickered on his face, his eyes so soft they disarmed her. "What are you saying?"

He got up and arranged the blanket more snugly against her before moving toward the fire. She watched the shadows play over his broad back as he added another log to the pit. The pile shifted and fell in upon itself like old bones returning to dust. He moved to the other side of the pit, staring at her over the flames. She felt the deep stillness of him.

She waited, her breathing shallow.

She didn't have long to wait.

"I'm saying I'll never find another who moves me the way you do. I want you to stay with me. *Forever*."

A small cry escaped. She fought with the blanket to try to stand and go to him, but he was by her side before she could get free. He ran his hands down the sides of her head, then put his finger to her lips, his eyes luminous in the shadows.

"I *will* have your enthusiasm. But first, I need to say this."

She could barely breathe. She wanted to rain kisses all over his body and make love with him under the stars. But she nodded. There'd be time.

Forever.

His teeth suddenly gleamed, the wicked smile heating her blood. She thought he'd reconsidered talking. But he sat back on the grass, stretching his long legs out in front of him like this was gonna take all night. *Hurry up, already. I can think of better things—*

His laugh burst free, and hers nearly did, too. Luckily she quickly caught herself and frowned at him. "Hey! You're not supposed to do that!"

"How can I help it when you think so loud?"

"Clod."

"I like seismic jackass better."

They smiled at each other as night bugs danced among the tiny embers that floated high above the pit. He leaned forward and with the gentlest of touches, feathered his lips against hers until she was breathless. His eyes promised secret pleasures.

"So I've been thinking a lot this week. Obviously with the bombing damage, I'll be relocating Samuel's offices to another property downtown. A bigger property. I'm sure you know it—the historic building across from the bank."

"Are you serious? The brick four-story?"

He nodded.

"It's gorgeous. You *own* that?"

Another nod with a smile. "We have a lot of other properties, too. John loved real estate about as much as he enjoyed construction. Anyway, I figure since I'm going to need the services of an interior designer, and you're probably going to be looking for another sponsor for the foundation..." His words trailed off expectantly.

Hot tears welled in her eyes, overflowing faster than he could wipe them away.

"An organization like Project Broken Wings is essential for people of all ages and walks of life. Let me help you with this."

He'd told her about finding his father's body. She bowed her head, trying to comprehend his gift. His character in the wake of—*in spite of*—his broken childhood.

He raised her chin. "Before you get too excited, I want you to know that I have one stipulation for this deal."

She sniffed, trying to bring her emotions under control. He smiled lopsidedly and pushed an errant strand of hair behind her ear. "God, I love you, Goldie."

"I love you, too. More than anything," she whispered.

"I'll give you everything I have. *Marry me.*"

"Hell, yes!" She launched at him, toppling them both to the soft grass where the fire's warmth dried all her tears as they kissed. She shivered when he broke away, cool air replacing the heat of his body. But only for a moment. He reached for the blanket, then gathered her into his arms.

Where I belong.

Yes.

He laid her back against the soft fabric, smiling into her eyes. The fire popped and crackled in harmony with the cricket songs and the wind sifting through the trees. He ran his hand down her flank, his broad palms stoking another fire within her. "Seems to me you had some good ideas earlier. Something about making love under the stars?"

He got his answer when she pulled him down on top of her.

Bodies entwined, his lips slanted across hers, his consuming hunger a welcome aggression. Her last articulate thought was how she'd found peace on the banks of a timeless river. In the arms of a man who saw all her shadows, and loved her just as timelessly.

Dear Reader,

Thank you for spending time with Zack and Sloane! If you enjoyed their harrowing journey, please consider posting a review on your favorite bookseller's site.

If you're ready for another sexy story, check out FLIRTING WITH FIRE, a fun contemporary romance. And if you're *really* feeling the love, please sign up for my newsletter (mistydietz.com/newsletter) for alerts on all my new releases!

Hugs & happily ever afters to you always, *Misty*

MistyDietz.com

Misty Dietz loves her man, her kids, kayaking, and Dean Winchester (oh yeah, Supernatural super-fans unite!). She writes paranormal, suspense, and contemporary romance, but she reads anything she can get her hands on, usually with her fur baby on her lap.

She spends her days writing sexy, adrenaline-fueled stories, enjoying family and friends, and praying her children don't come home with math homework. ☺

FLIRTING WITH FIRE by Misty Dietz

Walking through fire will either burn them...or forge a bond that will last a lifetime.

All work and no play has left hunky firefighter Cole Castillo's poetic soul floundering. Contrary to his meddling sister's fairy-tale wishes, romance is the last thing he deserves, and a week-long getaway at a luxurious mountain resort won't atone for the grievous mistake that haunts him. So he's ready to bail...until he finds a sexy little number jumping on the bed in his assigned suite.

Free-spirited school teacher Ivy Bradford has issues – parent issues, phobia issues, work issues – but one look at her sexy, tormented roommate, and those problems fade to black. To get him to stay for the week, Ivy poses a bet that Cole can't resist. But bratwurst eating and beer drinking aren't the only things that will challenge the delicate bond they forge during the week.

When obligations from Cole's past come a-knocking, will their steamy connection withstand the heat or go up in flames?

www.ingramcontent.com/pod-product-compliance
Lightning Source LLC
Chambersburg PA
CBHW051415170626
46809CB00006B/2177